PREDATORS & PREY
BY EDWARD J. MCFADDEN III

SEVERED PRESS
HOBART TASMANIA

PREDATORS & PREY

1

Drew Locke held his breath as he plummeted, his ejection seat twisting in the wind as he broke free of the clouds and a lush green tree canopy raced up to meet him. Slices of blue, green, and white spun across his face shield, the whir of his helmet fan like a drill digging into his skull. His stomach churned with the sensation of falling, the icy fingers of fear massaging his back.

The ejection seat deployed the parachute, and canvas fluttered, metal tinkled on metal, and Drew was jerked up as the seat harness dug into his spacesuit. He let out the breath he'd forgotten he was holding as pain lanced his chest and the parachute opened and slowed his fall.

"Reek! Reek!"

The shrill cry came from behind and Drew struggled to turn in his seat and locate the source of the call, but his harness held him fast and the helmet impeded his peripheral vision. "What the hell was that?" he said.

The metallic voice of his suit computer burst from a speaker in his helmet. *That data is currently unavailable. All connections to the Triumph have been severed.*

"Right," Drew said as he gripped the side rails of his seat, running his hands along their lengths until he got hold of the chute's steering toggles.

Ribbons of cloudy mist streaked the sky, droplets of moisture inching over his face shield like ants, the carpet of green below getting closer. He was coming in hot, and he needed to find a place to land because crashing into the forest could be deadly.

Drew pulled hard on the steering toggles, arcing toward what appeared to be a bare patch in the jungle next to a lake nestled within the shadow of a tall rock face. The clearing was far-off, but that gave Drew some distance to slow his fall. Coming in on a narrow-angle was the best way—only way he knew—to slow his descent. As he got closer to the forest canopy, he saw that many of the slender conifers were over a hundred feet tall, and the clearing he was aiming for looked to be no bigger than a football pitch, maybe two.

Rays of sunlight broke through the clouds, and Drew saw two red parachutes floating in the distance. They appeared and disappeared within the finger-like columns of mist that reached out from the underside of the clouds. Drew tracked the chutes as they floated beyond the cliff face and out of view.

Prepare for impact.

"You think!" Drew's arms ached from working the steering toggles, but he was still coming in too fast, and he needed to gain altitude. He eased back and raised his arms, which released the tension on the steering lines. That didn't help, and with a sickening dread that churned his stomach and sent daggers of pain racing to his extremities, Drew realized he wasn't going to reach the clearing.

The tree canopy was a hundred yards beneath him and coming on fast, the clearing still half a mile distant. Tall evergreens packed the forest, their thick limbs crammed with needle-like leaves. Animal paths crisscrossed the forest like an interstate highway system, but hitting one would be next to impossible given their size and his limited maneuverability.

A *womp*, like all the air had been sucked from Drew's spacesuit, filtered into his helmet, followed by the faint *pop* of an explosion.

Drew lifted his legs in a futile attempt to buy more distance and time.

Branches snapped as they got caught in the seat's undercarriage, treetops shrieking and breaking as the ejection seat plowed through the tree canopy.

He was wrenched in his seat harness, sharp green leaves scratching his face shield. The right maneuvering toggle got caught up on a branch, and the seat swung left like Drew was on an amusement park ride. As he slowed, the parachute sagged like a deflating balloon.

Drew's heart galloped as he looked down, but he couldn't see the ground as he plunged through the tangled mess of green.

The ejection seat burst from the trees and Drew screamed, the clearing stretching out before him. With not enough air in the parachute, his fall to the hardpan would be fast and his landing hard.

In the distance, beyond a steep escarpment of rock, a stream of black smoke trailed into the cloud-streaked sky.

The squeal of rending fabric rose above the shriek of bending tree limbs and the crackling of evergreen leaves, and the parachute's suspension lines sang and bitched as they went taut. The ejection seat swung back like a pendulum, Drew's face shield a blur of dark sand, gray rock, green leaves, and clouds.

With a thunderous crash that sent a tremor of pain rippling through Drew's body, the seat reached the tree line and knifed between thick trunks before slamming into a massive conifer.

Then Drew was falling again, tree limbs reaching out to grab him, the sound of cracking wood and the hiss of bending branches filling his helmet.

Drew was yanked up, the chute's suspension lines tangled in the trees at the edge of the clearing, and the seat dangled thirty feet from the hardpan, twisting in the breeze.

Nothing moved in the clearing, which Drew now saw was a boneyard. Tall rib bones arced over piles of skeletons whitened by the elements and time, vines winding through the area like giant green snakes.

The packed greenery of the jungle was at his back, and small bat-like beasts sprayed from the forest, fluttering around him, squeaking and hollering. Drew's heart hammered as his gaze fell on tendrils of black smoke that billowed over the escarpment, inched down its face, and crept over the lake toward the boneyard.

Drew closed his eyes and took several deep breaths as he waited for his nerves to stop jackhammering his spine. He shifted in his harness and the spacesuit chafed his armpits, sweat dripping down his back despite the climate control system in his suit going full tilt. He said, "Status report."

All suit systems are operating at one hundred percent efficiency. Suit integrity is one hundred percent. Bioanalysis shows subject has an elevated heart rate, and increased blood pressure, but both are within normal parameters given recent events. Exterior atmosphere is twenty-six-point-seven percent oxygen, and no contaminants have been detected. Current exterior temperature is ninety-two degrees.

"Any word from the Triumph?"

All connections to the Triumph have been severed.

"Are we…"

On Earth?

Drew said nothing.

Current GPS location is unknown because the estimated land masses don't translate to the current land formations within an acceptable error margin, but based on all known data you have arrived in the Cretaceous.

"Not the way we were supposed to," Drew said. "What the hell happened?"

That data is currently unavailable.

"Is that smoke from the ship?"

That data is currently unavailable. All connections to the Triumph have been severed.

"Is the sun in the south?" If he didn't get some information his head might explode.

Southeast, and based on the sun's current position sundown is estimated at 1834 hours, which is ten-point-three-four hours from now.

Perspiration stung his eyes as Drew undid the hasps securing his helmet to the suit's neck collar. The clicks echoed faintly, then a soft *pop* followed by a *hiss* as the positive pressure was released from the suit. Drew inched the helmet off his head and the scent of manure-like waste, moisture, and the rich smell of decaying earth filled his nostrils. It was hot, and he pulled off his gloves and stuffed them in the helmet. He thought of tossing the helmet to the ground, but decided that was a bad idea.

His suit was more advanced than the Extravehicular Mobility Unit (EMU) spacefarers had used for years. The new suits were much lighter, had a sleeker life support backpack, and could provide air into perpetuity via advanced oxygen scrubbers. Everything was powered by a battery locked into the life support backpack.

Drew used a carabiner attached to his suit to secure the helmet as he judged how far it was to the ground. He figured thirty feet, which was too far to jump. If he broke his leg, he'd be dead inside a week, and any injury could mean disaster. He could unsnap from the seat harness and attempt to cut some of the parachute's suspension lines and use the rope to climb down. A utility knife with a seven-inch carbon fiber blade, black rubber polymer handle, and a saw-notched back was in a sheath attached to the spacesuit's right thigh, but if he fell as he tried to cut the ropes…

Another approach was to pull the release lever, which would detach the ejection seat from the parachute. He might have better luck with the metal of the seat protecting him, but he thought the jolt would be severe.

As Drew considered which bad option to attempt, a gentle tremor ran through the tree trunk and the metal ejection seat vibrated.

He waited.

The tremors grew in strength and pace, like an approaching battle.

Drew had screwed up his courage to take the plunge in the seat when a green lizard-like head with a yellow stripe running between two glassy black eyes poked from the top of the tree canopy at the eastern edge of the boneyard.

A titan strolled from the band of jungle that separated the boneyard from the lake and rock escarpment beyond, moseying along one of the wide trails beaten into the hardpan. Bones of all shapes and sizes lay scattered about the area, and among the bleached skeletons, the carcasses of freshly dead animals littered the landscape.

Drew was no paleontologist, but he knew the huge beast was some type of Titanosaur. Tree trunk legs supported a massive elephant-like torso, and a long serpentine neck ended in a flat, narrow snake-like head. The beast's long tail swung back and forth, breaking and toppling bones, clouds of dust and grit clouding the air.

The ejection seat vibrated like a tuning fork as the gigantic beast strode across the clearing. The titan was at least fifty feet from its nose to the tip of its muscular tail, yellow and green skin rippling over undulating muscles. The beast paused, its head rotating at the end of its long neck like a periscope. Glassy black eyes scanned the clearing, and Drew felt the beast's stare, though the creature didn't appear to see him. The titan threw back its head and bellowed, a deep mournful cry that sounded like a sad ferry horn.

Drew didn't move, the wind twisting the ejection seat, the parachute's suspension lines squeaking and popping under the strain.

The Titanosaurus churned forward, the thump and rumble of its passage like concussion bombs detonating. When the beast reached the opposite end of the boneyard it stopped, its neck bending as it brought its head low to the ground. The dinosaur mewed and opened its huge mouth, railroad spike teeth barely visible within deep green gums. The creature munched on the lush tropical undergrowth that grew at the feet of the conifers, the snap of branches and the crunch of vegetation filling the boneyard.

Despite the dinosaur being a planteater, its sheer size, the power of its huge jaws crushing foliage, sent a ripple of worry down Drew's spine, pain settling in his lower back like relatives who just won't leave. Vegan or not, if the dinosaur decided it wanted to try meat, what could he do to stop it? He glanced down at the knife in its sheath and held back a chuckle.

He waited until the dinosaur had eaten its fill and moved on, and with the tremors of the beast's receding footfalls rattling the ejection seat, he yanked the release lever. Metal tapped on metal, and then he was falling. Drew gripped the armrests of the ejection seat and closed his eyes, his mind flashing back to his fall to Earth.

The seat hit the hardpan, and Drew was tossed in his harness, air rushing from his lungs as his stomach tried to force its way out of his mouth. Pain danced just beneath his skin, his head ringing like he'd been smacked with a bat, his back on fire. The seat toppled and Drew hung in his seat harness, the spacesuit's helmet dangling from its carabiner.

He released the safety harness and rolled out of the ejection seat onto the ground. Drew felt like he had been beaten within an inch of his life, and as he sat up the world spun in a kaleidoscope of color, starbursts of white speckling his field of vision.

The ground no longer shook, and a thin layer of dust and grit hung a foot above the ground, leeching into the forest like smoke. Drew pushed to his feet, stretched his back, and wiggled his fingers and toes. Everything worked, but he'd be sore for a week.

A stainless-steel water bottle was affixed to the ejection seat and Drew pulled it free. He drank deep, but when his thoughts drifted to finding more water, he pulled up and capped the container. He shook the bottle and judged it to be about half full. Twelve ounces, at best, and he had no idea how long it needed to last.

Drew recalled the lake just beyond the trees, but making a fire to boil water would take time, if he could manage it, and there was no way he was drinking untreated water unless he had no other options.

To the east, a column of black smoke rose above the cliff face. The source had to be the Triumph, and even if the ship was damaged beyond repair given current resources, there might be supplies; rations, water, meds, and purification tablets.

Then there were the two parachutes to consider. There had been six people aboard the Triumph. He pushed thoughts of who might have survived from his mind. Drew had more pressing problems. He needed rest, and then he'd trek in the direction of the smoke in search of the Triumph. Perhaps the communication system would be repairable, and he could call for help, but even as that fart of hope stank up his head, he knew communication home was impossible.

Drew ducked into the forest, found a shady spot, and stripped off his spacesuit. He wore a blue jumpsuit beneath, and since he had no shoes, he put the spacesuit boots back on.

He tied the arms and legs of the spacesuit together and created a makeshift backpack, then stuffed in the helmet, gloves, and water bottle. There was still some space in the bag, so he went back to the ejection seat and cut off the seat harness. There was nothing else of use, and Drew slipped on his spacesuit pack and held onto the blade.

The boneyard was silent, nothing but the whisper of the wind, and the distant cries of beasts. Several animal trails converged at the clearing, but he didn't think walking on the trodden paths was safe. Drew looked down at his blade. It wouldn't do much against the larger beasts, but perhaps he could find a straight stick and make a spear? Give himself more reach? He didn't know what he'd use to secure the knife to the pole—maybe the seatbelt—but that was a problem for another time.

Skeletons ranging in size from a Titanosaur to a house cat littered the clearing, most decayed and broken. Drew ran his hand along a huge rib bone as he picked his way across the animal graveyard, and it disintegrated to dust and grit under the pressure of his touch. Some of the bones still had darkened flesh clinging to them, but most of the remains looked old. He knew whales and other beasts often went to a certain place to die, but Drew thought it odd that there appeared to be many species in the boneyard.

He reached the eastern end of the clearing, the tree line so dense the dark maw of the trail the Titanosaurus had used looked like the entrance to the Holland tunnel. Drew flipped the knife in his hand, blade out. Visibility beneath the tree canopy was twenty feet, and if something came at him from the shadows, he wouldn't see it until it was on him.

The animal trail was fifteen feet across, the undergrowth along its edges thick and unyielding. Drew slashed his way into the underbrush, avoiding the path, his blade singing, muscles screaming. He trailblazed forty feet, the undergrowth a mix of weed-like trees and huge ferns with thick trunks and massive elephant ear leaves. Drew almost tripped twice, and he was making so much noise that he decided cutting through the underbrush wasn't worth the effort, and he was alerting every beast within a click of his position.

Yellow flies with blue eyes buzzed him, and the rustle of smaller creatures darting about within the undergrowth made his skin crawl with terror. He hacked his way toward the path, which he could barely see through the thick jungle. A surge of worry ran through him. If he got turned around and lost his sense of direction in the dense vegetation it might take hours to find his way out.

He slipped from beneath the cover of a wide conifer branch and worked his way up onto the trail. If need be, he could hide in the forest. That assumed he heard the predator coming.

As if on cue a primeval roar carried over the jungle.

2

The animal trail twisted through the jungle and judging by its easterly course Drew figured the path led to the lake he'd seen. Lakes are usually fresh water, but he still hadn't figured out how he was going to boil the liquid. He needed to, and soon, or he'd have to drink the unpurified water and hope some microbe didn't kick his ass, or worse, kill him.

Drew couldn't see the escarpment because of the jungle, but he knew a tall cliff face loomed beyond the lake, so he'd have to climb it or find a way around. Either way, he needed to drink. He could struggle through without food, and the hope of rations at the crash site spurred him because eating game, even if he could kill some, could be dangerous. The beasts of the Cretaceous could have adapted to some disease or microorganism that he'd never been exposed to, so watching what the creatures ate didn't prove definitively that a particular meat or plant was safe.

He considered putting his spacesuit back on. It was scorching hot, the air thick, and the suit's climate control could provide some relief.

A sharp *caw* pierced the day. It came from the jungle to his left and Drew dove off the path into the vegetation. Pricker vines grabbed at his jumpsuit as he went to the ground facing away from the trail. Thick green tropical-like undergrowth packed the jungle floor beneath the conifers and tree ferns, dead vegetation, twigs, and fern leaves blocking his view.

Large red ants marched across the ground before him, but Drew didn't move. He tuned his hearing, but heard only the push of the breeze, the hum of insects, and the occasional clicks and chuffs of the larger beasts. He counted in his head, perspiration dripping down his back and forehead, his nerves tap dancing on his spine. When he reached twenty, he slowly rolled onto his side and looked back toward the road.

Nothing moved within the window of crushed vegetation created by his leap from the path. A thin cloud of dust hung over the trail, but otherwise, there were no visible threats. Drew sat up, and when his head didn't get bitten off, he pushed to his feet, the spacesuit backpack dragging him down. He let the pack's straps fall from his shoulders as he crept back to the road, his stomach grumbling for food and water.

There was no sign of the cawing creature and Drew wondered if he'd overreacted. His gaze fell on the suit where it rested in a knot within the undergrowth. The suit would provide an added layer of protection, but it was awkward and restrictive, and with the helmet on, his field of vision was limited, but could be enhanced. The climate control system would make things easier on his body, and he wouldn't sweat as much and give-up precious water.

With the unknowns and problems stacking up, Drew decided he'd be better off in the suit, at least for now. As he retrieved it and untied the knots that transformed the legs and arms into pack straps, he felt the fool for being in such a hurry to take the suit off. He might know what time period he was in, but that was about all he knew for sure. The bigheads back in his time had made fabulous guesses and generated specific estimates based on the fossil record, the composition of the rocks and soil, and the air molecules contained therein, but Drew still didn't know for sure what he'd find on this alien world that was also his home.

When he had the suit on, Drew slipped on the helmet, secured the seal latches, and pulled on his gloves. Red numbers and computer code that looked like a foreign language scrolled over the inside of his face shield, and he heard the whirr of the helmet fan snap on, cool air filtering through the suit. He clipped the water bottle onto its carabiner, sheathed the knife, and hung the ejection seat harness over a shoulder.

After he'd cooled down, Drew continued his trek down the animal trail. He felt unseen eyes watching him from the shadows beneath the dense tree canopy and chuckled. He couldn't help himself. What must he look like traipsing down a dirt path through the primordial jungle in a white spacesuit? This certainly hadn't been the plan.

"Has the Triumph come back online?" he said into his helmet mic.

All connections to the Triumph remain severed.

Drew thought to ask the computer about the terrain, but remembered without a connection to the ship his onboard suit computer couldn't do much.

The path plunged into a shallow bowl packed with stunted palm-like trees, their spiked leaves casting knife-like shadows across huge elephant ears splashed with a myriad of colors. Vegetation packed the floor of the bowl, and mist eddied and swirled above the lush emerald tree canopy, the animal trail a dark line through the greenery. Creatures squawked and brayed from within the dell, but Drew saw no large predators from his elevated position. Clouds of insects hovered over the path, alighting on his suit, but unable to bite him. Drew didn't want to think about the diseases and germs the little vampires might carry.

Walking downhill is always easier than walking uphill, just ask anyone who's trekked to the bottom of the Grand Canyon, and Drew felt refreshed when he reached the bottom of the dell. Water reeds poked through the thick underbrush of weeds and broadleaf plants that reminded Drew of the calla lilies his mother had planted each summer when he was a boy. The plant's blood-red flowers were huge, their white stamens reaching out like snake tongues.

Drew rolled his shoulders, angst running through him as he examined the ground. His thoughts had focused on the famous beasts of the Cretaceous, but the fossil record showed insects, snakes, and all types of potential hazards within the food chain, right down to ants that could devour an animal carcass in twenty-four hours.

The suit fan was whirring at top speed when he reached the rim on the opposite side of the hollow, a narrow band of forest between him and the lake beyond. The surface of the lake shimmered, and the glare on the helmet's face shield made it difficult to see beyond the lake, so he pushed it up.

His face was blasted with heat as his suit computer admonished him, a gentle breeze redolent of pine, earth, moisture, and burning rubber filling his helmet. Hazy smoke filtered down the cliff face and leeched into the jungle. The escarpment was two hundred feet high if it was a foot, and it extended to the north and south as far as Drew could see. Not that he could see very far with the jungle crawling up the rock face like a fungus.

A cloud of insects engulfed his head and Drew pulled his face shield back down. Bright green flies alighted on the face shield, and his skin itched with imaginary bug bites. He heard a buzz in his ear. One of the little buggers was in the suit. Drew swiped at the air before him as he plunged forward, the cloud of insects dissipating as he pushed through it, his suit computer prattling on about the restoration of suit integrity.

The jungle thinned, and the land fell away to the lake. There were several clearings carved from the vegetation all around the lake where beasts came to drink, and creatures bathed in the shallow waters at the lake's edge. "Enhance vision fifty percent."

The spacesuit's face shield blurred, then cleared, and Drew's field of vision narrowed but sharpened.

Beasts that looked like a cross between an eagle and an ostrich waded in the shallows like a flock of waterfowl. The six-foot bird-like beasts half jumped, half flew into the lake, their short arms acting like gliding wings. The half-wing-arms ended in three-fingered claws, and the beasts balanced on two muscular hindlegs. Brown and black feathers covered the creatures, and they yipped and yammered at each other as they plucked tiny silver fish from the water.

The helmet fan sputtered, and the side of Drew's face was sprayed with the remains of the fly that had snuck into his suit. He cringed, his hand going to his face shield.

"Reek! Reek! Reek!"

He turned toward the sound and his face shield blurred for an instant as the magnification adjusted to accommodate the longer distance.

Two huge dragon-like beasts circled above the cliff face, their elongated shadows falling over the placid surface of the lake. The Pterosaurs, which are commonly referred to as Pterodactyls, appeared to be circling above the crash site, and the beasts swooped and soared like planes doing an airshow, their massive sail-like wings extended, their narrow heads ending in elongated jaws packed with teeth.

Drew sat just within the tree line beyond a black, muddy clearing pocked with paw prints of every shape and size. The watering hole was a daily destination for most of the creatures, and though he wanted nothing more than to take a swim in the crystal-clear water, he didn't dare reveal himself. Though he didn't see them, Drew felt the watchful eyes of predators locked on the lake, lying in wait, patient in their instinctual knowledge that most living things needed water regularly to survive.

He inched off his helmet and put it on the ground beside him. As Drew wiped bug remains from his face with his gloved hand, he was assaulted by a symphony of smells. Earth, moisture, rust, and a honeysuckle-like scent that brought Drew back to his days running around in the field behind his childhood home with his brother. His nose itched from the memory as Drew took a long pull of water from his stainless-steel bottle. He had maybe a mouthful left.

From within the shadows Drew watched as three beasts he could only label as Velociraptors eased off the trail onto the muddy strip of shoreline, their eyes focused on the lake as if waiting for something to emerge. Drew didn't know if the beasts were raptors. He knew there were several types and they ranged in size from a baby T-rex to a turkey, but there were also many other species that looked similar.

None of that mattered because knowing the genus wouldn't change the fact that the beasts were clearly predators that were big enough to take him down. Especially three on one, and Drew only having a blade.

The creatures had brown skin with red streaks, and their heads bobbed like a bird's, their hindlegs taking hesitant steps. The creatures clicked and argued as they got closer to the water, the largest of the three hanging back and screaming at the two smaller beasts.

With the caution of a cat stalking a bird, the dinosaurs inched into the lake, drinking, and dipping their heads below the surface.

Three guttural caws exploded from the forest behind him, but Drew had his back to a tree trunk, and he resisted the urge to locate the source of the cries. The braying continued, but got no closer.

Out on the lake, the raptor look-a-likes were taking turns drinking and bathing, one of the beasts always watching the trail and tree line for approaching trouble. If the creatures were concerned about whatever was shrieking in the jungle, they didn't show it, so Drew peeked around the tree trunk.

Nothing moved on the trail, but behind him in the dusk beneath the tree canopy a field of yellow eyes glowed within the undergrowth. The beasts appeared content to leave him be as they pulled pieces of fruit that looked like giant white raspberries from short palm-like trees.

Drew clipped the bottle containing his last mouthful of water to his suit and put the helmet back on. He secured its clasps as red writing appeared on the inside of his face shield, and he shifted his position and focused on the creatures behind him.

"Increase magnification one hundred percent." The face shield blurred, then went green as Drew stared at the underside of a leaf. He moved his head slowly, brown branches, dark bark, and yellow fanleaves cycling across his field of vision, and coming to rest on a closeup of one of the odd creatures.

The beast looked like a buzzard, but instead of feathers it had scales like a lizard, and a round shell sat atop its head like a hat, two red eyes focused on its work. The beast tore open one of the odd pieces of starvation fruit, and hope flooded through Drew as the beast stuffed the white bread-like fruit into its needle-tooth-filled mouth.

Bubbles popped at the center of the lake, whitewater leaking up from the dark depths and churning the placid surface.

The bird-like ostriches and the three raptor beasts snapped their heads toward the center of the lake and froze, the trill of the jungle insects going silent, the tap and snap of the creatures breaking open the odd fruit going still.

Far off a ferocious roar echoed over the jungle, and it was answered by a stronger statement of dominance. The beasts harvesting the breadfruit continued eating, crushed porridge-like goo dripping through their claws.

The lake settled and bubbles popped on the surface.

Slowly the creatures in the water resumed their drinking and bathing, and the trill of insects once again buzzed in Drew's head.

3

The raptor-like beasts bolted down the animal path and disappeared into the jungle, running right by Drew like he was invisible. He thought maybe the spacesuit was containing his human stink, and since his back was to the tree and his heat signature was subdued by the spacesuit, perhaps he was invisible to the creatures.

Great advances had been made in the study of dinosaurs thanks to new technology that allowed scientists to estimate not only the shape and behaviors of the creatures, but their color, what they ate, and what social structures they lived in. By studying the prehistoric footprints and tracks of dinosaurs, much could be gleaned about how they lived and interacted with their environment. What the bigheads knew little about, was what the creatures saw, though scientists believed because most dinosaurs' eyes were on the sides of their head, they had a wide view of their surroundings, and the general consensus was dinosaurs saw color like birds and modern reptiles.

Along with the evidence supported by guesses and extrapolations came fanciful notions associated with the unknown and lost civilizations, promises of elixirs, and the elimination of disease. One of those fanciful notions was the impetus for his mission, and now his home, his time, seemed a galaxy away, and the crushing finality of his situation sent a tremor of fear and sorrow racing the pathways of Drew's stretched nerves.

He gazed out on the lake, the sound of popping bubbles and churning whitewater carrying over the water. A rolling fist of whitewater drove across the lake as a massive leviathan rose from the depths, a mountain of bubbles and churning foam spreading over the surface of the lake. The face shield magnification was still enhanced a hundred percent, and Drew adjusted it, but with the sun's glare on the water's surface it was difficult to see any detail.

Drew pushed to his feet and reached for his knife, but even as he did so every warning light on his mental dashboard flashed red.

The jungle had gone still, and the ostrich beasts that looked to be an ancestor of Deinonychus, but didn't have plumes of feathers atop their heads or flat elongated tails, were backing out of the water. All eyes were locked on the knot of whitewater bubbling over the lake like a bleeding wound.

An explosion of water rocketed from the lake, a long flat mouth with rows of teeth surging from the tumult.

A crocodilian-like beast missiled from the lake, its massive, hinged jaws clamping down on one of the ostrich-like creatures. Feathers flew, and the other beasts bolted, leaving their comrade to its fate. Dark black scales rolled in the bloody whitewater, and the sound of cracking bone and tearing meat carried on the wind.

The beast was at least twenty feet long, and it twisted and squirmed like a sea serpent, its long narrow tail whipping around, its pectoral fin-like arms and legs driving the creature's huge body from the water. The two beasts fought and struggled, but the conflict didn't last long.

The predator sank beneath the surface of the lake, cherry bubbles popping, a blood slick dotted with strands of gristle, muscle, and chunks of fat spreading over the water.

Drew hadn't been chosen for the mission because of his expertise on dinosaurs, but every crew member regardless of specialization had spent time studying the various creatures that had lived during the Cretaceous, and though he wasn't certain, Drew believed he'd just seen a type of Mosasaur, an alligator-type beast that appeared way back in Earth's history and has survived in several forms to modern times.

His hands were shaking, his heart pounding in his chest. Drew couldn't get lost in the mythic surroundings or he'd get killed. He wasn't wandering through an amusement park or zoo. The beasts were real, he was an outsider, and he was moving through their world, and respect and caution was constantly necessary.

Drew picked a few of the odd starvation fruits and filled his water bottle, then he made his way around the edge of the lake, staying within the cover of the trees. The water settled, the blood slick trailing across the surface like a boat wake, clouds of flies and gnats swarming the area, but there was no sign of the sea monster or its victim.

No animal trails ran to the cliff face, so Drew was forced to bushwack with his knife. He looked over his shoulder every few steps, images of the raptors stalking him making his nerves jump. It was claustrophobic in the dense underbrush beneath the thick tree canopy, and the vegetation was so dense a beast could be hiding ten feet away and he wouldn't know.

Unlike the standard gray that typically depicted the skin color of dinosaurs when presented in film and books, the beasts he'd seen so far had varied skin colors, almost like natural camouflage, which made much more sense. Like humans, he was now certain the dinosaurs adapted to their environment, the pigments in their skin becoming darker and colorful based on what the creature ate and where it lived.

The Mosasaur had dark scales and black ridges on its gray tail, adaptations that allowed the predator to sneak up on its prey. How the giant beast had ended up in the lake, he didn't know. Mosasaurs lived in the seas, but perhaps the lake was fed by a spring, was the remnant of an inland sea, or possibly volcanic, that allowed—

A roar carried on the wind and Drew froze, heart racing, skin crawling with perspiration. He looked back, but saw nothing moving, even when he increased the face shield's magnification.

The sun dropped to the horizon at his back, the cliff face a half a mile distant. It was time to start thinking about where he would spend the night. He was exhausted, starving, and he wasn't prepared to trek through the primordial jungle in the dark. He coughed, the sound echoing inside the spacesuit helmet. With no light pollution, he hoped for a full moon, otherwise he wouldn't be able to see his hand in front of his face. He had no flashlight, no means to make a torch, so travel by night was out of the question, at least until he got to the remains of the ship.

His skin itched like millions of bugs covered his body. What would he do when he got back to the ship? He'd seen two other parachutes, so it was possible he wasn't alone.

When he reached the cliff face the sun had dropped below the tree line and dusk crept over the land. The smell of burning rubber was thick in the air, which meant the crash site was close, but thanks to the escarpment it might as well have been a hundred miles away.

The path ended at a wall of brown rock streaked with black and dotted with specks of gleaming quartz. Up close he saw that the cliff face was at least three hundred feet high. Without help, and rope, there was no way he could climb it. He'd have to take off his suit, and boots, and climb barefoot, which felt like the stupidest thing he could possibly do. Aside from the fact that he could plummet to his death, he could get bitten, scratched—a host of things could take him down.

Drew looked south, then north. The cliff face ran as far as he could see in both directions, and vegetation encroached to the wall's base, vines climbing up the jagged stone. Within the tangle of greenery, small creatures hid in their nests and burrows, and they squawked and fought as Drew considered his options.

He had no coin to flip, so he went south. There was no reasoning, no rationale, other than standing around wasn't going to get him anywhere.

Unlike many cliff faces he'd seen, this particular escarpment had very few tumbled boulders at its base, and it looked like the flat shard of rock had knifed from the ground without resistance.

Some of the tension drained from Drew's shoulders and back as he walked. It felt good having a solid wall as protection on one side, and the vegetation that led up to the escarpment was so thick he'd hear any beast coming, regardless of its size. The strip of jungle to the west emitted a symphony of shrieks, hoots, screams, bellows, chuffs, and odd bark-like screams, and the faint gleam of the lake fought through the densely packed trees.

Thick dusk settled over the land, Drew's muscles protesting from overuse and lack of sustenance. He considered drinking the unpurified water because his mouth was as dry as a moth's ass and his muscles were cramping, but he wasn't ready to take the risk. He had nothing to boil the water in, and—

He stopped short when he realized he could use the water bottle. It was made of stainless steel and could withstand the heat.

With his new revelation driving him onward, Drew collected dried twigs from the deadfalls that littered the base of the cliff face. He used the safety harness from the ejection seat to tie his bundle together, and he threw it over a shoulder. Now all he needed was a secluded spot.

From a nearby conifer a beast squawked, and Drew jumped. The bird-like creature stared at him, challenging him, but Drew moved on. It would be nice to have some meat to cook over the fire, or boil in the water, but throwing his only knife at the skinny animal didn't make sense. If he lost the blade, he'd be... what? Screwed? He was already screwed. What was worse? Beyond screwed?

A large deadfall of tree branches and lifeless vegetation blocked his way, and Drew eased into the jungle to get around it. The collection of debris was bigger than the others he'd seen because beyond it there was a wide crack in the cliff face, its dark maw a black gash in the mountainside.

Drew inched into the ravine. Darkness filled the crack, but as his enhanced gaze ranged toward the sky, he saw mountain peaks disappearing into the clouds to the east. With a creeping dread that tossed his empty stomach, hunger pains knifing through him, Drew understood that the escarpment was nothing more than the first upheaval of stone and was no more than the big toe of a huge mountain range beyond.

There were fallen boulders within the gorge, remnants of the geological upheaval that had formed the area. The effects of the final breakup of supercontinent Pangea created all types of hazardous environmental situations that forced life on Earth to adapt. A world with no borders, where all the land masses were connected was a thing of the past. There was no longer a single vast ocean, but instead narrow seas and inland oceans shaped the world.

The team had chosen a landing location on what was believed to be a stable portion of the post Pangea world, a section that would someday become North America, though Drew had no idea where he'd ended up. No ash floated in the air like snow, and he didn't smell the stringent scent of sulfur, so he was confident there was no volcanic activity in the area.

Drew found a secluded spot just within the ravine behind a large stone to make a fire. He had decided hunting for food was beyond him at the moment, the thought of rolling around on the ground with a varmint not even remotely amusing.

He stacked some of the dried branches into a teepee, then went about stripping dry wood from one of the sticks with the knife. When he judged he had enough shavings, he put them under the wood and searched for a flint stone.

The ravine floor was covered with rocks, and he looked for dark stones with a high concentration of quartz. He needed a rock slightly softer than his blade, and he found a perfect angular stone that looked like a large arrowhead, its edges tapering to a dull blade. Drew placed his flint stone atop a boulder and checked its hardness by hammering it with a much larger rock. When it didn't shatter or chip, he knew he had his flint.

Wind gusted down the ravine, stirring dust and grit, but Drew was shielded by the boulder. He struck the rock a glancing blow with the carbon fiber blade and a spark skidded over the wood shavings. He worked for fifteen minutes, and got plenty of sparks, but no fire.

Drew took off the spacesuit helmet, stripped off his gloves, wishing he had a lighter, even a match. After half an hour, he gave up and went to look for dried leaves, which he thought might catch better than the wood shavings.

For the first time since he'd ejected from the Triumph, he had some luck.

The leaves caught right away, then the shavings, and soon flames licked the growing darkness, shadows dancing on the canyon walls. He found a flat stone for the water bottle to sit on, and he placed it just beyond the reach of the flames. In minutes the water within the stainless-steel bottle was bubbling out its narrow mouth, and Drew moved it away from the fire. Ten minutes after that he was drinking lukewarm water.

He drank slowly, just a few sips at first, and when he didn't feel any adverse effects, he drank deep, leaving only a few ounces for morning. Drew looked out the mouth of the gorge at the dark expanse of jungle he'd trekked through, and thoughts of more water filled his mind. The fire popped and cracked, Drew's eyes closed, and he dozed off.

4

The ground trembled and Drew came awake. Plumes of black smoke poured off the fire's dying flames, and a rasping gurgle echoed through the ravine. A massive shadow fell on the wall of the chasm, an elongated head with triangular spikes cutting down its center. A cough-sniff, and the ground shook again as the mighty beast came forward.

Drew didn't move. His back was to a boulder, and he was partly hidden in shadow, the glow of the fire fading at his feet. The knife was in its sheath, the water bottle hanging from the suit via its carabiner. The spacesuit helmet was on the hardpan beside him, the remainder of the ejection seat harness wrapped within.

He inched out his hand and gathered up the helmet.

Two glowing eyes appeared and disappeared in the rolling waves of black smoke that blended into the stygian darkness. Moonlight angled into the ravine, and the fire flickered as a gust of wind tore away the smoke, revealing a full-grown apex predator.

The beast stood twenty-feet tall and was at least fifty feet from the end of its elongated snout to the tip of its powerful snake-like tail. Its slick skin was black with streaks that looked white in the dim light, one of which twisted up the creature's muscular neck. Powerful shoulders bulged from beneath taut skin, and the dinosaur's forelimbs were large and stocky, three sharp taloned digits on each claw. Tall neural shield-like spines marched up the beast's back, the long sail-like spines largest at the center of the beast's back and shrinking in size as they fanned out to the tip of the creature's tail and to the top of the beast's head.

The dinosaur's narrow snout fell open, rows of conical teeth glinting in the waning light. The beast swung its slender head, sniffing, its searchlight eyes falling on Drew. The beast threw back its head and roared, an earsplitting scream of anger and dominance that echoed off the stone walls.

Drew vaulted to his feet and ran deeper into the ravine, darkness engulfing him.

The ground shook, growling and huffing filling the canyon as he threw himself forward, helmet in hand, perspiration dripping down his face. Boulders appeared in the darkness, tough cactus-like plants sticking from every hole and crevice.

He ran into a massive spider web, its silky strands sticking to his face. Drew powered through it, arms up, helmet out before him like a shield.

The ravine narrowed, and more rocks appeared on the canyon floor, large boulders running along the walls. Darkness filled the ravine, the sliver of moonlight above the only indication that Drew wasn't underground.

The hardpan trembled, the crack of tumbling rocks like thunder, dust clouding the air, but the time between each footstep had lengthened, and the huffing and growling of the beast had faded.

He spared a glance over his shoulder and saw nothing in the inky darkness.

Drew's foot snagged on a stone, and he pitched forward, arms out to break his fall. Sticky spider web tightened on his face and sweat ran down his back as he hit the ground in a tangle, pain radiating out to his extremities. He heard the rip of fabric and a jarring pain rocked his right leg, his shin smacking a stone. Drew sucked back a scream, hot blood dripping down his leg into his boot.

The ground shook, but the rumble was faint.

He rolled onto his back and crab walked deeper into the canyon as he stared into the darkness. Of the dinosaur there was no sign except its rancid stink which hung in the air and drove out the smell of woodsmoke. Drew's shin throbbed and bitched, but as he gazed up at the line of gray light marking the lip of the chasm, hope flooded through him. The top of the ravine was much closer than it had been.

Drew forced himself to his feet, and he found a spot behind a stone that sat within a column of moonlight. He felt his leg and found a large rip in the spacesuit. Until he could repair the hole, the spacesuit was useless except to keep the insects from dining on him. He unsheathed the knife and stabbed it into the hardpan, then slipped off the suit.

The right leg of his blue jumpsuit was black with blood. He pulled up the pantleg, revealing a bloody gash just below his knee. It hurt like a bitch, its throbbing accompanying his galloping heart. He cut away the jumpsuit, being careful not to touch the cut with the dirty blade.

Drew knew he couldn't allow the wound to fester. Just like the air quality, and parasites and microbes in the water, plants, and animals, an open wound was an invitation to disaster. He cut two clean pieces of fabric from an arm of the jumpsuit, one for a bandage, and another as a rag. He wet the cloth with some of the remaining water, and with the darkness pressing in on him, the hoots, shrieks, moans, and buzzing of the night symphony leaking down the ravine, he cleaned the cut.

The gash throbbed, but the bleeding had mostly stopped, and Drew realized the abundance of blood had made the cut look much worse than it was. When he'd cleaned the wound the best he could, he cut the wet cloth into two strips, and laid the second piece of fabric over the cut. Then he tied the bandage off with the strips of fabric and leaned back against the ravine wall.

Drew jerked forward, the memory of the spider web elbowing its way to the front of his mental line. He examined the fissures and hollows in the stone behind him, found nothing, and leaned back again.

Most people, himself included, thought only of dinosaurs when considering the Cretaceous period, when in fact there was a variety of mammals and insect life, many similar to the creatures that inhabited the Earth in present day. Spiders had been around for three hundred million years, flies two hundred and forty million years, mosquitoes seventy-nine million.

Even though the suit's climate control system wouldn't be operational, Drew decided he'd be able to sleep better with the suit and helmet on. The thought of snakes, bugs—who the hell knew what—creeping over his face as he slept was too much to bare.

So he put the spacesuit back on, again, pulled on his boots and gloves, and secured the helmet, red writing and numbers scrolling across the face shield.

Suit integrity has been compromised. Life support system down. Climate acclimation system down. Bio rhythm—

"Got it," Drew barked. "Cease update."

The mechanical voice fell still.

Drew wedged himself between a boulder and the wall of the gorge, making himself small. Pain ran through him as he pulled in his legs, laid his helmeted head on his knees, and closed his eyes. The dull roar of the creatures of the night sang their disjointed tune, his wound throbbing in unison with his charging heart. For the second time on this night, Drew drifted into a troubled sleep.

Sunlight angled into the ravine, a thin layer of dust covering the helmet's face shield, and when Drew woke, he thought he was home. As he climbed from sleep, hunger pains churning his stomach, his reality came crashing down on him like the worst hangover he'd ever had. The crash, the parachutes, the smoke from the ship's wreckage, the Mosasaur, and the massive shadow of the prior night.

He leaned forward, rolled his shoulders, and cracked his neck. The ravine was much narrower than he'd thought, and only ten feet separated the walls. Tumbled stones littered the ground, and there were footholds and ledges he could use to climb out. He got to his feet, his leg wound throbbing, but he was able to put full weight on it. The squeak and trill of beast song floated down the gorge, and he considered backtracking, maybe all the way to the lake. He needed food, water, and he drew out one of the two starvation fruits he'd picked.

The white raspberry-like fruit had been crushed, its avocado shape now flat, but it hadn't busted open. His stomach growled, but he put the fruit away. He was desperate, but not that desperate, and the thought of backtracking and giving up all the distance he'd fought for seemed crazy, but there was no way to know when he'd get water again. Still, what real purpose would going back to the lake serve? Yes, he'd get more water, but then he'd have to drink it to get back to the cliff face. He could spend the rest of his life making that circular trip.

No. He needed to press on. The only hope was getting to the ship.

He drank some water, leaving only a mouthful, and put the helmet back on and stood at the base of the wall, planning his path, each foothold, every ledge. There were two spots that looked particularly challenging, and Drew wasn't sure he'd be able to get past them with the awkward spacesuit hampering him.

Tension stroked the cords of his nerves. He really didn't want to expose his bare feet to the stone, and what might be hiding within, so he decided to attempt the climb with the suit on, even the helmet. If he fell, perhaps it would cushion his fall. He knew the helmet was crash rated, so at least he'd be alert and cognizant when he died.

He tied together the two pieces of the ejection seat harness, and that gave him roughly ten feet of belt to use as rope. Drew flung the belt over a shoulder, checked the knife in its sheath, and mounted a large boulder pressed against the ravine wall.

It took an hour, and several times Drew had to use the knife as a piton to secure the harness line. Climbing in the cumbersome spacesuit boots did prove difficult, but he managed. When he reached the top, he was panting, and as he rolled over the lip of the ravine onto his back a wave of relief ran through him.

It didn't last long.

Giant slabs of ancient stone formed huge natural steps that led down to a thick jungle, the spaces between the rocks packed with barbwire-like plants. Tiny lizards darted around, flies divebombed his face shield, and odd lizard-like birds sprayed from the forest. Beyond the tangle of conifers, ferns, and broad leave trees, a gray mountain range cut across the distant horizon, its peaks disappearing into the clouds. Thick underbrush packed the ground, but several animal trails crisscrossed the carpet of green.

"Increase magnification one hundred percent."

Drew scanned the jungle below, saw only the deep green of the forest canopy and the occasional dirt strip. Beasts trundled along the paths, dust clouds obscuring the creatures. He was beginning to despair when his gaze ranged over a trail of bent and broken trees that angled through the jungle. He followed its path, and something glistened in the sunlight.

"Increase magnification one hundred and fifty percent."

Buried beneath a tangle of broken trees, torn up plants, and dirt, the gleam of metal could be seen. The ship.

Drew hooted like he'd won some prize, but gloom settled over him as he calculated the distance to the wreckage. It was at least ten miles. And none of the animal paths he saw went anywhere near the site, though one of them crossed the path of destruction laid down by the crashing ship. He stood there a long time, gazing down into the jungle, the heat of isolation leaking through him as he tried to memorize the primordial roadmap.

His parents hadn't wanted him to come on the mission, and it wasn't only that they'd never see him again regardless of whether the mission was successful or not. No, it was much more than that. They hadn't believed in Dr. Lokker, thought he was a nutter. A rich nutter, and Drew hadn't been able to resist the lure of visiting Earth's ancient past, seeing the famous dinosaurs in their habitat. The doctor had gotten him to the Cretaceous, so Mom and Dad had been wrong to some degree. As to the rest of it, his eyes found the gleam of the spaceship again, perhaps they'd been right.

Drew sat on a nearby stone, and said, "Increase external auditory sensor."

A splash of static, and the buzz of the jungle increased, the push of the wind like crashing waves. He listened hard and filtered all that out. Drew smiled, the faint tinkle of water echoed beneath the crush of the jungle noise. He closed his eyes, slowly turning his head in the direction of the running water.

When he opened his eyes, he was facing southeast, and he picked a large tree to mark the direction. Drew grabbed a twig and sketched a crude map in the hardpan before him, cementing the layout of the land before him in his mind. The trail that led to the crash route, the wreckage, the major animal paths, and the direction of the water. He stared at his work, committing it to memory before noting the position of the sun and descending the natural stone steps to the cover of the jungle.

5

It was dim and shadowy beneath the thick tree canopy. The hardpan between the tightly packed trees was studded with stones, and the underbrush was swollen with weeds and vines that had stiletto-sized thorns and large red leaves running along their lengths. Creepers climbed the trees and choked out the other plants in their endless search for light, and the gentle sound of water gurgling over stones carried on the breeze, accompanied by his footfalls that crunched dead leaves as he cut through the vegetation.

Drew's mouth was dry as cotton, the swallow of water he'd had upon waking a distant memory. His leg muscles were cramped and tight, and despite getting some sleep, a debilitating weariness bled through him.

Ants and beetle-like insects crawled over the toes of his boots, and every few seconds a loud cackle would erupt over the jungle cacophony. It was as if invisible kittens frolicked within the undergrowth, and it took several minutes of standing still before Drew caught a glimpse of the chipmunk-like beasts. They had black fur and yellow eyes, and the prehistoric varmints darted about so fast they were a blur.

The sound of running water grew louder, and thin fingers of mist pushed through the jungle like smoke. The cooing and clicking of animals floated from the mist. Where there was water, there were beasts.

Drew slowed and picked his way around trees. He ceased hacking at the underbrush, and instead moved with more stealth, slipping under huge elephant ear leaves, and avoiding vines and stubby weeds with long white flowers. He tried to maintain his southeast heading, but it was difficult because he was constantly shifting his course to avoid trees and thickets of dense vegetation. Green moss covered the northern side of some of the rocks and trees, which helped.

When Drew reached the thin river, he almost missed it. The stream was nothing more than a trickle of water running through a mostly dry riverbed of gray stones covered in dried yellow moss. The river ran southeast, and he followed the trail of water until the stream disappeared below ground.

Given the recent geological upheaval, the source of the water was most likely a spring deep underground. He found a spot where the thin stream of water, no bigger than a weak bathroom faucet, spilled over a flat stone and he filled his bottle.

With the sun obscured by the thick tree canopy, Drew set about starting a fire. Despite the learning curve, it took twice as long to spark a tiny flame than the day before. All the twigs and even the dead leaves were damp from the moisture bleeding off the stream, but he finally sparked a flame, and an hour later he'd knocked back three bottles of water, tended to his leg wound with hot cloth compresses, and prepared a bottle for the road like he was a newborn. He searched the tree canopy for coconuts—or something like them to make water containers out of, but then remembered coconuts weren't around in the Cretaceous, and he saw nothing else to serve that purpose.

Drew trekked along the riverbed, the water settling in his stomach like a rock. Acid crept up his throat, and though the hunger pains eased, his head thumped with a dull pain that sprinted up and down his spine, knotting his neck and lower back as he thought of the starvation fruit.

He hadn't gone far when he reached a clearing where a massive hardwood that looked like an oak tree had succumbed to rot, and its fallen trunk left a channel of destruction in the thick forest.

Within the clearing Drew saw the sun arcing toward noon to the south, and he determined the stream was still running roughly southeast, away from the cliff face. He called up the map he'd drawn in the dirt. If he was remembering correctly, there was a wide animal path east of his position, but to get to it he'd have to bushwack through the dense jungle.

The terrain reminded Drew of Madagascar, which was originally part of the ancient continent Gondwana. The island, together with India, pulled away from Africa a hundred-and-fifty million years ago, stretching and thinning the Earth's crust on the island's west coast before it finally snapped off. He recalled the escarpment of stone, the way the land cycled down to the feet of the tall mountains on the eastern horizon, and thought the land was similar to that ancient place, though the flora and fauna were different.

He decided to stick with the water source. If it petered out, so be it, but as long as he was moving in the general direction of the crash site he'd stay as close to the H2O as he could. It's strange how water had always been a given, always taken for granted, even when—

A faint tremor ran through the land, and the rocks in the riverbed clinked and tapped as they

vibrated. The thumps of giant footsteps thundered through the jungle, the crack and pop of stones like gunshots. The forest went still, and even the clouds of flies moved on.

Drew's heart fought to escape his chest, the approaching creature getting closer with each heartbeat.

The dry riverbed opened up ahead, and black sand with specks of sparkling quartz covered some of the stones and the ground in-between them, and only a dribble of water ran between the rocks.

A lizard-like head poked from the tree line that boxed in the stream, its golf ball-sized eyes searching, mouth hanging open in a smirk, dark gums sliding over rows of sharp teeth.

Drew eased back slowly, slipping behind a large fan leaf. Despite not knowing for certain exactly what spectrum of light the beast saw, he couldn't help but think his dirty white spacesuit would stand out against the deep green of the primordial vegetation like a leech on a baby's ass. He pictured himself with the suit off, covered in mud to hide his scent, and he almost laughed.

The beast's head dropped low to the ground as it sniffed, its dark eyes ranging down river.

Drew's skin crawled under that stare.

The dinosaur pushed from the trees onto the riverbed, rising to its full height, its long tail jetting out and tumbling stones and cracking tree branches. The creature looked like an adolescent T-rex, but there were so many species within the Tyrannosaur family that the beast could be any number of the T-rex's relatives.

Like the most famous theropod dinosaur, the beast balanced on two muscular hindlegs, its thick tail pressed to the riverbed for support. Two fingered hands hung from stunted arms, and claw-like feet with razor-sharp talons raked at the river stones as if the beast was spoiling to run. The thick black hindlegs supported a green, yellow, and black-streaked torso, and muscles heaved and pulled beneath leathery skin. The dinosaur's thick neck pointed down river, its head lurching back and forth in spasmodic jerks like a bird.

Moving as slowly as his jumping nerves would allow, Drew made sure his water bottle was hanging from its carabiner, checked the knife in its sheath, and wrapped the ejection seat harness over his shoulder. He felt the lumps of fruit in his suit pocket, and his thoughts ranged to steak, shrimp cocktail and wine, his imagination antagonizing his stomach which grumbled with hunger pains.

The T-rex eased back with two thunderous steps and bent over, its jaws chomping and searching the underbrush. The beast surged forward, pushing through the tree branches that hung over the riverbed, its powerful legs knocking aside stones.

Drew stayed still.

The dinosaur lowered its head, jaws flexing open and revealing sharp four-foot teeth. It roared, its hot breath stirring the leaves and twisting the vegetation. The beast bit at the air, and the snap of its jaws was too close for comfort.

Drew plunged into the forest, using the cover of the tightly packed trees, not paying attention to his direction, what lay before him, or what might be waiting within the dark confines of the jungle.

The dinosaur bellowed again, and rose to its full height, whipping its tail in a wide arc that cracked against a tree as Drew slipped through the forest.

Wood splintered, and tree branches fell all around Drew as he ran, leaves falling like rain. The earth shook, rocks smacked and cracked, and the pounding of great footfalls filled the world. Vines and leaves ripped at his faceplate and spacesuit, and each step became more labored.

Drew tripped over a tree root as thick as a python, and he tumbled to the ground, his leg wound wailing, his stomach in a knot. Thick green leaves hid him, and every impulse told Drew to get up and run. What if the beast stepped on him?

Full-grown T-rexes weighed upwards of seven tons, and this version, though much smaller, would still crush him like a bug. But then he remembered how tightly packed the forest was, and he heard no snapping trees, or the crunch of underbrush being trampled.

He looked back, but saw nothing except the underside of large yellow leaves with dark black veins running down their center and disappearing into a thick red petiole that ran to a stem the color of the sea.

The ground stopped trembling.

Drew pushed to his knees. Through the thick cluster of greenery, he saw the dinosaur standing at the center of the riverbed, its body shifting as it searched. The predator threw back its head and roared, but when Drew didn't run screaming from the forest, the beast turned away and continued down the stream, rocks clicking and snapping, the ground shaking again.

When the creature was gone Drew picked his way along the stones at the edge of the stream bed, steadily heading east. If his memory was right, he would hit an animal trail that ran diagonally southeast. The one that cut over the path of destruction left by the ship.

The stream bed broke up and the sound of running water died away. As he'd speculated, Drew figured there was a spring in the area, and hopefully there would be other streams throughout the jungle. The river that had supplied him with water hadn't been crowded with wildlife, which meant there were other, most likely better, options.

He sniffled. The rank smell of his body odor filled the spacesuit, and he longed to pull off the helmet and feel the hot wind on his face, but the enhanced vision was too helpful in the shadowlands beneath the tree canopy.

Stunted palm-like trees and huge ferns gave way to slender pine trees with branches that splayed out from thick trunks like spokes on a bicycle wheel. Drew considered climbing one of the taller trees to get his bearings and make sure he was going in the right direction. He couldn't afford to get lost, and his stomach growled for emphasis. Still, the climb had its dangers, and he was confident he was going in the right direction, so he decided against the climb. He could always change his mind if he got lost.

Drew wanted to boil the breadfruit when he made camp for the day, but to do that he needed a better vessel than his water bottle. He knew turtles of all sizes and types lived in the Cretaceous, and there were bones, pieces of tree bark, and other things that might be used to make a fireproof bowl, and he made a mental note to keep an eye out. That reminded him of his need for a stick to make a spear. Such a weapon might help him catch game, which he could char black to minimize the effects of possible contaminants.

He trudged on for three hours, slipping through the jungle instead of bushwhacking. He was forced to traverse fields of boulders embedded in the jungle, and several times he had to change direction to avoid nasty thickets of vegetation and stands of evergreens and tropical broadleaf trees packed so close together a snake couldn't get through them.

The sun started its fall to the horizon, pinpricks of orange light leaking through the tree canopy, when Drew hit the animal path he was looking for. It was definitely a thoroughfare, and as he inched from the jungle, his thigh wound screaming in protest, Drew slipped off his helmet, pulled off his gloves, and drank some water. The faint smell of burnt rubber carried on the breeze.

Dust hung over the trail, the scent of rot carrying on the oven-like breeze. He buttoned up his suit, including the helmet, checked his meager belongings, looked in both directions like he was crossing the street, and headed southeast on the trail that would take him one step closer to finding the ship.

6

A great braying and squawking and roaring thundered from the forest, and Drew was forced to leave the animal trail several times to avoid larger predators. Insects, mammals, and lizards of all shapes and sizes went about their daily business, the food chain rattling. Pterosaurs shrieked above the tree canopy, the static of crashing water filtering through the jungle.

The Cretaceous was teeming with life, all the beasts blissfully unaware of the giant space rock barreling toward Earth that would end the party. If the bigheads' calculations had been correct, that extinction event wouldn't occur for several million years, but bending time isn't an exact science, even he knew that.

Drew was sweating profusely when he arrived at the watering hole, which was picturesque in its magnificence, like an illustration in a children's book. This was no muddy hole with brackish water. A thin waterfall cascaded through loosely packed stones into a pond, the edge of which was packed with beasts of all types. If it wasn't for the constant threat of predators, a casual observer would think all of nature was in harmony here. While that was true, harmony meant different things depending on the situation, and the circle of life was harmony in its purest form.

He found a large fern with wide leaves and planted himself beneath it where he had a good view of the pond. He took off his helmet and drank some water, leaving only a mouthful. His hair was soaking wet and matted to his head, and his tattered blue jumpsuit was drenched through. Clouds of mist rolled off the pond, the falls knifing into clear water as Drew's body cooled.

A lizard the size of a cat bolted through the foliage on its hind legs and hissed at Drew as it tore into the thick underbrush and disappeared.

His nerves danced on a wire, oppressive heat forcing all the moisture from his body. The ejection seat harness fell off his shoulder and clattered to the hardpan. He stared at it like it was a snake, his stomach in a knot from the water, his weary mind struggling to pull up information that was right below the surface.

He could use the belt as a tourniquet. If he tied it off above the tear in the suit, he might seal it enough to restore suit integrity, which would allow the climate control system to function.

A fight broke out along the watering hole, two giant bird beasts pecking and swiping at each other. There was no way he could get water, and starting a fire was out of the question. He judged he had three hours of daylight left, and as he'd already decided, Drew had no intention of walking around the prehistoric world in the dark with no weapons except a knife. He'd love to take a swim, but this location was probably a twenty-four-hour rest stop, and eventually the big boys would arrive.

It was too early to make camp, so Drew decided to push on. He wrapped what was left of the ejection seat harness around his calf, just above his leg wound and the tear in the suit, right below the knee. He pulled the harness tight, but not so tight that it would impede blood flow.

Drew clamped on his helmet, and the suit computer came to life. The helmet fan whirred, the usually annoying buzz a welcome sound.

Suit integrity is at eighty-one percent and rising. Bio—
"That'll do."

Like going outside in summer and then coming home to a house cooled by air-conditioning, a chill ran through Drew as he slinked into the jungle and followed the edge of the animal trail. His wet jumpsuit was icy, and he shivered, but the chill didn't last long. Fifteen minutes of hiking through the dense forest left the suit struggling to keep up. Drew tightened the strap on his leg every few minutes, and that helped, but the suit was struggling to maintain temperature.

It was still better than no suit. The spacesuit boots were cumbersome, but their soles were thick, and he didn't need to worry about what he might step on. Flies, mosquitoes, and a host of dragonfly-like beasts buzzed his helmet and alighted on the suit, and his skin itched at the thought of getting bitten.

Hunger was his constant companion, thoughts of the nasty white raspberry-like breadfruit he carried in his pocket like a splinter in his brain. Soon, he told himself. Soon.

When the sound of running water fell to a faint tinkle, Drew left the path and headed northeast, where he hoped to run across the stream that supplied the watering hole. The western horizon was buried behind the tall trees, but Drew knew the sun sat on the western horizon because of the way the orange light angled through the tree canopy.

When he came across the stream gurgling through the forest, gray dusk had settled over the land. Drew hadn't found a good place to camp. There were no fallen trees, no crags in the piles of boulders. It would take too much time and energy to construct a shelter, so he decided to start his fire, eat, and drink, then climb into one of the large conifers and make a simple platform in its boughs. Being off the ground had its advantages, though based on what he'd seen so far, there were plenty of creatures that could pluck him from the tree like a ripe apple.

The stream was running strong, the water clear and cold, but the stones above the waterline were covered in dried yellow moss, which told Drew the river sometimes ran higher. The dried moss made it easy to light a fire, and as the inky darkness settled over the jungle Drew prepared and drank three bottles of water.

He'd been unable to find a turtle shell, or similar vessel to cook the starvation fruit, so Drew decided to use the water bottle. It would be a hassle, but he had no other options.

The outer skin of the starvation fruit was crushed, but there was a thin layer of dense skin, almost a shell, just beneath the fruit's white dimpled skin. He used the knife to cut the fruit in half, its white bread-like insides dotted with large dark seeds. The cut fruit smelled like dirty socks and yeast. Drew cut strips of the stuff and stuffed the pieces into the water bottle. When he'd filled the container with as much of the fruit as he could, he added water from the stream and put the bottle next to the heat.

Drew was no oatmeal fan, even when brown sugar, cinnamon, and other flavor enhancers were added, but the brown goop that oozed from the water bottle tasted better than any oatmeal he'd ever had. The stuff thickened to a glue-like paste as it cooled, but the issue was easily resolved by adding more water.

He slurped down three batches of bread goo, rinsed the bottle, prepared fresh water for the morning, and put out the fire. Drew put his helmet and gloves back on and leaned against a tree trunk, relaxing, the helmet fan purring, the suit having an easier time maintaining temperature now that the sun had gone down.

The trill of the night symphony filtered into the helmet as the creatures of the day gave way to the beasts of the night, and roars and answering calls rang through the primordial blackness. His stomach hurt with the familiar pains of having eaten after not having eaten in a long time, but the feeling passed, and relief flooded through him. At least now he knew he could eat the fruit when properly sanitized by cooking, though Drew hadn't seen any more of the unique cactus-like trees that bore the starvation fruit.

Drew had the onboard computer do a complete status report, and other than the suit being at eighty-three percent integrity everything was within normal parameters. He secured the knife and mounted the lowest branch of the tree he'd selected.

The climb, though only fifteen feet or so, was arduous and tiring. His limbs felt like they were filled with concrete, the breadfruit settling in his stomach like a brick. A good brick, but still a brick.

He didn't want to be too far from the ground in case he somehow managed to fall from his perch while sleeping, so he'd chosen a conifer with thick branches that splayed off the trunk at even intervals. Each branch was roughly a foot above the one below it, and about twenty degrees around the trunk as the branches climbed up the tree.

Drew chose two branches that were close together because the tree next to it had encroached into its space. He didn't want to expend unnecessary calories, but he needed to reinforce the natural platform created by the two branches.

Using the saw back of the utility knife, Drew cut three branches. It took an hour, Drew's arms turning to jelly, his head ringing with exertion, but as stark moonlight filtered through the trees, he was able to comfortably sprawl across his bed of evergreen branches fifteen feet above the hardpan.

Moonlight shone like a spotlight through a gap in the tree canopy, and Drew focused on it like it was a window to another world. Clouds fleeted past, and stars twinkled against the deep black backdrop. With no light pollution, the night sky was crystal clear. His stomach grumbled, but it was a call of digestion, not hunger pains or food poisoning.

The jungle was alive around him, and branches snapped, leaves rustled and tore, and beneath it all the steady vibration in the earth as the predators of the night stalked their prey.

A primal wail of pain, chuffing and crying, then the crack of bones breaking followed by the rip and tear of meat. A low growl carried through the tree canopy. Another beast was attempting to home in on someone else's kill.

Drew closed his eyes, and though his nerves trembled, and the purring of the helmet fan sounded like a chainsaw, he was so exhausted, sleep took him.

The French Quarter reeked with the intoxicating aromas of baking bread and charred meat. The crowd sauntering along the sidewalk was lost in their merrymaking, yellow light shining on them from classical light fixtures that hung from ornately decorated black poles. Drew had never been to New Orleans before, and he was uncertain he was going in the right direction. He asked an older woman carrying a bag of groceries and she said she'd never heard of the bar he was looking for, The Snail.

He tapped his temple and brought up his retinal display, the glowing rectangle of a holographic screen appearing in the air before him. He called up the Zap he'd gotten from Dr. Lokker and expanded the attached directions. Not only was he going the right way, the place was close.

Cars floated along the street in bumper-to-bumper traffic, crowds of partygoers leaking onto the road from the packed sidewalks. He was looking for an alleyway called Escargot Lane, and he never would've found it had it not been for a small black sandwich board with the picture of a white snail on it. There was no name, no list of specials, or any contact information, just the snail holding what looked to be a martini with an olive.

The alley was dark, and the braying and laughing of the crowd died away, the smooth sound of jazz piano pushing down the lane like a gust of wind. Murals of huge dinosaurs and ancient woolly mammoths covered the red brick of the buildings that pressed in on the lane. There were doors with numbers on them, but they appeared to lead to private residences. Deep in the darkness, at the far end of the side street, a white neon snail blinked in the blackness.

Drew inched down the alley, the sound of music growing stronger.

Like its sandwich board, The Snail had no identifying marks except the snail. The door was red, and small porthole-like windows stood on both sides of it. He pushed the door open and slipped inside.

His senses were assaulted by cigar smoke and the smell of stale beer. Soft lighting glowed in the ceiling, and a long bar ran down one side, a line of booths down the other. Professor Lokker waved him over, and the doctor called over a waitress.

Drew sat, ordered a whiskey, and waited.

After a bit of research Drew learned that Dr. Lokker was a rich and famous archaeologist who studied ancient civilizations. He believed a civilization of homo sapiens had existed during the Cretaceous, and when he reached out to Drew, he'd claimed to have proof.

Drew was a fossil mercenary that specialized in logistically difficult extractions, and he was one of the best on any planet. Given the doctor's world-famous reputation, Drew was surprised the old man had sought him out because Drew did whatever needed to be done to secure the prize, and sometimes that got messy.

The whiskey arrived and Drew took a long pull, still waiting for the old man to speak. The guy was bent and withered by time, but he appeared spry as he lifted his drink and took a sip.

The low murmur of the bar settled over them and still Drew said nothing.

"So, you're wondering why you're here?"

Drew nodded.

Lokker reached down and lifted a photograph off the seat beside him and slid it across the table.

The picture was of a mountain, tall peaks filling the background. In the foreground, a group of people excavated a structure from the gray stone of the mountainside.

"So?" Drew said.

"That structure is at least eighty million years old."

"That's not poss—" Drew's head snapped up to find the old man smiling at him in the half-light.

7

Morning in the jungle was a gray haze of twilight, stray sunray spotlights, and ghostly shadows. The creatures of the night slithered and crawled into their lairs, and the beasts of the sun rose to greet another day of survival. The clear blue sky was a distant memory, hidden by a thick ceiling of green life that fought for every sunbeam. Vines competed with trees for supremacy, while giant ferns, mosses, and broad-leafed weeds shared the ground, which was perpetually drenched in a netherworld of dusk.

As his small fire heated water, Drew did a search of the area looking for starvation fruit trees. He didn't find any, but he tracked the scent of rot and the intense buzz of insects that carried on the wind.

Downstream half a click from the conifer Drew had slept in, beneath a fallen fern, Drew found the remains of the beast he'd heard killed the prior night. It was the size of a large dog, its snout longer and thinner, and an armor plate jutted vertically from the center of the beast's crushed skull. The creature's torso had no plating, and cracked ribs stuck through jet black fur. Entrails spilled onto the loam that covered the jungle floor, the corpse partly obscured by a thick cloud of insects. Long claw marks raked across the beast's hindquarter, and both rear legs had been torn free and were nowhere to be seen. The meat reeked of rot, so even if the stuff had been safe to eat, it was already spoiled.

The helmet fan whirred, and his leg wound throbbed. The cut was doing fine and had scabbed over, and pain no longer shot up his leg with each step. Beyond the animal corpse to the east the trees were spaced further apart, tall palm-like behemoths that rose two hundred feet, large fan leaves packing the tree canopy. He increased the face shield's magnification and saw that the undergrowth was also thinner.

Drew called up his mental map. If he struck out east, he should hit the trail of destruction left by the crashing ship.

Purified water bubbled up the neck of the water bottle when he got back to camp, and he let it cool while he found and trimmed a straight six-foot branch. The wood was green, had a one-inch diameter, and it was strong, the pole hardly flexing when he swung it like a staff. It was a simple thing using a piece of the ejection seat harness to secure the knife to the staff's end, and when he was done, he had a spear-knife with longer reach he could use to fend off smaller animals and perhaps nab some meat.

He drank, imagining it was tea with a shot of bourbon and cream, his thoughts drifting to his dream the prior night. The images had been so clear, so vivid, like he'd been in the rustic bar just yesterday. When had the meeting taken place? Drew couldn't recall exactly. All he could remember was wanting to go on the mission so badly he hadn't heard much else he'd been told that day.

Drew managed to force out a weak stream of urine, and with the warm water bottle dangling from its suit carabiner, he pulled on his helmet and got the standard status report. The connection with the Triumph hadn't been restored. He rested the knife-spear on his shoulder and followed the riverbed until he passed the rotting corpse, then worked his way into the forest.

The undergrowth had been flattened in spots. Morning mist hovered above the ground, the chill of night still hanging in the air. Something big had slithered through the jungle. He knelt, examining a section of ground. Drew had seen gators make similar markings. They left flattened vegetation as they half-slithered, half-walked, but this beaten trail was wide.

A gentle breeze heavy with the scents of earth and rot rattled leaves and stroked the undergrowth, and a sharp hissing leaked through the jungle. Drew searched his memory and concluded the trail could only have been created by the fabled Titanoboa, one of the largest snakes to have ever slithered on the surface of Earth. The fossil record suggested Titanoboa thrived for most of the age of reptiles, and that the creatures grew to upwards of fifty feet long and could weigh over two thousand pounds. It thrived in warm climates, and though Titanoboa was considered an apex predator, Drew knew the creatures were more complex and lived in greater numbers than originally believed.

The hissing sound drowned out the rumble and buzz of the jungle. Ahead, the woods ended at a clearing, and Drew's breath caught in his throat like a chicken bone.

The clearing was roughly the size of a sports field, and the area had gone through some type of geological upheaval. Drew thought perhaps the area had been a tar pit, or quicksand back when Pangea was dividing the world like a pie, and the Earth belched through its crust. The ground was a mix of black and brown sand, and creepers reached out from the forest and ran over the charred earth.

At the center of the clearing, coiled like the thickest piece of rope Drew had ever seen was a huge snake. Its serpentine body undulated as it sucked down something hidden by its massive girth. The beast was at least forty feet long, and its black and brown skin rippled as prey passed down its gullet.

Drew dropped to a knee and peered through a huge fern.

The snake's head jetted upward, shards of thick brown shell flying. The creature was dining on eggs, and suddenly everything made sense.

Sauropods and other species laid their eggs in nests spanning several hundred miles, so the eggs would've been like meatballs for the snake. It was common for Sauropods, Triceratops, and other types of dinosaurs to bury their eggs in loose sand and cover them in a thin layer of sediment or dead vegetation such as leaves.

The ground trembled, and a loud *snap* reverberated over the jungle.

The hissing ceased, and the massive snake turned its head, its doorknob-sized obsidian eyes searching for the source of the noise.

A Triceratops poked its armored head through the ferns, thick horns curved to the sky, its eyes dark balls rimmed in white. The three curved horns were the size of a man's arm and they protruded from the dark green shield that surrounded its head, thick legs supporting a huge sagging torso.

Drew stayed still. Most likely it had been his noisy trek through the jungle that had aroused the Triceratops interest. The dinosaur shrieked, the piggish call ending in a high-pitched wail that sounded like a horse whinnying. The beast jerked its head up and down, stomping its right foot as if preparing to charge. It roared again, inched forward, and threw its head in the air and snorted.

The Titanoboa appeared unimpressed, and the snake's eyes locked on the Triceratops, its forked tongue lashing out like a bullwhip.

Triceratops was an herbivore, but mothers and their young broke through all normal barriers, and with a thunderous roar, the huge, armored dinosaur lunged forward, its massive spikes surging up and down as it crossed the clearing.

Whether the giant snake had eaten its fill, or it just didn't want to tangle with the tank of a creature, the Titanoboa lifted its narrow flat head and hissed at the gray monster barreling across the black and brown sand. The gigantic snake uncoiled and slithered into the forest with a speed that surprised Drew given the creature's size.

The Triceratops skidded to a stop before its destroyed nest. The armored beast was the size of a full-size SUV, and the beast hung its enormous head. Puffs and squeaks emanated from the beast, then it threw back its head and wailed, the sound unmistakably sorrowful.

It was time to leave, because Drew didn't want to be the next living thing the Triceratops saw after finding its destroyed nest and the remnants of its eggs.

The iconic beast stood with its huge, armored head down, stomping its feet and kicking up dust and grit.

As Drew moved through the forest the Triceratops saw him, the eyes on the sides of its head giving the creature excellent peripheral vision. Drew was protected by the densely packed trees, yet he still felt exposed with eight tons of muscle, horns, and aggression aimed in his direction.

The beast growled and rumbled toward him.

Exploding earth and sand filtered through the trees and passed over Drew like a gust of wind as the dinosaur slammed into the forest. A cacophony of cracking wood and fleeing creatures echoed through the woods as the Triceratops' massive shield got stuck between two tree trunks. The beast churned forward like a locomotive, digging into the wood and tearing up the ground. The trees bent and swayed, but didn't break.

Drew bolted into the underbrush, juking around trees, fronds lashing the face shield. The rumble of the Triceratops faded, and the ferns thinned as he ran on.

When the ground no longer vibrated beneath his feet and the sounds of pursuit had died away, Drew stopped to rest beneath the boughs of a tall evergreen that rose above the surrounding fern trees like an overbearing parent. His stomach screamed for food, his knees pulsed with pain, and his leg wound thumped in rhythm with his pounding heart. He popped off the helmet and drank some water, his stomach gurgling and whining like a baby sucking on a rubber nipple. Tiny white stars danced across his vision, and shadows slithered through the undergrowth.

He trekked east for most of the day, the angle of the sunrays fighting through the tree canopy growing shallow as they marked the passing hours. Each step hurt his legs, every joint protesting, hunger pains wracking his body. He'd seen no starvation fruit trees, and he cursed himself for not picking more when he'd had the chance. Squirrel-like beasts with rat-like furless tails and dark beady eyes raced around beneath the underbrush, and Drew thought if he had the energy, he might be able to catch one, but he felt like he might fall on his face at any moment.

Narrow escarpments of stone only a few feet high cut through the jungle, the green moss-covered black stone barely visible within the greenery that packed the forest floor. Broad leaf plants that thrived in shade and grew with minimal water filled every empty space, the ancient parents of the hard to kill hostas and calla lilies. White orchid-like flowers grew from the cruxes of trees, and dried lichen hung like gray hair on some of the lower branches.

The forest gave way to devastation. Claw prints large and small marked the ground, and several smaller animals paused to stare as Drew inched from the jungle.

Insects hummed and buzzed, and a ribbon of blue cloud-filled sky could be seen over the ship's trail of destruction. Huge creatures with tent-like wings glided in circles above, and rodents, small dog-like animals like the corpse he'd seen, and several plump duck-billed Hadrosaurids watched him like he'd just dropped from space.

8

Bulky beasts with long, laterally flattened tails and heads with duck-like beaks and round cranial crests studied Drew, heads bobbing as the smaller creatures scurried back into the jungle. The planteaters were large, the size of juvenile elephants, and Drew thought the beasts were a genus of Hadrosaurids, perhaps Edmontosaurus, which was among the largest of the Hadrosaurids. Like others of its kind, the creatures' forelegs were smaller and less muscular than their hind legs, but they were long enough to be used in standing or moving on all fours. The beasts had brown skin, with green stripes running down their backs, and long flat blade-like bones rose parallel from the beasts' spine. The herbivores' skulls were roughly triangular, with the front forming a spoon-bill shape. The beak was toothless, but Drew knew there were teeth for munching vegetation in the creature's upper cheeks.

The planteaters screeched and bitched at each other. Drew wanted to tell them to keep it down. He was dead on his feet and the last thing he wanted to do was draw attention.

The trail of destruction ran southeast, a plowed freeway of broken and torn up trees, crushed underbrush, and knotted vines. There was no question which way the crashing ship had been traveling. All the bent vegetation and fallen trees pointed southeast, dark burn marks standing out on some of the tree trunks like black scars. The scent of burnt rubber and wood pervaded the air, and birds played and fought, flying beasts of all sizes spraying from the jungle and darting across the clearing like deer traversing an interstate. Birds evolved from the early dinosaurs, and along with the horseshoe crab are direct descendants of prehistoric creatures that still inhabit the Earth in the present day.

Drew stared down the trail, enhancing magnification of the face shield to maximum, but there were too many fallen trees and bunches of tangled vegetation, and he couldn't see the ship.

The planteaters stood watching him, not coming closer, but not backing away. Drew was something new, an oddity, and the creatures were most likely judging what to do about the stranger, if anything. Yes, he was a shiny new thing, but he was their size, and as far as he knew, the dinosaurs didn't eat meat.

The red parachutes floated through his thoughts like a dream just beyond reach at waking. He had seen them, and he now knew they'd been traveling east, so theoretically they should have landed closer to the crash site. If they were theoretically alive.

He turned three hundred and sixty degrees, scanning the jungle and eyeing the pack of Edmontosaurus, who appeared content to let him make the first move. Drew activated the suit's external annunciator system and yelled, "Hello! Anybody? Hello?"

The insects didn't pause in their trilling, the birds frolicked and chirped, and the creatures of the Cretaceous went about their day like strange spacemen walked amongst them every day.

He went through the ritual of drinking water, tending his wound, but he decided to hold off on making a fire in hopes of finding more starvation fruit, or better still, the ship. Drew eased down the plowed path, climbing over cracked and split tree trunks, and blazing a trail through scorched greenery.

The ground trembled faintly, and a roar echoed over the jungle. It sounded too close for Drew's liking, and he picked up his pace, sweat dripping down his back, the hum of the helmet fan trying to keep up a constant static, like a fly caught in his ear.

Drew had only gone about half a mile when he found a chunk of burnt and twisted metal at the center of the blackened trail. Burned leaves and twigs crunched under his spacesuit boots as he went to examine the metal. It appeared to be one of the ship's heat shields, which he knew covered the underside of the Triumph like scales.

A cry, like a huge chicken in pain, pierced the day, and Drew snaped his head around in search of the noise.

The group of Edmontosaurus was following him, hiding behind fallen trees, their heads bouncing around like birds. The beasts squawked and brayed, their calls becoming more aggressive with each strident step they took, and as the ground trembled beneath his feet, Drew took cover.

Wind gusted down the trail, stirring the vegetation.

The ground stopped trembling and the pack of herbivores froze, their brown and green skin rippling.

Drew eased further into the shadows.

The planteaters stood a hundred feet away, and with the show seemingly over, the beasts turned their attention back to gathering food, and judging by the size of the beasts, they needed a lot of it. A baby elephant can consume over five hundred pounds of food per day. The creatures strode around, pulling leaves from the flattened vegetation, unaware of the danger Drew felt creeping down his spine like a disease.

The midday sun angled onto the path of destruction and bird song carried over the scene like a lullaby.

On the opposite side of the path a tall creature stood within the shadowed tree line at the edge of the trail, its glowing hockey puck-sized eyes sparkling with hunger and eagerness. The bulbous eyes hung in the vegetation thirty feet above the ground, and they were the only sign the beast was there, its green scaly skin perfectly camouflaged. The huge eyes constantly shifted, scanning the area, tracking the herbivores who were still blissfully unaware of the predator.

The T-rex came forward with a burst of violence, a glassy-eyed monster that bounded from the underbrush, a streak of green. The lurking Tyrannosaurus Rex was bigger than a tractor-trailer, and at least forty-feet long from its nose to the tip of its elongated snout. The ground shook like thunder, the beast's massive hindlegs churning as the creature exploded onto the path. A mangy fuzz covered the beast's back, its alligator skin covered in quill-like spikes that looked like the beginnings of feathers. Dark black streaks ran across the beast's torso and down its long muscular tail, and the T-rex's stocky legs pumped, its short muscular arms meek and absurd by comparison.

Drew's mouth fell open. The T-rex was the tyrant king, the largest land predator to ever live on planet Earth, and it was the ruler of the Cretaceous. Fear crept up his spine, but it was awe, excitement, and exhilaration that kept his feet cemented to the ground, seeing something no human had ever seen.

The apex predator lunged toward the nearest planteater headfirst, jaws flexed, rows of railroad spike teeth glinting in the sunlight. Jaws with an unimaginable crushing strength clamped down on one of the unaware planteaters, and crunching bone, tearing flesh, and squeals of anguish carried over the jungle.

The T-rex reared back, its main weapon, its head, falling away as the tyrant king lost its grip on the struggling animal and the dying beast managed to free itself. Blood splattered the crushed vegetation, but the herbivore was smaller, faster, and more agile than the T-rex, and it escaped into the forest.

Frustration rolled off the T-rex in waves as it turned its attention to the remaining planteaters that were frozen with fright like spiders caught when the light comes on. The giant beast threw back its head and screamed, the sound of its angry call ringing through the jungle like a fire alarm.

The ground trembled, leaves fell, and Drew felt his heart inch into his throat. Clouds of dust filled the air, and for a heartbeat everything was still, even the trill of the jungle.

The angry carnivore surged forward, the smaller dinosaurs scattering before it, and for an instant it looked to Drew like all the beasts might get away, but the T-rex was too fast, the strike of its viper-like head too deadly.

Teeth met flesh, and bones splintered and broke as the T-rex tore an herbivore apart, blood spilling from the beast's neck.

Leaves burst from the tree line across the path from where Drew sat, like a great exhalation blowing through the forest. Trees bent, branches snapped and twisted, and as Drew watched, three more green monsters, mouths open in toothy grins, inched from the jungle.

Drew noted that the new arrivals were slightly smaller than the alpha, and as they surged onto the path, eyes aglow, he realized the T-rexes were a pack, and big boy was the group's leader.

The four meat-eaters brayed and chuffed, celebrating the alpha's victory. The smaller beasts frolicked, nipping and biting at each other in anticipation, the blood lust driving them into a feeding frenzy as they positioned themselves for the prime pieces of meat.

Big boy went first, the beast's serrated teeth tearing and ripping into flesh, blood pooling on the hardpan between the crushed vegetation and fallen trees. After the alpha had taken a few bites, it stepped back, letting the other three killers take their turn.

The three smaller T-rexes pushed and shoved like children in line at the holo shows, biting and taking chunks of the big boy's catch.

Drew watched with wicked fascination as the Hadrosaurid was devoured, and the kings of the jungle lost interest and wandered off, leaving a lump of bloody gristle, broken bones, and chunks of fat. The rusty scent of blood wafted over the scene, and as the dust settled, the jungle orchestra came back online, and the beasts of the day continued their daily grind.

He cowered in his hiding place for half an hour, his nerves jangling, his stomach a knot of excitement, fear, and hunger. When Drew had judged enough time had passed, he slipped from cover and pulled his knife.

Drew gazed up at the blue strip of sky above the trail. Beasts with sail-like wings circled lower and lower, zeroing in on the T-rex's leftovers. Drew cut a large fan leaf from a nearby plant and used it as a wrapper for the chunks of meat he salvaged off the dead animal. He took a clump of fat also, and he tied it all together with a green creeper vine he cut off a tree.

The smaller blades on the dead planteater's back closest to the end of its python tail were the size of a small dinner plate, and they were slightly cupped in the center. It took some work, and he made a racket, but Drew managed to cut one of the blades free to use as a skillet. It was bloody, caked with fat and dried muscle, but it would work.

He sheathed the knife, set the face shield's magnification at standard, collected his bounty, and continued down the trail of destruction. His hands still shook from the spectacle he'd seen, and Drew had never felt so small in his life. He was an insignificant ant when compared to the beasts he'd seen on this day. Even the Triceratops, which was an herbivore like the Hadrosaurids, had sent a tremor of fear through him, though he doubted the T-rex would be eager to attack those armored tanks.

The sun disappeared and tendrils of dusk inched over the forest when he found the charred leg. A thigh bone, femur, tibia and the smaller fibula, and the remnants of a spacesuit boot like the ones he wore. Small maggot-like bugs covered what was left, which wasn't much. All the skin and muscle had been burned away, leaving a tar that stank like a butcher's dumpster.

Thoughts of burying the leg flitted across his mind as he wondered whose leg it was. Whoever it was, there would be time to mourn when he wasn't fighting for survival.

As if it had heard his thoughts, somewhere a dinosaur roared.

9

At sundown, Drew made camp for the night beneath the boughs of a conifer wrapped in the suffocating embrace of strangler fig. The tree's long branches hung low, half dead under the weight of the spidery vine-like strangler fig plant, and this created a natural roof beneath the main canopy. He prepared a fire and used his bone skillet to cook the chunk of dinosaur meat he'd scavenged until it was super well-done. If there were microbes that could live through that, they could have him.

He ate the meat, which tasted like duck or the dark meat of a ranch chicken, and when he was done, he boiled some of the fat. It tasted like ass, but when it cooled, he slurped the brownish sludge from the bone shield and drank some water, leaving an ounce or two for morning. He was close now, and tomorrow he'd make one final push to get to the ship. If there were no supplies to be salvaged there, he'd cross that tar pit when he came to it.

Drew settled into his cozy natural shelter, his back to the conifer, its bark loose and falling away. It wouldn't be long before the ants and other insects joined the strangler fig in its battle against the large tree, and eventually the evergreen would fall.

He wouldn't be around to see it. What would he be around for?

The jungle sang, the creatures of the dark starting their day. Moonlight angled into the forest, tiny spotlights piercing the strangler fig and dotting the ground with points of white light. A beetle-like insect with a yellow carapace and red-streaked shell worked its way over a tree root bulging from the ground. It paused within a column of moonlight, turning its luminescent eyes on Drew, then continued its trek. When it got to the end of the root and could go no further its head swiveled, and it clamored off the root and disappeared into the darkness.

Drew tossed more wood on the fire as he burped, a gentle nausea massaging his stomach. His eyelids sagged, the cacophony of the braying jungle fading, darkness pressing in on him. The fire popped and crackled, flames licking the blackness, shadows dancing on the green leaves of the strangler fig. Smoke rolled off the fire as a piece of wood broke, firefly sparks funneling into the tree boughs, and in those surging flames, Drew saw a memory.

Waves of invisible heat rolled over the Badlands, the sun a blister overhead, the sweet wind carrying the scents of sagebrush and smoke. Drew powered up the windows, killed the air generator, and the hovercraft settled on the brown and red sand. He hated pulling fossils at the Hell Creek Formation. There were so many hunters, tons of rules and procedures, and it was sometimes hard to navigate, which was why collectors and even desperate researchers paid for his services.

There was a bluff of striped stone ahead covered in a hair of devil grass, scrub pine, and sagebrush. A small excavator sat covered in a camouflage tarp next to a camper half buried in sand. Drew sighed. He didn't even know what he was digging for. Some type of Jurassic beast that a professor in Norway thought was buried beneath the remains of the Cretaceous.

He got out of the vehicle, grabbed a copy of his dig permit, and shuffled off to find history.

The miniature backhoe was churning through the iridium rich primordial dirt when the call symbol appeared in the air before him. He cursed to himself because he thought he'd turned off all incoming communication, but there were exceptions.

It was Julie, and *she* was definitely an exception.

Drew shut down the machine and leaned back in his seat, 'Answer Call?' hanging in the air before him. With a roll of his eyes that nobody could see, he tapped his earpiece to accept the communication as he took a pull of water.

"Drew?" said Julie.

Drew said nothing. What was there to say?

"Are you there?"

"What can I do for you, Julie?"

"What are you doing?"

"Working."

"Where?"

"Can I help you with something?" His daughter's mother only called him when she needed something, which sounded horrible, but was actually his fault. He'd been an ass, jetted off to Russia to provide security for a fossil hunting team, leaving her behind when she needed him most. That was a thing with him—he'd been told several times—when relationships got tough, he got going. He'd also been told he acted that way because he feared letting people down and was scared of the possibility of losing someone he cared about more than anything else in the world. Both things could be true, and that equaled him alone.

"Yeah, I'm sure you're busy," Julie said.

He waited, the insinuation that his work was always more important than anything else hanging out there like a fart in church.

"Kimmy told me you'll be away for a while. Some crazy mission to she wouldn't say where, and that you might not see her for a long time."

Drew said nothing.

"That true?"

"I haven't decided." That was a lie, he'd decided as soon as Dr. Lokker had explained the mission parameters.

"What's more important than Kimmy?"

"That's not fair."

"Isn't it?"

"I have to work."

Julie laughed. "Right, there's no other jobs available? What happened to the list you're always bragging about?"

She had him there. There were other jobs, opportunities that wouldn't potentially take him away from his daughter forever. The harsh truth was he loved the excitement, the change, and challenges more than he liked being a father. That thought brought bile up his throat and made him feel like the biggest dick ever born, but he was what he was, and change came to him reluctantly and slowly.

Drew justified his feelings with the idea that he'd never wanted to have children—shit, or a girlfriend for that matter. But strange things happen in the middle of a winter storm when people are trapped in a hotel with unlimited supplies of booze.

Not that he didn't care for Julie, he did, more than anyone else, except for Kimmy, but he was a loner, always had been, and he always would be. Anything more made him uncomfortable, and then he always overcompensated and made things worse.

But when he'd seen that pink mealworm of a child enter the world, when he'd held Kimmy in his arms, she captured his heart, and from that moment forward everything he did, he did for her, or at least that was the line of shit he tried to sell himself.

Truth was, he wanted to go on the mission, and the pile of credits the doctor was paying him was going in an account for Kimmy, so that let him justify the trip, and his entire solitary life.

A dinosaur roared, and Drew's gaze shifted from the fire to the wall of green strangler fig, the memory fleeing like a ghost. He pictured Kimmy in his mind, her dark hair, chocolate skin and hazel eyes. The way she watched a person like she knew everything that person was thinking. He'd felt that stare, and his daughter had seen right through him. Yet, she loved him, and set him free, telling him an opportunity to visit Earth's past was a chance that couldn't be passed up. She would go and leave him behind, she'd said, if she'd been given the opportunity.

Drew sighed and burrowed into himself, pulling his arms tight to his chest, the hum of the helmet fan an ever-present annoyance. He closed his eyes and let the jungle serenade him to sleep.

The stink inside the spacesuit was becoming ripe. He noticed when he took the helmet off to drink the last mouthfuls of water. The suit was dirty, ripped, and having the seatbelt wrapped around his leg was less than comfortable, but it was better than dealing with the intense heat. Despite the climate control system doing its job, he still sweat from the exertion of trekking through the jungle and running and hiding from the forest's inhabitants. His jumpsuit was perpetually soaked through, his hair matted to his head, but wearing the suit was still the safest option.

Morning sunrays angled into the wide trail as Drew walked the edge of the strip of destruction that knifed through the jungle, staying just inside the tree line so as not to draw the attention of lurking beasts. The way T-rex had prowled prior to its attack coincided with what researchers back home believed. Images of the massive beast chasing down cars and planes were for the holos. The scientists had been right. T-rex stalked its prey, and not alone, but in packs, an idea that took three generations of paleontologists to take hold.

The final stage of his quest, though easiest from a predator and terrain perspective, was the hardest mile of his trek. He hadn't gotten sick from the overcooked meat he'd eaten, but his stomach begged for water, and his muscles were done waiting.

Drew was staggering and out on his feet when he saw a glimmer of metal in the distance. He stopped short, staring like a man who's seen a mirage, a huge pond of fresh water with a table full of food sitting on its shores. The light wavered and disappeared, and Drew lurched forward like he'd missed some opportunity, like failing to alert a rescue ship.

He doubled his pace, pushing his body to the limit as he eased under fallen trees and around tangled vines and charred underbrush.

As the wreckage got closer Drew's heart sank.

The destroyed foliage that made up the path was charred black, fingers of burned vegetation exploring the edges of the jungle.

Chunks of black metal littered the area like onyx rocks, and tension ran through Drew as he realized what he was looking at was only the front of the ship.

The Triumph had resembled a jetliner, but with two notable exceptions. Instead of tiny rear stabilizer wings, the ship had two rear wings almost as big as its forward wings, and they were gone, along with the forward wings. Also, unlike traditional airplanes, the ship's undercarriage had a variety of landing options that allowed the ship to touch down vertically in a small area like the helicopters of old he'd seen in museums.

Tension stroked his nerves. The entire back of the ship was gone. Metal twisted like an angry giant had ripped the ship in half, the nose of the ship smashed and burnt. Drew's breath caught in his throat like a fishbone as he surged forward into the wreckage, his suit snagging on a sharp piece of melted metal, the sound of tearing fabric echoing inside the helmet.

Suit integrity dropping. Please take—

"Shut it!" Drew screamed as he picked his way to the crew area.

Hope flooded through him. It looked like the forward ejection seats had jettisoned. The two parachutes he'd seen. Two of his crewmates had gotten out.

He let out a long breath, his tension easing. Maybe he wasn't alone, but... Drew gazed around, didn't see any footprints. His teammates could be anywhere within a grid of hundreds of miles and finding them would be akin to locating a needle in the proverbial haystack. But there was a chance, a distant hope, that perhaps he wouldn't have to face his nightmares alone.

The moment of relief didn't last long.

A gust of wind brought the nasty scent of burnt flesh, and Drew tracked the smell to the forward section of the wreckage. Ripped and blackened chunks of metal created a maze around the ship's nosecone, where Drew found the remains of two people charred to cinders.

Drew lowered his head, heart hammering, pulse racing. He recalled the ship's pilot and co-pilot, a husband-and-wife team recruited for the mission because they had no children, no ties to the new world other than their marriage.

He reached out and ran a gloved hand over the black corpses, one of which was missing a leg. Like most people, he needed to touch death, look into its eyes, and stare it down. He hadn't killed these people, yet he felt a responsibility to honor their memory because that's what civilized people did.

The bodies were black bones wrapped in charred leather, their suits burned away, the remains of their helmets fused to their skulls. Only the teeth were white, and they shone through the melted face shield like a string of pearls laid across their black and hollowed out faces. The pilots looked like mannequins that had been tossed into the incinerator because the new motion activated mannequins had arrived. The remnants of fat and skin hung from the charred bones, the corpses like melted black candles.

The seats were black, all the equipment that was used to pilot the ship was burned to slag, and the forward cabin was nothing but a tomb. He made the sign of the cross and bowed his head again as he considered why the pilots hadn't ejected. Going down with the ship had always been a dumb concept, but pilots were pilots, regardless of what type of ship they captained.

He didn't believe in God, not many people did anymore, but as he stood there alone, his heart racing, his stomach clamoring for food, he prayed for the other three team members who had been on the ship with him, though he knew it would do nothing except maybe bring him some peace.

Wind gusted over the destroyed ship and a twig snapped.

Drew spun around, staring at the wall of trees and underbrush that packed the southern side of the path.

From within the wall of green a red pupil rolled against a black cornea and settled on him, then narrowed.

10

Drew inched back behind a black chunk of slag.

A narrow tooth-filled snout inched from the wall of green, red eyes appraising Drew. A bird-like creature the size of a large dog stepped from the undergrowth. Drew stared in awe at the Velociraptor, the creature hardly resembling the dinosaurs depicted in the holo vids and classic films.

The raptor was skinny and lightly built for a carnivore. Measuring six feet long, the beast walked on its hindlegs, its narrow head ranging back and forth. The Velociraptor's sickle-shaped claws clicked on stones and chunks of charred metal as it advanced, undeterred by Drew's toothpick with a knife fastened to its end. Slender arms hung from the beast's narrow torso, each hand equipped with a smaller talon. Black feathers ran down the beast's spine, and they transitioned to brown and gray as the feathers blended into the beast's white chest.

Drew put his back to the chunk of metal, raising his knife-spear, readying to strike. He had no intention of attacking the dinosaur, but as the raptor inched through the wreckage Drew realized that a confrontation was inevitable.

The raptor clicked and chuffed, its head jerking around, its red eyes narrowed and focused on its prey.

Drew had the size advantage, and though they'd never discussed or drilled an encounter with a predatory dinosaur— because the plan was to have advanced weapons—he did know how to deal with bears in the forest back home. Even the big grizzlies were usually scared of people, unless they were starving, or you were messing with their cubs.

He inched into the open, spear out before him like a lance, and he yelled, "Yo dinosaur! Yo dinosaur!"

The raptor stopped walking, its head still, eyes wide.

Drew took a slow step forward, yelling and screaming, waving his spear around. He glanced over a shoulder, wondering if the theory that Velociraptors hunted in packs was true. The green wall of the tree line was still, and no eyes peered out from the undergrowth.

The raptor squeaked and took a hesitant step forward, ten feet separating the beast from Drew.

Yelling wasn't working, so Drew did the only thing he could. He lunged forward, spear out as he stabbed at the dinosaur.

The raptor's eyes went wide, and its mouth fell open, revealing a row of tiny knife blades.

Drew thrust out his spear blade again, screaming so loud his throat hurt.

The Velociraptor threw back its head and screeched, but when help didn't arrive, the raptor darted away and disappeared within a tangle of vegetation and fallen trees.

Drew's heart raced, and as the adrenaline fled, he fell on his ass, all energy gone. At some point during the confrontation the helmet fan had stopped whirring, and the climate control system had shut down. The second tear in his suit was too large, and the climate control couldn't keep up. Drew popped the release hasps and took the helmet off. A warm breeze massaged his face, the sweet scents of earth and flowers tickling his nose.

The metal water bottle tinkled on its carabiner, and Drew reached for it, remembered the bottle was empty, and let his head fall into his hands. What the hell was he going to do? The remains of the ship were useless, and whatever hadn't dropped into the jungle had burned.

He pushed to his feet and gave the destroyed ship a full search. The cockpit was one-piece of blackened metal, and the right side was missing. Drew knew there had been a supply cabinet, and each team member had a personal storage locker, but if they were still part of the ship they'd been melted and burned beyond recognition.

Birds sprayed from the forest, knifing under and around the fallen trees that covered the ship's trail of destruction. The flying creatures had claws at the ends of their thick legs and looked much different than modern day birds. The little black rats that filled the air now looked more like large insects.

Drew found a spot where he could easily construct a shelter, and that thought made his stomach boil. What other choice did he have but to hang around the crash site and hope his crewmates showed up? The idea of staying in one spot didn't appeal to him, but without the aid of the ship's central computer he didn't know what else he could do.

This plan was complicated by the fact that the two parachuters might hike to the rear of the ship, wherever it ended up. There could be supplies there, but Drew had no clue where the back of the ship was—even if it was on land. The rear portion of the fuselage could be in one of the many slender oceans that split the land masses. Or it could've burnt up.

Drew stripped off the spacesuit, turned it inside out, and hung it to dry as he went in search of water.

The temperature dropped beneath the dense tree canopy, and gnats, flies, and mosquitoes buzzed his head. He picked a large fan leaf and waved it before his face to shoo the insects away and it worked well enough. It felt good to not be confined within the spacesuit, and the jumpsuit and boots kept most of the smaller critters from getting to his skin.

He didn't find water, but he did find several useless pieces of the ship in the surrounding forest as Drew worked his way back down the burnt-out trail.

The sun was an orange ball on the western horizon, the last light of day angling through the jungle, and still Drew hadn't found water, or anything of use. Stomach screaming, muscles aching, his head ringing like someone was drumming on his brain, he gave up for the day.

Since he had no food, no water, Drew decided to forgo a fire, and instead bundled back into the spacesuit, and this time he used two green vines to tie-off his leg and arm where the suit was ripped. After some adjustments, the suit computer declared that suit integrity had been restored to sixty-six percent, and the fan in the helmet buzzed to life.

He crawled beneath a twisted piece of blackened metal, and lay on the ground, sweat dripping down his face despite the climate control. The inside of the suit still stank despite Drew airing it out, and the ripe smell of his body odor made his stomach gurgle with nausea.

He laid his spear-knife on the hardpan beside him and closed his eyes. Despite the pounding of his heart, his partying nerves, and the thump and pain of his leg wound, Drew fell into an uneasy sleep.

Drew felt like he'd been used hard and put away wet, and hunger pains wracked his stomach, his knee joints protesting with each movement. Errand rays of morning sun sliced from the jungle as he rested in the shadow of the black hunk of metal he'd slept under. Small rodent-like beasts scurried about, insects tittered and sang, and every few seconds the roar of an apex predator would carry over the jungle like the noon bell, reminding every living thing within earshot who was in charge.

Finding water was top priority, and he changed his search grid. Instead of following the path of devastation, he circled outward from the wreckage in an expanding circle. He came across more pieces of the ship, what looked like a forearm and hand burned to the bones, a chunk of seat cushion, and a lot of other blackened junk, but nothing useful, and no water.

After several hours of fruitless searching Drew discovered the blackened remains of a metal box caught in the crux of a large conifer tree. It was hard to tell from the ground, but since beggars can't be choosers, he decided to climb the tree and see what the item was, and while he was up there survey the area.

He stripped off the spacesuit, but put the boots and gloves back on. The bulky boots would make the climb more difficult, but there was no way he was attempting the ascent barefoot.

Getting to the blackened item was easy, and Drew nudged it with his foot and dislodged it. The charred box plummeted to the ground and disappeared into the green undergrowth. The rest of the climb was more difficult, and as he got higher the trunk tapered down in thickness, the top of the tree swaying gently in the wind. Drew knew there was no way he was heavy enough to snap the top off the flexible tree, but his stomach still fell and twisted with each swing of the treetop.

To the south there was a dark line in the tree canopy. Most likely a stream or river. It didn't look far away, but that wasn't what made Drew's nerves dance like his skin was on fire.

About two klicks away to the southeast there was another large chunk of the ship. Its trail of destruction was much smaller, and though the piece was charred, Drew also saw portions of shiny metal glinting in the sunlight. He started down, then stopped.

Drew scanned the forest canopy for several minutes, wishing he had the enhanced vision of his helmet, but he finally found what he was looking for. Due east about a klick, there was a low grove of trees that looked similar to the starvation fruit trees.

Hope surged through him as he climbed the rest of the way down.

He thought maybe starting a large fire could work. His crewmates might see the smoke. Or, if there was a way he could make a loud sound, like breaking stones, perhaps he could tap out a rhythm that would draw in his crewmates. But that was for later.

The burnt box was nothing more than a hunk of metal, so he left it where it was.

Water was more important than food, so he donned the spacesuit and headed south. It was tough going, and he had to stop several times to avoid conflicts with the native fauna, but when the sun reached its zenith Drew arrived at the banks of a wide stream that tumbled over stones and ran through the dense jungle.

Drew made a fire using the flint rock he'd been carrying since day one. Then he boiled water and rested as he drank, the day falling away. The starvation fruit trees couldn't be reached by nightfall, so he'd do that first thing in the morning and maybe do a little hunting.

The small mammals didn't have much meat on them, and he'd abandoned his bone skillet, but Drew was sure he could spear one of the little rascals because the creatures didn't appear to fear him. Drew was just another animal, even if an odd one, going about his business, and since he wasn't three stories tall and roaring, for the most part they let him be. Except for the flying vampires. They were larger and more aggressive than the mosquitoes of the twenty-second century, but their probosces weren't strong enough to pierce the spacesuit.

He headed for the second piece of the ship he'd seen. Thick conifers packed the forest, their boughs so dense little light managed to penetrate their canopy. Drew marched on in the perpetual half-light, eyes down to avoid tree roots and stones. The underbrush was thin due to the lack of sunlight, so he made better time, but shadows gyrated behind every tree trunk and under every bough, teasing his nerves. He moved as if he was under the watchful gaze of a predator hiding in the greenery, waiting for the perfect moment to strike.

Drew overshot the second chunk of the ship, but he saw its path and was able to backtrack.

A large piece of the spaceship's midsection lay tangled in the destroyed forest, most of it charred and useless. He found no bodies, no supplies, nothing.

Drew's confidence fell and the heat of worry and fear crept through him like a disease. He searched the forest around the wreckage and wasn't surprised to see other smaller pieces of the ship gleaming within the deep green. He'd have to search the entire area, but not today.

Darkness crept over the land and Drew hid in the shadows, lying in wait like a T-rex, spear at the ready. He sat like that a long time. Drew had never been a hunter and he'd only gone fishing once as a novelty because his father had oversold the experience. Sitting in the hot sun, bobbing around on the ocean, and waiting for a fish to come along and take his bait wasn't Drew's idea of fun. He didn't even eat fish, though he'd take one now—even a blue fish or a sea robin.

A low crunching sound, like an animal chomping on leaves and sticks, carried through the jungle. He waited, the sound getting closer. Drew laid the shaft of his knife-spear on his shoulder, ready to fire his makeshift weapon at the first sign of prey.

When a turtle the size of a toilet seat cover pushed from the undergrowth Drew chuckled to himself. The beast's long serpentine neck lifted its lizard head above the weeds, its dark eyes scanning the jungle. The creature didn't look much different than the beast that prowled Earth in modern times.

Drew got to his feet, slowly inching from his hiding place until he stood before the prehistoric beast.

Upon seeing him, the turtle snapped its sharp talon-like mouth, and Drew threw his knife-spear at the beast's head and missed.

The creature hissed at him and tried to run, but even in the spacesuit boots Drew could move faster. He retrieved his spear, approached the turtle from behind, and used the weapon to flip the turtle onto its back. The creature's legs churned and struggled as Drew plunged the spear-knife into the turtle's belly and it fell still.

With darkness blanketing the land, Drew decided to sleep within the chunk of ship he'd found. Within an hour of spearing the turtle, he'd cleaned and butchered the creature, made a fire, and using the beast's shell, was boiling turtle meat. He took the helmet off and ate and drank, the nourishment sending waves of weariness through him.

It had been a long one, but tomorrow was another day.

11

Mist shrouded the jungle, the trill of the night symphony dying away as the growls, buzz, chuffs, and roars of the daylight inhabitants carried over the jungle. Dusk before dawn is a dangerous time in any forest where there are predators, so Drew waited until sunlight filtered into the jungle before he went back to the river to rinse off, clean his new turtle shell pot, purify water, and cook the last of his turtle meat.

Morning chores completed, he left the spacesuit hanging from the wreckage to dry out, and with spear in hand, set out to search the area. There was more debris around the second piece of the ship, it was less burned than the cockpit section, and he'd found the chunk of metal in the tree. All of that made him wonder how many other pieces he'd missed because he'd kept his eyes pasted on the ground before him.

The ground trembled, but whatever massive dinosaur was trundling to get coffee was far off. Small beasts scurried about within the undergrowth, strange bat-like black birds darting around the trees. Drew hacked and sliced with his spear-knife, and it was slow going, not only because the vegetation was thick, but because he didn't want to miss something useful hidden beneath the blanket of weeds and broadleaf ferns.

He'd been searching about an hour when he found several shards of metal sticking from the ground like someone had been playing lawn darts. The torn and blackened strips were oddly shaped and roughly the size of a baseball. There were six of them, and three of the pieces had round notches in them and Drew figured the metal had run along a seam of the ship. He plucked them from the ground, and found they were roughly a half-inch thick, all sides sharp.

The breeze brought the fragrant scent of flowers, and he recalled that colored plants were relatively new to the world in the Cretaceous. He hefted one of the shards of metal, threw it at a tree, and it stuck in the hardwood like a throwing star. Drew smiled. He had six weapons.

Sunrays angled into the forest from the south, the sun climbing toward noon, when he found the shiny piece of aluminum alloy embedded in the hardpan. It was nothing more than a piece of the fuselage, but when Drew saw his haggard reflection in the smooth metal his breath caught.

His short brown hair was matted to his head, and dark bags hung beneath hazel eyes. Dirt smeared his face, and the salt and pepper stubble that covered his cheeks and chin made him look older than he was.

Drew mentally froze, his mind spinning backward. What the hell had happened? Based on what he'd seen so far, the crash had been caused by an explosion, but how had he escaped? And the others? He knew that under certain conditions the onboard computer would jettison the ejection seats, and everything had happened so fast, but like the survivor of a car crash when others have died, Drew was left wondering why he was spared. He struggled to recall the details of the crash, but his brain only gave him images of takeoff. The last time he'd seen Kimmy and Julie.

The ship had been a marvel of human innovation. Something scientists for centuries had said wasn't possible. A warm breeze stoked Drew's face as he stared at the piece of the ship, and he was back there, nerves jumping with anticipation.

Rain beat the roof of the hovercar as the vehicle dropped below the cloud cover, the tapping and snapping filling the car with static. Drew drove, and Kimmy sat in the passenger seat staring forward, her cheeks taut, eyes wet with building tears. Guilt swept through him, but Drew couldn't let that rule his life.

"I'll be back before you know it," he said, knowing even if things went perfectly, it would be a long time before he saw his daughter again.

Kimmy didn't look at him.

"What if something goes wrong?" came Julie's voice from the backseat. Always helpful Julie was.

"What if a hovercraft lands on me? Or I fall in a sewer? Or—"

"Dad," whined Kimmy and he fell still.

Drew drove on in silence, the whistle of the air jetting from the underside of the hovercar accompanying the pounding rain. There was really nothing left to say, and any platitudes he offered up to assuage his guilt would be shot down with the reality that he didn't have to go, and there was a good possibility he wouldn't make it back.

His daughter agreed this was a once in a lifetime opportunity. That he would be crazy to pass it up. All of that was true, but the fact that he was putting himself—his wishes and dreams—above his daughter, ate at him like maggots.

The spaceport appeared out of the fog and torrential rain, the gleaming silver spaceship sitting on its yellow pad. It looked like a jetliner of old, except for the large rear wings and lack of visible engines. As it had been explained to him, the ship bent space, but Drew would believe it when he saw it.

"Are you sure that thing will fly?" Kimmy asked.

Drew chuckled. His daughter had seen only modern transport ships, which were hovercars and used forced air to jet through the sky, leaving no noxious fumes, and needing nothing but the sun's rays as fuel.

As the hovercar touched down, the rain stopped like a spicket had been turned off, and the wet starship gleamed in the half-light. Drew inched the car into a parking garage, killed the blowers, and let the vehicle settle to the ground.

Drew and the remains of his family sat in silence, the absence of the rain beating the hovercar's roof bringing on an unreal stillness. He reached into the backseat and gave the car fob to Julie, and she accepted it without a word.

He glanced at his watch. Takeoff was at 0900, and it was 0808.

A tear leaked down Kimmy's face and Drew leaned over and took the child in his arms, his chest burning with an unbearable heat. He hadn't cared about much in his life, but the two people in the hovercar were the exceptions.

"It's time," Drew said as he peeled off his daughter.

"Good luck, Drew," said Julie, and she got out of the car so she could take over the driving.

"I'll see you soon, O.K.?" he said to his daughter.

Kimmy nodded as she fought back tears, but she lost the battle, and when the waterworks came Drew felt like his heart was being torn from his chest. He took her in his arms again and hugged her tight, and for the first time he considered not going on the crazy mission.

Julie opened the driver's side door and Kimmy pulled away as she wiped away tears, her face rigid and defiant.

"I love you," he said.

Kimmy said nothing, and that final stab, that final appeal for him to understand how upset she was despite her agreeing he should go, sent a tremor of sorrow through Drew that weakened his knees.

"You going?" Julie said.

Drew forced himself to get out of the car, and he stood there like an idiot as the hovercar lifted from its pad, eased out of the garage, and disappeared into the rain.

Up close the spaceship looked much larger, three times the size of a transport hovercraft, and as he was greeted by workers in gray flight suits, he saw that the lights were on inside the ship. "Is everyone here?" Drew asked one of the ground crew.

"Everyone except Ms.—"

"Gina," came a voice from behind. "Dr. Gina Teallie."

As Drew turned and shook the woman's hand, he recalled she was the team's leading paleontologist, and the resident expert on the Cretaceous and the event that ended that glorious period of Earth's history.

Gina was stunningly beautiful. Her jet-black hair was pulled back in a loose ponytail, and her brown eyes were aglow, her mouth perpetually twisted in a half smirk. She was shorter than him, slender, and her blue jumpsuit showed off her amazing figure. For some odd reason Drew felt no attraction to the woman.

"You just gonna stand there? Or are we going to get this show on the road?" she said.

Drew smiled and swept his arm toward the staircase that led up to the ship's access hatch. "Ladies first."

The coo of a dove that belonged to a killer the size of a turkey with a narrow snout and teeth like a chainsaw blade snapped Drew from his reverie. The beast watched him from the cover of the underbrush, its wet eyes blinking, head still.

Drew pulled one of his makeshift throwing stars, his thoughts clouded with the daydream of Kimmy. He needed to get home. For her. He had no idea how he'd manage that because he didn't know where the emergency return pod was, if it was in one piece, and even if it was, he didn't know if it would function. He didn't see his daughter in the flesh much, but they spoke regularly and their vidcalls were the highlight of his life. He missed talking to her, hearing about school, sports, and seeing her grow into a woman before his eyes. It all hurt in places he hadn't known he had. For the first time in a long time, he considered what it would take to get back together with Julie. Would she ev—

The dinosaur squawked and stepped forward.

He threw a shard of metal, and it whizzed through the air, hit the beast on its flank, and fell to the ground. The creature's head rotated down and it stared at the shard. The dinosaur yelled again, spun around, and bolted into the forest.

"Hold up now," Drew said as he gave chase. The beast's torso was plump, and Drew had visions of roasting the beast over an open flame.

Branches whipped his face and arms as Drew pushed through the undergrowth, and soon he'd lost the creature. He stopped, panting as he looked around, trying to get his bearings. The second piece of the ship and the spacesuit waited to the south, but he had no idea how far he'd gone. Judging distance and direction in the dense jungle was next to impossible, but he'd left a few slashes on extra-large trees to mark his path should he become lost.

A great braying and snorting and screaming filtered through the jungle and the forest gave way to a small clearing created by a piece of ship debris. Broken trees, torched vegetation, and scorched earth created a blight in the greenery. At its center a charred supply chest sat unopened, and turkey dinosaurs protected it like mother hens protected their eggs.

As if on cue, a roar resounded over the forest and all the beasts froze. Drew chuckled to himself. When the big boys spoke, everything listened. The pause didn't last long, and with the echo of the roar still hanging in the air the beasts continued to bite and yap at each other, all of them unaware of his presence, except one.

The beast Drew had been chasing stared at him, head bobbing, its gray feathers on end as it puffed itself up. The beast screeched and yelled, and the commotion drew the attention of its flock. Soon seven sets of eyes stared at Drew like he was lunch.

Sweat dripped down his back as he inched out the tip of his knife-spear. Like with the Velociraptor, Drew decided being the aggressor was the best option.

He burst forward, screaming like a nutcase, waving his arms, and brandishing his spear.

The dinosaur paused, staring at him like he was a fly that had just landed on its food.

Drew slung one of the warped throwing stars at the nearest beast, the one he'd chased through the jungle, and it hit the creature in the chest, but didn't penetrate the dinosaur's thick quill-covered hide.

The beast yelled, but took a step back as the other creatures stared at Drew in amazement.

"Yo dinosaurs. Shoo. Yo dinosaurs!" he screamed, thrusting the spear forward as he advanced. He threw two more shards of metal, missed both times, but the clang of the steel hitting the storage chest rang over the clearing and the turkey-dinosaurs scattered like birds after a gunshot.

The hum of the jungle paused, as if the forest itself was watching and listening.

Drew waited, catching his breath, his skin tingling with anticipation, excitement, and fear.

Black eyes with yellow corneas stared at him from within the wall of green, and Drew picked up a stone and tossed it into the jungle. Breaking branches, the rip and tear of leaves, and then the eyes were gone.

Slowly the buzz of the forest returned, and Drew went to examine his prize.

The piece of metal was definitely a supply chest, though it had been burned badly. Streaks of white and silver ran through the charred metal, and Drew was unable to make out the writing on its tag.

Drew's heart did summersaults as he imagined what the supply trunk might contain. Rations, weapons, parts for the suit, maybe a data bar, or radio. He didn't know what good those last items would be, but there was no way to know unless he got the chest open.

He nudged the trunk with his foot. The thing was heavy, and both the hinges and front latches were frozen. Drew looked around for a stone, and when he didn't find one big enough, he sat on a fallen tree and wiped his brow with the back of his hand as he eyed the chest.

The lip of the trunk's cover could still be seen, and if he could work the knife into the gap—but no. He couldn't afford to break the knife. If that happened… he didn't want to think about it. He'd have to find a piece of debris and use a stone as a hammer, and those ideas brought forth another idea. If he could find two round stones the size of golf balls, perhaps he could cut some vines and make a bolas?

He unclipped the water bottle from a loop on his jumpsuit, the click of the carabiner like the tap of a lock falling into place. He drank deep, confident in the fact that he knew where to get more water. The jungle was alive once more, the primeval creatures having moved on to their next task. The ground trembled, and Drew thought the vibration that ran through the land was constantly there, but he'd become used to it. He brushed back his hair and stared at the blackened chest. Nothing is ever easy. He pushed to his feet and went in search of stone age tools.

12

Drew found the perfect wedge, a piece of angled steel from the fuselage that he was able to jam into the crack at the lip of the storage chest. He pounded on that spike with a stone like the burnt piece of metal was the cause of every wrong, every injustice he'd ever suffered. After forty-five minutes he gave up and tossed his rock into the jungle.

Click click clak clak.

Wind gusted from the forest carrying the rank scent of unwashed flesh.

Across the clearing, thirty feet from where Drew stood, two raptors inched from the underbrush, heads bobbing, mouths hanging open in toothy grins.

A rustle behind him, the snap of a tree branch, and Drew spun to find two more beasts creeping from the jungle. These specimens were larger than the first raptors he'd seen, and Drew thought they were Utahraptors. Their black, brown, and gray feathers were covered in mud, and the reek of dung pressed over the clearing like a wave of invisible heat. Drew shifted his gaze between the two pairs of predators, his spear-knife out before him like a sword, but what good it would do against four raptors he didn't know.

He remembered the shards of metal and he pulled one of the makeshift throwing stars from his jumpsuit pocket and hefted it in his hand.

The largest of the Utahraptors stepped away from its partner, clicking and chuffing, muscles rippling under its feathers, its black glassy eyes locked on Drew. The other pair divided as well, and soon Drew was surrounded on four sides.

Muscle cords flexed and spasmed as the raptors inched forward on their powerful hindlegs, their narrow heads ranging back and forth. Drew eyeballed the Utahraptor's sickle-shaped claws and saw one of the beast's feet were covered in blood. Slender arms flexed, talons glinting in the sunlight, the tension in the air like electricity before a storm.

The leader of the pack bent low, bringing its narrow head to the ground, sniffing, its mouth falling open. It hopped and shrieked as it came forward, the beast twenty feet away, but to Drew it felt like twenty inches.

Like skipping a stone over a lake, Drew slung his shard of metal, aiming for the beast's face. The shard whizzed through the air and struck home, the makeshift throwing star thumping into the beast's right eye. Blood spilled down the raptor's face as it surged forward, moving with incredible speed as it charged.

He fished out another piece of metal, but held his fire.

The alpha Utahraptor slowed, its head falling as its tree trunk legs stopped churning. With a shuddering cry that faded to a whimper, the beast came to a slow stop and appeared to deflate. The raptor swayed on its feet, went rigid, and fell to the ground, blood puddling around the head of the corpse.

Everything went still for a heartbeat.

Drew held his breath, sweat dripping down his face and back, tension poking his skin.

The remaining three Utahraptors appeared just as stunned about the fall of their leader as Drew, and the beasts didn't advance. Instead, they looked to one another, that primal dance of leadership that's often settled by someone... or something standing still as all their fellows stepped back.

An inrush of air, and the corpse of the alpha raptor jumped, muscles flexing as the creature received its last burst of energy, its dying brain sparking one last time. The other three dinosaurs looked on, surely hoping their leader would get up and shake off the four-inch piece of metal sticking from its head. Smaller creatures peered at the scene through the underbrush, waiting for the battle to be over so they could peck at the dead.

Seconds dripped away as the three remaining raptors spread out, filling in the gap in the containment circle left by their fallen mate. Undeterred, the beasts came on, heads moving like a boxer, mouths clicking.

Drew heaved another star. Missed. Another, and this one hit home but bounced off the lead beast's chest and fell to the ground. The blow only served to aggravate the creature, and it bounded forward in anger, leaving its two mates to circle around behind Drew.

He lashed out with this spear, the knife blade inches from the advancing raptor's chest as the dinosaur skidded to a stop. Like a bird pecking at a corpse, the beast came at Drew with the only weapon it had. The Utahraptor's mouth and head were its main weapons, its thick muscular tail an afterthought.

Drew threw the spear with everything he had, and the stick with a seven-inch carbon fiber blade attached to its end plunged into the raptor's mouth as it flexed open. The beast's momentum carried it forward, the spear sticking from the raptor's mouth like a giant toothpick. The scent of shit filled Drew's nostrils as the creature's bowels gave out, and the dinosaur fell forward.

The stench of waste overwhelmed him as Drew rolled away from the mountain of quivering, feather-covered flesh as it hit the hardpan.

Dust and black soot clouded the air, and the tangy smell of blood and the bitter stench of dung wafted over the clearing.

The remaining raptors didn't hesitate as their prior two leaders had. The Utahraptors came at Drew from two sides, and there was nowhere for him to run, and no time anyway. With his spear still impaled in the raptor, all Drew could do was pull his last shard of metal, but the beasts were too close. Before he could get the makeshift throwing star from his pocket the lead raptor plowed into him, and Drew went to the hardpan in a knot of arms and legs.

His leg wound screamed as the air rushed from his lungs and he struggled to breathe. His attacker threw back its head in triumph, screeching and roaring as if ringing a dinner bell. Sucking for air, pain paralyzing him, Drew tried to scramble away, but the raptor shifted its position, straddling him where he lay pinned to the ground.

The Utahraptor gazed down at Drew, its mouth sliding open, drool dripping through razor-sharp teeth and landing on his face. A cackle that sounded too much like a chuckle leaked from the beast's open maw as it coiled to strike.

Drew covered his head with his arms, an image of Kimmy's melting face mocking him as the shadow of the raptor fell over him, a freight train of teeth heading right for him.

Two gunshots rang out in fast succession, and the Utahraptor's head exploded, spraying blood, bone, and brains onto Drew as the shadow of the headless raptor fell toward him.

He had a moment to consider the irony of death by falling dinosaur, but self-preservation isn't a reasoned response. Drew rolled to his right and the falling beast landed beside him with a thud.

The remaining raptor didn't hang around to see what had killed its buddies, and it darted into the forest.

Drew lay on his back, staring at the sky, his mind spinning. He glanced over at the headless raptor, recalled the gunshots, and sat up.

Dust and ash eddied around Allan Walls as he eased from the jungle, pistol in hand.

At first Drew thought his shipmate was a mirage. He'd been alone so long, seen things within the shadows that weren't there.

"You O.K.?" the big man said as he strode forward and offered a hand.

Walls was the Swiss army knife of the team. He specialized in security, fossil digs and labor, as well as survival in harsh environments, and his military experience made him a perfect complement to a team of scientists and dinosaur hunters.

Drew took Walls' hand, and the big man pulled him to his feet. Walls looked much different than the last time Drew had seen him. His red hair and full beard were tousled and caked with dirt, and he wore his spacesuit helmet, but the suit itself had been cut away, leaving only the helmet collar and life support backpack and its harness. His blue jumpsuit was in tatters, and he had a bloody bandage pasted to his right side. He wore spacesuit boots and gloves, and a pouch hung from a vine belt that wrapped around his waist.

Walls patted Drew on the back and said, "I'm so happy to find you, mate."

Drew's nerves danced beneath his skin, a cold sweat creeping over him as he caught his breath. "Thanks," he said. "If you had arrived just a bit later, I'm not sure what would have happened."

"You would've been that guy's lunch." He pointed at the headless raptor.

Drew chuckled. "Thanks again, and nice shooting."

Walls bowed, smiling behind his face shield, and said, "Have you seen anyone else?"

"No." Then he remembered the burned-out cockpit and the two pilots. "Actually, nobody alive. I found the front of the ship, and what was left of the two pilots was burned beyond recognition."

Walls' chin dropped to his chest. "What of the others?"

"I saw two parachutes, and I assume one was you, but the other…"

In the distance a dinosaur roared.

Drew used his shirtsleeve to wipe the blood off his face as he said, "Where did you get the gun? Got any food?"

"I had an emergency pack." He held up the pistol. "Rations and first aid supplies are gone, and I've got eighteen bullets left in this baby. You?"

Drew shook his head. "My pack wasn't on my ejection seat." He pointed at the black supply chest. "There might be something in there, but I couldn't get it open."

Walls nodded, his blue eyes gleaming.

"What happened?" Drew pointed at the blood-soaked bandage on Walls' torso.

"Had a disagreement with the local fauna. You?"

"Same."

The two men stood in silence, the surrounding jungle a cacophony of life.

"Do you know what happened? To the ship, I mean?" Drew said.

"Not exactly, but when we came out of the bend something wasn't right, like we hit something, like an invisible barrier."

"How did you know to come this way?"

"I've just been trekking in the general direction where I thought I saw a piece of the ship go down. What have you been eating? Do you have water?" Walls tapped his empty stainless steel water bottle where it hung from his vine belt via its carabiner.

"There's a river to the south of here. It's not far, and I've been boiling my water. As far as food…" He sighed, then told

Walls about the starvation fruit and the turtle meat. "I've got a turtle shell back at camp, and I've been using that."

"You can make a fire? I've been drinking untreated water, and I've been fine."

Drew asked, "Where's your knife?"

"Lost it in the fall." Walls looked around, sizing up the raptor corpses. "Do you think we can eat these bitches?"

"Don't see why not," Drew said. "I take it you didn't see any other emergency packs in the jungle?"

Walls shook his head sullenly inside his helmet and said, "They either burned up, or they're lost in the jungle."

"No communication with the ship?"

"Nope."

"And I assume no sign of the emergency pod?" Drew asked.

"Zero. I don't even know if it jettisoned." He left the obvious unspoken. Without it, there was no way they could get home. "I see you're not wearing your helmet and suit."

"They're back at camp. What happened to yours?"

"Ripped beyond repair when... this happened." He motioned toward his wound. "I only have the helmet on for enhanced vision and to keep the damn mosquitoes off my face. At home I live... lived, next to a swamp, O.K.? So, trust me when I tell you these flying bastards are bigger, their bites worse, than any flying vampire I've ever seen."

Drew chuckled. He knew very little about his shipmate. They'd barely spoken during mission prep and the brief period before takeoff. He recalled the man being gruff, sullen, and distant, but emergency situations made friends of the most dissimilar people. Drew needed to get to know this man, befriend him, because their survival depended on it. "You have a lot of bug bites?"

Walls comically pointed out several large red welts on his arms and legs.

"At least they didn't give you a disease and kill you," Drew said.

"There is that."

Drew dislodged his spear from the mouth of the raptor he'd stabbed and set about slicing meat from the fallen beast as Walls collected several elephant ear leaves to use as wrappers. When they were done, Drew said, "Lets head back to the river and I'll cook you a welcome feast." He didn't bother collecting his makeshift throwing stars because they'd had no effect and had been more trouble than they were worth.

Walls popped the release hasps on his helmet and pulled it off. "What about that?" He pointed to the blackened supply chest.

"Unless you've got an idea how to open it, I give up. I was pounding on the thing with a rock and made zero progress. All the racket was what brought the raptors."

Walls nodded as he wiped sweat from his forehead with the back of his hand.

The partners headed south, Drew marking trees as they went. "I've been leaving a trail since I left the destroyed cockpit, so we should have a nice triangle map now, with the second crash site, the supply trunk, and the river at each of its points."

"There's nothing of use at the first site?"

"Not a thing."

The duo hiked on in silence, both men basking in the afterglow of having found each other, the comfort of just having another living thing near that could be trusted. Pain and survival are solitary affairs, but having some help, support, just someone to bitch at could be the difference between living and dying.

Walls bushwacked, Drew trailing after. The big man said, "Did you see anything odd after you jettisoned?"

"I got a good look of the eastern section of this quadrant." He explained the lake, the escarpment he'd traversed, and the various creatures and challenges he faced to get to the first crash site.

"Damn," Walls said. "All I've been doing is slinking through the forest, hiding from the local inhabitants like a rodent, which appear to be all over the place, by the way."

"Did you see anything notable on the way down?"

Walls said nothing.

Drew stopped walking and Walls turned.

The big man's eyes shifted to the ground, then jerked back up to meet Drew's.

Drew licked his lips, waiting.

"I saw something, or..." Walls looked up at the dark underside of the tree canopy. "I think I saw something."

"What?"

Walls sighed and shook his head. "We've got more important things to worry about."

"And nothing but time to worry about them," Drew said. "Now I'm intrigued. Out with it."

"You saw that huge mountain range to the east?"

"Of course."

"Their peaks disappeared into the clouds, but..." Walls shook his head again like he didn't believe what he was about to say.

Drew said nothing.

"It was covered in greenery, and I can't be sure, but I think I saw the professor's ancient structure on the mountainside."

13

Drew felt his insides loosen, an unreal heat spreading over him, his head ringing with excitement and confusion. The tasks of survival had dominated his life, and he'd given little thought to the purpose of their mission: to discover if the structure found in the twenty-second century existed before the end of the age of reptiles.

"I know what you're thinking. I was falling, my mind clouded, the mountains were a long way away," Walls said. "I get it, but there was something there."

"Something?"

"At first, I thought what I was seeing were vines that had covered the side of a cliff face, which would've explained all the right angles. I increased magnification, but I was falling, spinning through…" Walls paused. "You know all about that. Anyway, it was hard to focus, but there were several dark squares in the vegetation, like windows, and there appeared to be a path, or stairs. I don't know."

"And you're sure it wasn't just a natural formation?"

"Sure?" Walls chuckled.

"How far east of here did you land?"

Walls whistled. "Quite a ways. Maybe ten klicks."

"So about half way to the base of the mountains?"

"Roughly, but I—" His eyes went wide with understanding.

Drew started walking again as he said, "The professor or Gina could have headed for the mountains thinking that's where the other survivors would go."

Walls nodded. "That's probably what I would've done if I hadn't thought I might find supplies at the crash site."

The pair went on in silence, the forest singing at them as they slipped under huge fan leaves and traversed conifers, stunted ferns, and tall palm-like trees with wide fronds with purple stems. Huge red ants trundled over the hardpan, and spiders spun webs in the primordial underbrush. Walls bushwacked with the knife-spear, the slap and ring of the blade cutting vegetation carrying through the jungle.

Drew's back, which had been perpetually tight since the crash, had loosened, the presence of another person, not being alone, calming Drew's instinctual need to be part of a team, a pack, and as a loner he wasn't used to the feeling. Back home he always felt crowded, like people were too close, always whining and pushing and demanding. He rolled his shoulders, cracked his neck, and took a sip of water before passing the bottle to Walls.

"Thanks," Walls said.

"Drink it all. We'll be at the river soon and you look a little... pale."

The pair arrived back at the second crash site, Drew's spacesuit hanging right where he left it, the turtle bowl resting on its side against a burnt and melted chunk of the ship's fuselage.

Walls examined the piece of wreckage and said, "You said you found the cockpit, right? The nose of the ship?"

Drew nodded.

"So more than half the ship is unaccounted for," Walls said.

"Along with the emergency pod."

"Didn't that have an emergency beacon?"

"I don't recall, but our suits should be able to communicate with it if the thing was live, but they can't, so..."

"It could just need repairs."

"And all I need is beer and T.V. and I could call this place home." Drew frowned. It was a bad joke, and he knew it. Kimmy's stern face appeared in his mind's eye, and shame washed through him.

"Can you conjure a helicopter while you're at it?"

Drew chuckled. "No, but I think it's time to climb another tree. Find a really tall grove, and both of us go up and survey the land."

"We can check the mountains, also."

Drew nodded emphatically.

Walls collected firewood as Drew made wood shavings, and as sunlight turned to dusk, shadows flitting about in the perpetual grayness beneath the tree canopy, Walls and Drew sat down to eat. The raptor meat was cooked well-well-done, and it was chewy and had bone-like ossified tendons running through it which made it difficult to eat. Still, both men chowed and drank until their stomachs ached from the burden, and when Walls brandished a flask of whiskey Drew felt a thousand pounds fall from his shoulders.

"To getting home." Walls sipped from the flask, his face smoothing with pleasure. "Only take a sip. It's all we've got. Maybe forever."

Drew's chest ached as he accepted the steel flask. Maybe forever. He sipped the whiskey, relishing the hot burn, and as the alcohol worked its way through him, he felt better than he had in a long time. "How'd you sneak this onboard?" he asked as he handed the flask back to Walls.

"I didn't. It was right in my bag. The professor brought a case of wine." Walls smiled, capped the flask, and slipped it into his bag.

"He did, didn't he."

The night symphony tuned up, and as darkness fell over the jungle, and the temperature dropped, Drew and Walls threw more wood on the fire, the glow of a massive blaze creating a bubble of orange light that filled the clearing and bled into the forest beyond. Smoke stung Drew's eyes, sparks shooting into the sky.

Using sticks as skewers, Drew cooked the rest of the dinosaur meat as Walls searched out fresh branches with leaves still on them to use for their shelter. Walls braced the branches against a section of the wreckage, creating a lean-to.

The fire crackled and popped, smoke pouring into the sky.

"Do you think the fire might bring unwanted guests?" asked Drew.

"Possibly, but I'd say the odds are just as great that it scares them away," Walls said.

"Even in the dark? The beasts will be able to smell the smoke a hundred klicks away."

"And they'll run in the opposite direction, thinking the woods are on fire. And, if the professor and Gina are out there, they might see it, smell the smoke."

"Maybe," Drew said, but the idea wasn't new, and he was still far from convinced.

As if it had an opinion of its own, the fire popped, and a cinder shot across the hardpan, glowed orange, then faded to black.

Seeing how close the ember came to the jungle, Drew said, "But we don't want to burn down the forest. Trap ourselves within a forest fire."

Walls said nothing as if awaiting instructions.

"Don't put any more wood on it. It will die out soon enough."

Walls nodded and the two men cleaned and bandaged their wounds with fresh leaves before settling into their shelter. Drew wore his full spacesuit and Walls wore only his helmet and neck collar.

"So tomorrow we'll climb?" Walls asked.

"Yup. There are conifers out there the size of redwood trees. You ever see one of those?" The massive redwood forests were mostly gone, but a few of the giants had been protected, the four-thousand-year-old trees signposts of humanity's failure when it came to nurturing and protecting the Earth.

"So why did you come here, Walls? The money?" Drew asked.

The muffled sound of Walls sighing made Drew think perhaps he'd been a bit too forward, too fast. When Walls spoke, his voice sounded weak and despondent. "It was the money, of course, and I've always been an adrenaline junkie. Did you know I've kayaked lava flows on Mars? Been to the top of Everest and Olympus Mons?"

Drew shook his head inside his helmet, realized Walls couldn't see him, and said, "No, I didn't. How did you pay for all that? Passage to Mars alone is more credits than I'll earn in a lifetime."

"Yup," Walls said. "I was support on all those missions, so I got paid to do those things. I was like a tour operator that got to accompany his guests."

"So when you got a chance to see dinosaurs, you jumped at it."

"Yes and no. Part of me wanted to see the beasts, and I wanted to be part of what might be humanity's biggest discovery."

"Or biggest farce."

Walls said, "Do you believe that?"

Drew said nothing. He didn't know what he believed anymore.

"Anyway, it wasn't money, the thrill, or any of those things."

The screech and thunderous wails of two beasts locked in combat rose above the trill of the night symphony, and the ground trembled. Then the sound of breaking bones and ripping meat carried on the wind.

"Sounds like something's having steak for dinner," Walls said.

Aware that Walls still hadn't told him why he'd come, Drew said nothing.

In the void of silence those with the most to say usually stayed silent, but after a few minutes Walls said, "I have no one back there. No wife, no kids, and my parents are dead. So why stay?"

Drew waited, images of Kimmy and Julie staring at him through the endless void.

"This is a new world, unsullied by man. Our stink isn't all over the place, and I thought, hell, if things go south how bad could it be?"

"You've only got a couple of ounces of whiskey left."

"No worries. I can make beer from the breadfruit you told me about."

Both men laughed, and it felt good, the stress of the unknown leaking from Drew like diseased blood.

The next day dawned bright, and after eating some dinosaur meat and drinking their fill, the duo headed out into the jungle in search of tall trees. They brought everything they had with them, including the turtle shell, because there was really no reason to come back to the spot.

To the east the land climbed, so they headed in that direction, and they hadn't gone far when they came across a stand of tall conifers that rose into the sky several hundred feet. Their trunks were at least five feet around, and as Drew mounted the lowest branch of the tree he'd chosen, he said, "The first item on the list is the starvation fruit tree grove northwest of here."

Walls climbed the tree next to Drew's, and for the next forty-five minutes the two men picked their way up their respective trees, going limb to limb, being careful with their footing, and never looking down. When the conifer's trunk started swaying in the breeze, Drew paused and waited for Walls, who appeared to be less than comfortable with heights.

Wind gusted and argued, and the treetop shifted and swayed, Drew hugging the trunk which was only a foot around now. When Walls was level with him, the man gripping his tree like it was a life preserver and he was tumbling on a storm swept sea, Drew said, "We're at least three hundred feet up, so don't fall."

"That's your advice?" Walls said. "Don't fall? Perfect. That's just perfect. Thanks."

The pair climbed until the branches had grown thin and they had a good view of the surrounding area. The treetops swayed, the uneasy feeling that the top of the conifer was going to break off an ever-present fear.

"Shit," said Walls.

Drew turned to see the back of his teammate's helmet, and beyond, on the northwestern horizon, a ball of blackness rolled across the sky. "That looks like some storm."

"It's huge, but see how localized it is?" Walls said.

"Like a tornado or hurricane?"

Walls said nothing.

Drew found the grove of starvation fruit trees quickly, but that early success had to sustain them, because neither spacefarer found anything else of note. The tree canopy covered the ground like green gnarly hair, but Drew dialed up his face shield's magnification when he saw a watering hole at the base of the mountains.

There was a pond, and duckbills, Triceratops, and an assortment of other creatures could be seen moving around the water source, but when a T-rex entered the area all the beasts scattered, even the three horned tanks.

"You start scanning the mountains in the upper north quadrant, and I'll start at the base of the range in the south. That grid should minimize us searching the same areas."

Both men focused their attention on the mountain range to the west, their peaks perpetually shrouded in clouds. With their face shield magnifications set at maximum it was slow going. Drew's neck hurt from lack of motion as he slowly panned his gaze over the green covered hills of the lower mountains, the tree swaying gently. An hour slipped away, two. Drew's arms trembled and his knees were threatening to come unhinged when Walls called out.

"I... I think I found something." Walls described a large cliff of stone that stuck out from the mountain side roughly halfway to its peak.

Drew struggled to find the marker, but when he did, he followed Walls' detailed instructions, and when he found what Walls was looking at, icy perspiration slid down his back. There could be no doubts any longer. There was definitely something there.

The structure reminded Drew of the cliff dwellings found in the southwestern portion of the old United States. That land was part of Indogarden now, but thousands of years ago ancient beings who called themselves Paleoindians had built great cities of stone in the red striped cliffs of steep gorges that sliced through the landscape.

Green vines covered the entire structure, and black rectangles, windows in the green, stood out like sullen eyes, which struck him as odd. Why hadn't the vines and overgrowth covered the openings?

"Access suit computer," Drew said. He'd shut the system down when he'd met Walls.

Awaiting command.

"Identify the object within my visual scope," Drew said.

Walls watched, saying nothing.

There is insufficient data to draw a conclusion.

"What direction am I looking in? Exactly, degree point specific... please."

68.7345 degrees northeast.

As they climbed back to the ground, Drew said, "So what's say we go get some breadfruit."

"Then what?" Walls said.

Drew didn't answer. There'd been no signs of the emergency pod or their missing crewmates, and given what they'd just discovered he didn't think he could sit around in the jungle waiting for something to happen. If nothing else, they'd have a better view from high up on the mountainside. He said, "I think you know."

"Really? I mean… shit!" Walls popped off his helmet and took a long pull of water.

Drew knew exactly how he felt; lost, hopeless, alone, despite them having each other. He planted his feet before each step, making sure he didn't step on a thin or rotten branch. But he didn't come across one, and he was the first to the ground. He dropped on his ass, pulled his helmet, and drank deep as he watched Walls descend out of the greenery.

14

The breadfruit was plentiful, and Drew and Walls cooked, ate, and drank their fill. Thunder boomed in the distance, tendrils of dark clouds leaking across the sky. The forest was subdued, and the duo sat at leisure as the sun climbed toward noon and was consumed by the oncoming clouds.

"Feel better?" Walls asked.

Drew nodded. "We've been lucky. If we'd crashed in the middle of a desert, we would be dried bags of skin by now."

Walls said nothing as he clipped his water bottle to his belt and pushed to his feet. "I figured we'd make for the large animal trail we saw cutting across the bulk of the jungle. Maybe sneak in some time on the path and try and make it to that pond at the base of the mountains by tomorrow night, three days tops."

"Works for me," Drew said.

The men packed as much breadfruit as they could carry and headed east, helmets off, fresh air tousling their hair. The jungle was a tangle of conifers and huge fern trees, the ground packed with weeds and stunted palms, their fronds sharp as knives. Drew took a turn bushwacking, and Walls covered him from behind with the gun. In the tight confines of the forest, he didn't need to worry about the big guys, but insects, reptiles, and mammals of all sizes lurked in the greenery, and who knew what diseases they carried. So far, they'd been lucky; no food poisoning or infected wounds, but luck was made to run out.

Drew's wounds thumped dully as he walked, slicing and hacking large fan leaves and thick pricker vines.

"Whoah," Drew muttered. He had cut away a large leaf, revealing a shallow depression in the land. At its center, water reeds stretched their tender stalks, their fluffy heads twisting in the breeze. Branches snapped and hoots and hollers floated up to the rim of the depression. Thunder cracked, and an explosion of clouds blotted out the sun in the west.

"Won't be long now," Walls said.

The hole in the land disappeared into the vegetation on all sides. A thin animal trail knifed down slope into the shallow dell, and the duo followed it. Drew's muscles ached from the constant bushwhacking, and it felt good to walk unimpeded.

The partners were halfway to the bottom of the dell when the rain started. It came in sheets, gusts of wind tossing around the tree canopy, leaves and twigs dropping like hail. Drew's spacesuit was waterproof, but he had his helmet off and water leeched into the rips in his suit and around the neck collar. His jumpsuit was already drenched, so he trudged on.

Walls stowed his gun as he struggled to stay on the narrow trail, his boots slipping and sliding in the thin rivulet of water that ran down the center of the path.

The wind howled, and the rain grew heavier, a deluge of water that felt cleansing. The heavy rain made walking difficult because Drew couldn't see his hand in front of his face, though he held out his open water bottle as he powered forward. Lightning streaked from the clouds, the explosion of thunder like a collapsing building.

Walls screamed, and then he was gone.

Drew stumbled to a halt, peering through the dense curtain of rain, but he couldn't see anything beyond five feet. The ground trembled, and the storm snarled and argued, stones and sticks rushing past Drew's boots, the stream of water running down the center of the path now a foot deep. He inched forward, arms out, as if that would do anything. He saw no sign of his partner.

The ground gave way beneath his feet and Drew fell, sliding down the path on his ass in a river of mud. He was moving fast, and he reached out and grabbed for underbrush, and vines with two-inch thorns grabbed his suit, ripping and tearing at the existing holes. The spacesuit material was tough stuff, but the thorns were sharp stilettos, so Drew reigned in his arms and stopped trying to use the underbrush to stop his slide.

Walls screamed, but it was a cry of fear, not pain.

Drew still couldn't see his partner, and he eased back, letting the surge drive him forward, muddy water overtaking him, his face obscured with mud, his helmet filling with water and muck.

The sensation of freefalling knotted his stomach as the path ended and Drew slid off a ledge and plunged feet first into a quicksand-like mud puddle. He saw the flash of Walls' helmet as it sank into the morass, and Drew flailed, arms pounding the mud, but there was no resistance and he was slipping beneath the thick brown sludge.

Drew's legs churned as he tried to tread water, but he continued to sink, the mud up to his chest. The rain eased, and Drew saw Walls on his stomach, swimming in the mud like he was doing laps at his local pool.

What was good for the goose and all that rot—Drew tossed his helmet, flipped on his stomach, and swam, mud covering his face as he stroked, legs scissoring, arms pushing the gravy-like mud, his heart trying to escape his chest.

A muffled call worked its way through the haze, but Drew didn't have a moment to process what he was hearing before a vine struck him on the head. He reached out blindly, gripped it, and he was jerked forward as Walls pulled him from the muck.

Drew crawled the last few feet, rain beating on him and washing the mud away, bubbles of color dancing before his eyes, his wounds shrieking in protest.

Walls sat a few feet away, helmet off, head tilted upward as he caught the cold rain in his mouth.

The rain surged again, and the partners hid beneath the boughs of a conifer, nursing their bruises and egos.

"We were lucky," Walls said. Water leaked through the needle-like leaves, tiny rivers running through the bronze needles that covered the hardpan.

Wind gusted and sang, the rain coming in sideways, the dark gray lines in the tree canopy like black cotton candy.

After an hour the rain stopped, streaks of white and blue fighting through the thinning clouds. The partners continued down the animal trail, their suits dirty with mud, the jumpsuits chafing and clinging to their wrinkled bodies.

The forest thickened, the path nothing more than a thin line through ferns, weeds, and scrub pine. Broken stalks of bamboo fell across the pathway, and vines with dark green leaves clung to the dead stalks making a thatched roof over the trail.

A slash in the thick wall of conifers ahead was dark as night, and it stood out like a doorway in the greenery.

The sounds of chirping birds and bleating lizards faded, and the temperature dropped as Drew and Walls stepped into the gray half-light beneath the dense tree canopy. Bushes with mini tricolored elephant ear leaves and massive weedy plants with huge leaves and bark-like stalks boxed in the path. Cotton candy spider webs and yellow lichen clung to everything, the ground on both sides of the path uneven, dull black puddles shimmering in the gloom.

A rectangle of gray light glowed a hundred yards ahead at the end of the cavern of vegetation.

Walls stopped walking and stared into the thick tangle of vegetation.

A gentle hum pulsed through the jungle, like a tiny motor buzzing to life. Drew's stomach went sour, maggots wriggling and writhing as they climbed up his throat. He looked back, the vines hanging over the path swaying with his passage, the scent of rot and mildew assailing him.

The whine rose in pitch and volume. A massive shadow fell over the path, and the hum became a buzz, a single sound comprised of millions of tiny wings biting the air.

Two large birds with black feathers and white stripes streaked down the path, passing over the duo's heads as the two men ducked. The birds tittered and squeaked as if issuing a warning before disappearing into the rectangle of light at the end of the tunnel.

Walls yelled, "Run!"

A sheet of insects surged up the tunnel, a dense black cloud of mosquitoes swirling and undulating like a flock of birds.

Walls' spacesuit was gone, and he had only the helmet and the remains of his jumpsuit to protect him. Drew had his suit on, though there were many holes, and his helmet hung from its carabiner. He stared at the growing fog of tiny vampires, the worry maggots burrowing into his spine and neck.

The initial onslaught hit Drew like a million needles, mosquitoes alighting on every section of exposed skin, stabbing with their proboscis swords, injecting itchy poison.

He felt their hair-like legs dancing on his flesh as the bugs crawled on his face and into the tears of his suit.

Drew pulled on his helmet as he was encased in a cocoon of insects that pulsed and whined and bit, the shriek of millions of tiny wings cutting the air filling the helmet.

The skeeters multiplied exponentially, and Drew felt them working their way into the tears in his suit and fighting to crawl under his jumpsuit as the vampires inside the helmet bit at his face. He ran then, slapping at the air before him, stinging welts blossoming inside his boots and along his arms and legs where the mosquitoes had worked their way into the suit.

Drew stumbled forward, half running half falling, the air dark with the swarm of bloodsuckers.

Walls made it to the far end of the tunnel, and he stood silhouetted in the gray rectangle waving Drew on like an excited parent watching their child compete in a foot race.

A tree root snaked across the path like a boobytrap, and Drew toppled, clouds of mosquitoes filling the air. The tiny black vampires covered his face shield, and the skeeters that had worked their way into his suit delved into his ears and eyes, fighting to get into his mouth.

Terror gripped him, and the primal side of his brain came alive, bringing to bear the reserve of energy stored for survival and preservation when all other fuel is spent. He vaulted to his feet, bloodsuckers covering him, trickles of blood running along his torn spacesuit from the insects he'd flattened. The skeeters were under his clothes, and they bit and sucked on his legs and arms as the more adventurous vampires worked their way toward his groin.

He had twenty yards to go, and as he ran, the cloud of mosquitoes thinned, the air pressure from his rapid movement brushing away any vampire that didn't have its proboscis impaled in him. He itched all over, his muscles cramping, his knees threatening to come unhinged. The whine of the swarm rose, as if all the bugs were controlled by one small brain and it knew Drew was almost free.

Drew burst from the jungle tunnel into a small clearing and dropped to the ground like he was on fire, rolling and squashing skeeters. Walls helped him move away from the tunnel entrance, Drew's ears ringing.

"Are you OK?" Walls asked.

"Yeah," Drew said. "Good thing I had my suit on."

Walls held out his arms, which were covered in red welts, and a large red mosquito bite blossomed on the tip of his nose.

Both men took off their helmets and cleared out the skeeters, brushing them away like dead skin.

Drew drank water as he moved further away from the thick jungle tunnel. Stray skeeters still circled, and he enjoyed slapping them flat.

"We've got to…" Walls scratched his arms. "We need to do something about these bites. Any ideas?"

"What's different from all the other bites you have?"

Walls shrugged. "These itch like a bitch."

Drew bent and found a section of hardpan soaked by the recent rain that wasn't covered in plants.

"What the—" Walls shifted on his feet, his eyes going wide.

Drew applied mud to his bites, and he felt better immediately, and Walls did the same. Some of Drew's welts had started to fade but the itching intensified. Many mosquitoes had sucked his blood, but the fact that those beasts would soon be dead did nothing to ease his irritations.

The partners cleaned out their helmets and put them on, their faces painted with dirt, the face shields opaque with grime. Drew had never felt skuzzier in his life, and thoughts of a hot shower made every muscle in his body ache. Next time it rained, he was cleaning himself.

15

The climb out of the dell was harder than the slip-and-slide in, but the eastern side of the depression sloped gently up to grade level, so it wasn't a strenuous climb. It poured again, and Drew and Walls stripped down and bathed in the cool rain like cavemen, though they wouldn't inhabit this part of the world for millions of years, long after the age of reptiles. The forest was fragrant with moisture, that clinging natural perfume that seemed so much stronger after a heavy rain.

The pair sat in their underwear on a large stone at the center of a clearing in the thick jungle created by a fallen tree. The clouds had blown through, and Drew leaned back, face angled toward the sun. The warmth soothed his nerves and brought thoughts of better times.

"Can I catch a nip of that whiskey?" Drew asked. He wasn't feeling like crap, so he figured he'd up the ante.

Walls harrumphed, looked at him hard as if to say "Are you out of your mind?", then reached into his pouch and pulled out the metal flask. "A sip. One!"

Drew unscrewed the top and took a shallow pull. It was like medicine for the soul, and as heat warmed his stomach he handed the flask back to Walls, who capped it without taking a sip. Drew lifted an eyebrow.

"I get two tonight," Walls said as he got to his feet. "Are you putting your suit back on?"

Drew shrugged. "I feel like all I've been doing is taking the damn thing on and off. I feel clean, and that…" He pointed to where his dirty spacesuit and jumpsuit hung from a branch in the sunlight, "…is anything but clean. How is your modified setup working out?" All that remained of Walls' suit was the helmet collar and life support backpack and its shoulder assembly.

Walls lifted his arms, which were covered in red welts. Drew was much better off thanks to his suit. "I had no choice, and if you're asking me if you should cut away the spacesuit…" The big man shook his head, "I wouldn't, though I'm giving my helmet a rest today."

That settled it, and before Drew put on his jumpsuit, he covered his mosquito bites with a fresh coat of mud. The damn things itched like crazy, a constant strain on his mental state like back pain. He made a backpack from his spacesuit as he had the day he fell to Earth, and he stowed the turtle shell and extra breadfruits. He'd removed his knife from the end of its pole, and he reaffixed it, tightening the length of seatbelt.

Walls checked his pistol, which looked like a Glock, but it was smaller and had a tiny laser sight atop its barrel. He eased the magazine out, gave the cartridges the dirty eyeball, and slammed the clip back home and chambered a round. "Ready?" Walls asked as he stuffed the pistol in his waistband and hefted his helmet.

The partners reached the large animal trail at noon, and they drank water and ate breadfruit as they watched the path. Drew told Walls about how the T-rex had attacked, exploding from hiding like a huge green ghost.

"I didn't see the thing until it burst from the forest. It was perfectly camouflaged," Drew said.

"So it turns out many of the bigheads' guesses were right?"

Drew nodded. "The advent of computer simulation allowed anthropologists who had never been on a dig, never collected fossils, to make incredible extrapolations based on very little data. And now, with everyone pooling their information, the computers are painting a very detailed scene."

Walls said, "I've seen the old renderings." He shook his head and chuckled. "All the beasts were gray. What animal has ever been gray?"

"There are a few, and most of them are lizards. Think iguanas and such. Rhinos. Elephants."

"I suppose. But nobody thought T-rex was an ambush predator."

"Not until about seventy-five years ago when the simulators were able to analyze footprints."

"Like you said, does it make—"

The thunder of footsteps shook the ground, and dust clouds rose on the road to the south.

"Looks like rush hour," Drew said.

The partners delved into the undergrowth along the edge of the trail, positioning themselves behind a thick tree that looked like an oak.

The first to race by were the duckbills. All sizes and colors fleeing as if the Earth itself was trying to suck them under. The larger beasts galloped on all four limbs, while the smaller duckbills threw themselves forward, their forearms off the ground as their thick hindlegs drove them forward. Scale-like bones started at the end of the creature's spine and got larger as it cut over the dinosaur's scalp. The herbivores ignored the forest as they ran past, their tiny black eyes focused on the path, their long necks gyrating as they ran.

"A perfect example of what we were just talking about," Drew said. "The idea that duckbills, or Hadrosaurs, are semi-aquatic was as old as fossil hunting. But via simulation and the evaluation of all the new data, the bigheads decided Hadrosaurs were adapted for aquatic life, but were actually more terrestrial animals that walked the forests and ate plants such as conifers."

A layer of dust hung over the path and the next to arrive was an assortment of mid-sized dinosaurs. Like the partners were watching a parade of the food chain, giant lizards, birds, and raptors wove in and out of each other, species normally at odds now allies until the danger passed. It was like strangers standing on a lift when the lights go out. In that darkness, everyone is together, in the same boat... at least until the lights came back on.

To the north the smaller creatures were veering into the jungle, a thick cloud of dust and grit rolling south along the path like a storm.

On the path to the south, three T-rexes plodded along the trail, not even trying to catch the fleeing creatures any longer. Tyrannosaurus was fast, but not as fast as the smaller beasts of the Cretaceous who had been given speed as their top defense mechanism against huge alpha predators that needed hundreds of pounds of food each day to survive.

A pack of Triceratops emerged from the dust to the north, their horns spearing the air as the tanks filled the trail. Unlike other dinosaurs, the Triceratops' gray armored body did resemble how it had been depicted throughout history; a stronger, bigger, and more deadly hippopotamus.

The pack of Triceratops bounded down the path, no signs of stopping.

Coming on from the opposite direction the three T-rexes loped along, their weak little arms dangling against their scaly green skin.

To Drew, the game of prehistoric chicken lasted minutes, but it was only a few seconds. Time slowed as he peered through the undergrowth, the confrontation that was about to occur a common occurrence in the Late Cretaceous. T-rex might be king of the jungle, but Triceratops was a close second, even though it was a salad eater, and there were often more of them, like now.

Drew whispered, "It was originally believed the Triceratops was preyed upon by T-rex, but as you can see the beasts will fight the king."

Huge bony shield-like frills protected the Triceratops' necks, their sets of three horns surging up and down. Triceratops was one of the largest dinosaurs of the Cretaceous, up to thirty feet long and upwards of ten tons in body mass.

"For a long time, scientists believed the three facial horns and frill were viewed as defensive weapons against predators. Now we believe these features were primarily used in courtship and dominance display, much like the antlers on deer. But let's see."

"I hear you, but my money is still on the king," Walls said.

Neither species pulled chicken, and the pack of Triceratops and the three T-rexes clashed in a thunderous impact of flesh, bone, claws, and teeth.

The beasts snorted and screamed, the Triceratops nodding their heads as they attempted to impale the T-rexes, one of which had been knocked from its feet and was struggling to get up. Bloody mist filled the air, and bones snapped and cracked as two of the Triceratops engorged the fallen Tyrannosaur, their head spikes ripping into the fallen beast, blood leaking onto the path as the creature thrashed and wailed.

The other two T-rexes fared much better. One had clamped its massive jaws onto the neck of a Triceratops, directly behind its shield-like neck frill, and the beast growled and chuffed as it squeezed. The Triceratops whined and mewed like a pig, the crunch of bone and the ripping slap of meat being torn from bone carrying into the forest.

There were four more Triceratops that had blown through the T-rexes, and they skidded to a halt, kicking up dirt and dust as they turned around for another strike.

The unoccupied T-rex thrashed about, snapping its jaws and searching for prey as the ground shook, leaves falling from the trees.

As the four Triceratops came forward like a line of tanks, two veered off to deal with the T-rex chomping on their mate, the other two driving into the remaining Tyrannosaur.

Within the confines of the animal path the beasts fought.

A T-rex drove a Triceratops into the forest, and trees cracked and branches snapped as the two beasts plowed into the jungle.

On the trail, two Triceratops tried to circle a T-rex, but the beasts' movements were awkward in the tight space, not that the T-rex was moving any better. The beasts stumbled around each other, the T-rex's weapon-head darting forward like a bird, the Triceratops countering with thrusts of its five-foot head spikes.

The beasts screamed and yelled, T-rex tails clapping the undergrowth along the road, green leaves flying, pricker vines raking across the T-rex's undulating hide. The beast's awkward movements made the creatures look like they were moving in slow motion, despite the fact that their size didn't appear to slow any of the dinosaurs down.

The battle royale lasted for several minutes, and when it became clear the T-rexes were going to lose on this day, one of the two surviving Tyrannosaurs threw back its massive head and roared, before darting down the path into a storm of dust and grit. The other T-rex followed, blood covering its entire torso, large purple-red puncture wounds from the Triceratops' horns dotting its flanks.

When the dust cleared there was a dead T-rex, and two dead Triceratops.

"I wish we had a camera," Walls said. "Do you know how much money we could make with the footage for the holo channels?"

He did, but they didn't have a camera and the way things were going they were never going to make it home.

The victors abandoned their spoils, and the surviving six Triceratops continued on their way. As herbivores, the pack wouldn't eat their kill. Instead, the alpha Triceratops barked, as if calling all their friends to dinner. With its low head, Triceratops ate ground vegetation, though they sometimes used their size and brute strength to knock over plants and trees to get at the more appetizing foliage.

"Will you look at that," said Walls as the pack of Triceratops passed twenty feet from where they hid, leaving the battlefield ripe with meat for the smaller carnivores. "I didn't realize herbivores had such powerful jaws and big teeth."

Drew nodded as he inched back into the shadows, gripping Walls by the elbow. "Raptors and their kin will be showing up soon."

Walls nodded.

"Triceratops' mouth is beak-like, as you can see. Easier to pluck and tear plants," Drew said. "Did you know a full-grown Triceratops can have up to eight hundred teeth?"

"For leaves?"

Drew chuckled softly. "They shear more than puncture, and they're designed to handle large volumes of tough plant material."

It didn't take long for the smaller carnivores of the Cretaceous to appear for their free meal. Triceratops had done the hard work, and now the other beasts got to feast on their kill, as well as the two Triceratops' corpses. Raptors, insects, and an array of small mammals slinked from the forest, their wary eyes darting about as if expecting the Triceratops to make a curtain call. The tank-like beasts might not eat meat, but that didn't mean they wouldn't butcher anything that got in their way. Case and point being the dead Tyrannosaurus rex lying on the path with its entrails spilling out of its chest.

The shaking ground settled to its ever-present low vibration, and when all the new arrivals were fighting for position around the carcasses of the dead T-rex and Triceratops, Drew and Walls moved south along the edge of the trail. When they'd reached a safe distance, they cut across the path, heading due east toward the foot of the mountains.

Drew's entire body itched like he was one large mosquito bite, but the fresh air felt good on his face. His stomach was settled with food and water, and the rusty scent of blood and death soon faded. If only it was that easy to forget.

16

The partners left the crowded path and feasting beasts behind and headed due east. Bird chatter filtered through the forest, the ground trembling, and they'd been trekking an hour when Walls spied what he believed to be an odd opening in the jungle to the south. Cloud swept sky was visible through the thinning tree canopy, and with Drew hacking and cutting, and Walls watching his back with the gun, the partners headed for the clearing.

The thick forest underbrush ended abruptly, and a dead zone no bigger than a football pitch stretched out before him. There were no signs of fire, or lightning, and as Drew scanned the clearing the tingle of amazement tickled his stomach.

An unnatural stone formation sat at the center of the clearing.

The first thought to pop into Drew's head was the anomaly was the discarded skin of the largest snake ever, but the various sections had ninety-degree angles. The thing was slate gray and made of massive rectangular stones placed in the shape of a snake with its head lifted, each rock in the chain the same size. The formation appeared incomplete, and the edges of the multisided object were sharp. Someone had cut the large stones, even from fifty feet away that was obvious.

Walls and Drew exchanged a glance, their gazes shifting back to the odd formation. Drew's mouth dropped as he stared at… He had no idea what he was looking at.

The partners inched out onto the barren patch of ground, moving as if the earth might collapse beneath their feet. The hardpan was hard as rock and there were no animal prints crisscrossing the wasteland. Whatever had scarred the land had done its job well. No roots snaked over the ground, no dead vines. There were no signs life of any kind had ever sprouted from the earth.

"Maybe that thing is what's left from a crash, or an asteroid impact or something?" Walls said.

"Does the ground look like there's been an explosion? A fire?"

"It could have been thousands....millions of years ago and the charred stuff washed away."

"But the soil is still toxic? We've both seen burnt sections of forest where the creeper vines basically crawled around the hot embers to start their climb up burnt tree trunks."

Walls said nothing.

The sun was past noon, and the sky was clear. Pterosaurs, the huge dragon-things with sail wings circled above the clearing, their faint cries like ripping paper. Insects chirped and buzzed so loudly it sounded like the hum of a small motor, and Drew's heart played bass drum as he slunk across the clearing toward the odd formation.

The marker appeared to be made of stones, but closer inspection revealed they were made of a synthetic concrete-like material neither of the men had ever seen before. The blocks were smooth to the touch and had no discernable markings, each stone a different shade of slate gray. Drew examined the structure looking for notches or indentations. In his wildest fantasy he'd find an activation switch that, when initiated, would show some sign of technological advancement, but he found no such thing.

Drew searched the area as Walls did a thorough inspection of the formation, verifying every angle, double checking that there were no hidden compartments or faded writing or symbols etched into the odd stones. Neither man found anything of note, and as the midday sun started its fall to the horizon the partners sat in the shade just within the forest, eating breadfruit, sipping water, and staring out at the odd wasteland, the gray twisted finger of stone mocking them from its center.

"So, what the hell?" said Walls.

Drew didn't answer. Back home, he had to talk fast, jump into conversations at the slightest pause, otherwise he'd never get a word in edgewise. It had only taken a few days in the primordial jungle to strip him of the need to always be talking, always fighting for his point of view, making his case. He could fool himself all he wanted, but he didn't speak because the answer to the question made imaginary bugs bite at the tips of his fingers and toes.

Finally Drew pushed out, "Occam's razor."

Walls said nothing as he slurped a piece of breadfruit, cloudy viscus liquid running down his chin onto the remains of his blue jumpsuit.

"Do you know what that is?"

Walls wagged his head, then shook it no. "I've heard the term. It's some ancient history about easy being right."

"Sort of," Drew said. "It's a philosophical rule, really, that says the simple explanation for something is usually the right explanation. Simple deduction based on facts are more valuable than more complex explanations of unknowns."

"KISS," Walls said.

Now it was Drew's turn to be perplexed. He knew there'd been some crazy band that wore facial makeup way back in the day, but he had no idea what Walls was talking about.

Seeing his confusion, Walls said, "It's an old advertising term. Keep It Simple, Stupid."

Drew and Walls laughed.

"Definitely applies," Drew said.

The partner's laughter died away, the Pterosaurs above cackled and shrieked, and a stiff gust of wind carried bird song and the scent of earth from deep within the jungle.

Putting off answering the real question for fear of hearing the words spoken aloud, Drew said, "Occam didn't invent the theory associated with his name. Not sure why I know that, but there had been many philosophers and theologians that embraced the concept. It was Occam, though, that pounded it home. He used the idea to counter what he considered the fuzzy logic of his theological contemporaries."

Walls said, "So what the hell does Occam tell you about this?" He motioned at the clearing and the odd formation.

"It tells me what we're looking at isn't natural, and was constructed. The stones are unnatural and too even and unworn to be the crash site of a ship, part of a ship, or an astronomical object like a small asteroid. The ground has been, by all visual accounts, made sterile and is unable to support life of any kind. One must assume this was done to keep the jungle from overtaking the... sculpture."

"People make sculptures."

So there it was. Drew nodded slowly. "I think it's clear someone, or something beyond our understanding, made this.

But why it's here, who put it here and when, and what its purpose is or was, is beyond me."

"And Occam, apparently."

The pair finished eating in silence, the ground trembling under their butts, the steady band of creatures singing, piping, tooting, and yelling as they went about the daily chores of survival.

When it was time to move on, Walls said, "I wish we could take a picture."

"For the professor?"

Walls nodded.

"If we ever see him again, we can draw him a picture." The unsettling idea that the professor had jettisoned the emergency pod with him in it at the first sign of trouble had lodged itself in the back of his mind and wouldn't let him be, but he said nothing.

Walls shrugged and hefted his helmet.

"Let's walk the perimeter one last time and make sure we didn't miss anything," Drew said. He donned his spacesuit and put on the helmet.

As he surveyed, Drew realized the area was a perfect rectangle. It was as if someone had drawn a line in the jungle outlining a new sports field, the edge of the clearing a straight line that ran to a right angle in the southeast.

Walls shouted, "You might want to come over here!" The big man stood at the edge of the forest staring at the sculpture, gun at his side, helmet under his arm.

The tiny hairs on the back of Drew's neck stood at attention, his stomach dancing with fear, anticipation, and excitement. He crossed the clearing, and when he stood next to his partner, Walls pointed.

Drew jerked back, astonishment smacking him in the face. From his position in the southwest corner of the clearing, the sculpture came together to form a perfect triangle with an opening at its center. He laughed and patted Walls on the back. "It's an impossible triangle."

"Impossible? What the hell am I looking at then?"

Drew nudged Walls to the south, and as the pair moved the illusion fell away, and the stone snake with its lifted head reappeared.

"Shit," Walls mumbled.

The triangle was a solid object, made of three straight beams of square cross-section which met pairwise at right angles at the vertices of the triangle. When viewed from any other position the triangle became a line of blocks.

"Did you notice what's at the center?" Drew asked. That had been the part that made his knees grow weak.

Silhouetted in the triangular opening at the center of the impossible triangle a section of the tall mountains in the east could be seen.

Drew stared through the gap in the triangle, making sure the helmet was in line. He said, "What direction am I looking in? Exactly, degree point specific... please."

69.0348 degrees northeast.

"Close enough," Drew said.

"What did—"

Drew held up a hand. "Increase magnification to maximum." His face shield blurred for an instant as he stared through the gap at the center of the triangle.

Dark window-like openings stood out in the walls of green, and like the sculpture, he saw right angles, and the dark trail of steps up the mountainside. Drew pulled off his helmet and said, "At least we know the way."

"Do you think there are more of these things?"

"Occam would say so."

"Why not just build a triangle? Why the illusion?" Walls said.

That was an interesting question. One he didn't have the answer to, so he shrugged. He thought maybe whoever... whatever, had built the things had a different visual spectrum? Or it was part of some bigger puzzle?

"Whatever the reason, it's clear there were... intelligent creatures here," Walls said.

"Occam sees no other explanation," Drew joked, but neither man laughed. Their discovery supported the professor's theory that there were people, or at least intelligent creatures, on Earth during the age of reptiles. It was an enormous thought that was dwarfed by the partners' current predicament. It was hard to get excited about a scientific discovery, regardless of its magnitude, when going to the bathroom and wiping his ass with leaves were at the top of Drew's daily chore list.

With nothing left to do, the survivors left the clearing, following a course northeast that would take them to the foot of the mountains below the ruins. Drew thought if they didn't run into any major problems, it would be about a two-day hike to the foothills, but from then on he had to consider how they'd manage to climb the mountain, which had vine covered escarpments all along its lower edge. Drew hadn't seen a path to the alleged staircase notched in the stone, but he'd cross that desert when he came to it.

"We're going to need some rope," Drew said as he stuck out his chin in the direction of the mountains.

"Let me radio in for a supply drop."

"Vines, my boy. Keep an eye out for thick creepers with wide leaves, preferably those with thick bark skin. That stuff will be less flexible, but stronger."

Walls harrumphed. "From what I saw there's plenty of vines already there."

"Still, let's find a few lengths. It might be helpful."

"O.K., sure," Walls said. "I don't have enough to carry."

The clearing faded behind them, the forest closing in, the underbrush thick and tangled. Drew said, "Do you mind taking a turn bushwhacking? My arms are like bricks."

"Sure."

Drew exchanged the knife-spear for the pistol.

Walls said, "There's already a round in the pipe, but there's a safety you need to put in the firing position before the gun will function. But I'm sure you remember that from mission prep."

Drew nodded and located the safety. The gun felt good in his hand, like the weapon could solve any problem that might come his way. He usually carried a gun on missions and digs, but he hadn't fired a weapon in the line of duty in a long time.

There was a rustle of branches in the underbrush ahead, the tree canopy swaying, the ground vibrating as animals fled before them. The faint static of rushing water leaked through the forest, but it sounded far off. The prospect of water drove the partners forward, the sun falling at their backs.

The crack of a gunshot pierced the day, and Walls stopped walking and Drew bumped into him, the tip of the gun barrel digging into the man's back like Drew was holding him at gunpoint.

The wind whispered and the insects trilled.

17

"You heard that? Right?" Walls said.

"Yup." The gunshot still rang in Drew's head, the implications of all that it might mean sending his imagination on a roller coaster ride that screeched to a halt and left three people stranded in the Cretaceous instead of two.

"That was a gunshot? Not a thing barking or a branch snapping?" Walls said.

"I'd say so. Did you get a bead on the direction?"

Walls pointed northeast in the direction they were heading.

The frenzied forest noise hadn't paused, and Walls continued cutting his way through the jungle, Drew tight behind him holding the gun. The sound of splashing water filled the forest now, and Drew was convinced there was a waterfall nestled within the confines of the deep green primeval jungle.

Time marched on, and thin rays of sunlight angled through the tree canopy, the perpetual dusk fading to black. The waterfall sounded close, but traveling in the forest at night was a fool's errand. So they made camp, ate the last of their breadfruit, drank all their water, donned their helmets and what remained of their suits, and settled in under the thick boughs of a conifer for the night.

Drew couldn't sleep, the faint rumble of water and the growl and titter of the night symphony strumming his last nerve. He couldn't get the gunshot out of his mind, yet he knew it changed very little. Once the survivors were together, then what? Did it matter if the professor had been right if they were unable to tell anyone back home about it? Does a tree that falls in the woods when nobody is within earshot make a sound?

Walls was snoring ten minutes after he leaned against the thick reddish tree trunk, his head resting on the inside of his helmet, his red hair matted to his forehead, beard dirty and unruly. Not that he had ever seen the big man polished, but the man's scruffiness had reached new heights. How many days had it been since he'd taken a proper bath? Sure, he'd rinsed off in the rain, but with no soap or scrub brush or towel it had only been an exercise and cleaning off the top layer of filth.

He reached up to rub his beard, his hand hitting his face shield. Drew lay still, not moving, willing his body to slip into a temporary death.

As it often is when weariness overtakes all parts of the body, Drew was awakened by the shrill cry of a beast to find that he felt more tired than when he'd dozed off. He wondered if he'd actually fallen asleep at all, but instead had hovered in that middle place between waking and sleep that seemed to sap energy at a greater rate than being awake.

Drew's back screamed, and his wounds, which had scabbed over, pulled at his skin, pain leaking through his body. He popped off his helmet, reached for his water bottle, remembered it was dry, and instead pushed to his feet.

"We should've saved a sip," Walls said as he held his own empty bottle.

"Usually do, but…" The crackle and pop of running water filled the forest so there was nothing to be said, no plan to be made. The men collected their meager possessions and continued their search for the waterfall.

Mist snaked through the jungle like ghosts, swirling around trees and eddying below and through the brush. The land vibrated, its steady hum broken by the buzzing insects, the sound of crunching vegetation, and the occasional snort-bark. Something big was eating its breakfast of leaves nearby.

"Sounds like a swarm of locusts," Walls said.

"Anywhere there's water—"

A cackle-like bark, that started loud and slowly fell in volume, filtered through the forest, but none of the beasts appeared to notice. Like parents yelling at a child that had long ago learned to tune out the sound of their voices, the complaining beast continued to wail and chuff, but as far as Drew could tell the bitching got no reaction from the hollering creature's neighbors.

The mist thickened and the conifers were replaced by water reeds, stunted fern trees, and large weed-like plants with huge green tropical leaves variegated with patches of red and yellow, their stalks disappearing into a root system that was partly above ground like mangroves.

The partners trekked on and soon came across a thin animal path pounded into the soft ground by heavy traffic. Animal prints of various sizes and shapes could be seen imbedded in the dark mud all along the path.

Drew said, "The geek paleontologists would have a field day with this."

"Would it really tell them anything? I mean, any patterns that may have been there have been trampled."

Drew chuckled softly. "Not an issue. The programs pull apart the image, layer it, making each mark—not each print, but each mark—its own level, like a negative. Then the computer uses that data to extrapolate the whole."

"So they know certain species drank from the same pond. So what?"

"You're jaded because you're seeing this with your own eyes, in real time. Picture scientists sitting at their desks millions of years from now trying to piece together a major puzzle with only a few pieces. The fact that certain species shared watering holes is relevant to their behavior, an area in which our knowledge of dinosaurs is still woefully inadequate." The team had agreed to be debriefed upon their return, and there was sure to be a long list of budding scientists wanting to interview them.

"So let's go see for ourselves," Walls said.

Dark puddles glowed within the vegetation and Drew's mosquito bites itched and thumped in rhythm with his heart, reminding him of what had happened last time he entered wetlands.

"Hey," Drew said.

Walls turned, saw Drew putting on his helmet, and he did the same.

Huge flying bugs that looked like large dragonflies zipped through the water reeds, but none of them came close. The trees and ferns fell away, replaced by water reeds stacked on both sides of the narrow path like a wall. Drew didn't want to think about what might be hiding within the slender paper-like stalks, mere feet away, waiting to spring and end his adventure.

As he trudged along, an image of his corpse getting slowly consumed by the beasts of the Cretaceous filled his mind. He shook his head in an attempt to scare away the thought. It lingered, but as mist covered his face shield and the reeds fell away, Drew and Walls arrived at their destination.

A series of low, but magnificent, waterfalls spilled into a crystal-clear pond.

The path ended in a muddy bog, the thunder of the falls driving out all other sounds, waves of mist rolling over the water. The air looked clear of vampires, so the duo took cover in the water reeds. If they'd realized anything over the last few days, they'd learned the Cretaceous was never what it seemed.

Birds and insects alighted on the pond, the falls churning up whitewater that crashed over the surface and dissipated like waves on a beach. Duckbills packed the northern shore, and they frolicked and drank, feathers fluttering, their squawking cries sounding, not surprisingly, like ducks quacking. Smaller mammals and black beasts that looked like enormous rats with no tails plucked tiny fish from the pond. Above, Pterosaurs circled and occasionally one would dive like a pelican, smashing face first into the drink to snatch a fish.

Several paths terminated at the watering hole, but as Drew and Walls waited, no predators of note materialized. A beast that looked like a small T-rex stuck its head over the falls from above, but the creature didn't attempt to climb down and none of the beasts in and around the pond paid the beast any attention.

When Drew judged they'd waited long enough, the duo inched from cover, slopping through the black mud that sucked at their spacesuit boots. With Drew in the lead, gun in hand, the partners skirted the edge of the water until they reached a series of tumbled boulders at the edge of the nearest waterfall.

There were seven waterfalls in total, the largest at the center. The clear water cascaded over moss-covered stones, vines and underbrush crowding the river above. Drew stopped atop a flat stone, the spray of a waterfall dousing the black rock.

"The beasts are a natural alarm, and if we cover each other, I think we can rest here and rinse off. You game?"

"Sure," Walls said as he looked around, his face twisted. "You can go first."

Drew laughed. "What? Do you see something I don't? Everything looks fine."

"That's what scares me."

Drew nodded. His partner was right, and he repeated his new mantra to himself. Nothing is ever what it appears to be in the Cretaceous. "I hear you. Keep an eye out—except on my balls."

It was Walls' turn to laugh. "Not that there's anything wrong with it, but do I strike you as a lover of men?"

"No. No you do not." Drew stripped down until he was in his underwear and stepped under the cool stream of water that spilled over the moss-covered black stone escarpment.

The water was warm, and he opened his mouth and drank deep. Since he'd hooked up with Walls and learned the water wasn't tainted or filled with harmful microbes, they'd ceased worrying about their supply.

A low broken bellow echoed over the lake, but none of the beasts paid it any mind. The ground trembled, and the tree canopy to the south swayed, but still the duckbills and mammals didn't freeze or flee.

The largest of the paths that led to the watering hole was in the northwest corner, where the black mud of the lake bottom met a beach of pebbles of every color and shape. A huge flat head at the end of a long serpentine neck pushed from the foliage, the massive neck swaying back and forth as two donut-sized eyes scanned the pond.

Drew stepped out of the stream of water, his eyes locked on the newcomer.

Walls lifted the pistol, pointed in the direction of the dinosaur's head, then let it drop to his side when he realized they weren't in danger.

Yet.

A Titanosaurus emerged, each step a concussion bomb. Drew had seen the majestic beasts before, but Walls hadn't, and the tough guy stood with the gun at his side, staring open mouthed at the goliath as it made its way to the water's edge, creatures parting before the huge dinosaur like it was Moses.

"Amazing, isn't it?" Drew said.

Walls nodded slowly.

The Titanosaurus moved with the fluidity of water, despite its size. Dark leathery skin striped with a myriad of yellow and brown patches undulated, thick muscles churning beneath. The creature's thick tail swayed gently back and forth, but it broke no trees, flattened no underbrush, and when the beast took its place amongst the other creatures at the water's edge, its long neck dipping its turtle-like head into the pond, only a few birds protested. They squawked and screamed, but the Titanosaurus ignored them, the sound of the dinosaur sucking water from the lake like a massive pump draining a flooded house.

The huge dinosaur seemed unaware that two humans from the distant future watched like children seeing their first holo. After the Titanosaurus had drunk its fill, its narrow head slowly lifted in the air, water pouring from its closed mouth through spike-like teeth. The beast bellowed, its squeaky call odd given the dinosaur's immense size.

Two smaller Titanosaurs eased from the forest, the wet stone beneath Drew's feet vibrating, the suck and pop of the beast's huge feet pulling from the thick mud like the pucker of giant lips. The two smaller Titanosaurs joined their leader, and the creatures drank, their long necks bent low.

A calm settled over the pond and Drew covered Walls with the pistol as his partner bathed. Then they rinsed out the suits, laid them on a hot, dry boulder, and rested within the shade of the water reeds.

There was no breadfruit left, but there were small green fruit-like things the size of walnuts hanging off little trees with hosta-like leaves. Drew noticed several of the small rodent mammals munching on the ugly fruit, so he and Walls picked some and cracked them open. The things were mostly seeds, and the dark green flesh was so bitter it was hard to eat, but it didn't make them sick, and it filled their stomachs.

"That was a bit of luck," Walls said, holding up a cracked chunk of the nasty fruit.

Drew didn't respond. His gaze was focused on a patch of water reeds to the north where no paths worked their way to the water's edge. The brown firework tops of the reeds swayed, their slender stalks bending and crunching as something moved through them.

Walls turned to follow his gaze, and as the two men looked on, three pairs of yellow-rimmed eyes peeked out from the cover of the water reeds.

18

Every creature around the watering hole froze, their primal connection to the land and each other sending a rippling warning through the Titanosaurus and its young, the duckbills, birds, and mammals bathing, drinking, and plucking fish.

Everything stayed still for a heartbeat as a creature out of a nightmare crawled from the underbrush.

The beast moved on all fours, its tubular body shielded with layered black scales that gave way to sharp spikes that ran down the lizard's spine. Neck frills hung like ivy, the creature's yellow-rimmed eyes bouncing around as it surveyed the scene. The beast looked like a huge monitor lizard, its tongue lashing out, its short legs ending in long paws with five-inch curved claws.

Two more of the lizards inched from the water reeds as the wind gusted, the thunder of the waterfall the only sound, thick clouds of mist cycling over the pond and leeching into the water reeds.

The alpha Titanosaurus was the first to move. It swung its massive flat head toward the newcomers and stomped one of its tree trunk legs as it squealed, kicking up mud and water.

With stuttering cries that sounded like angry cats, the lizards got low, pressing themselves to the ground.

A roar echoed over the pounding of the waterfall, and all three of the Titanosaurs answered with a series of barks that sounded more vicious than previous cries.

The lead lizard looked back at his partners as if asking for advice, and when none came, the three newcomers turned and slunk back into the water reeds. They didn't move fast, or slow, and each looked back several times as if to say, "We're leaving, but we won't be far."

Commotion over and crisis averted, the duckbills, Titanosaurs and other beasts went back to their daily tasks.

The mountains grew larger as Drew and Walls fought their way east through the dense jungle. The trees were shorter, the vegetation less dense, and colorful rocks decorated the hardpan like monuments of a geological time not long ago when the entire planet had been torn apart. The partners heard many beasts, but saw very few due to the dense greenery, which was a good thing. If they had to change course every time a beast crossed their path, they'd never make it to the foot of the mountains.

Drew was feeling O.K. His stomach was full, his muscles and joints had given up complaining, and his two major wounds were healing fine, and neither cut hampered his movements any longer.

The morning mists had burned off, and the rumble of the waterfalls had faded, the constant hum of the jungle like static.

"What do you say we have some meat tonight?"

Drew nodded.

"Any idea what I should shoot?"

"Let's wait until we come across an herbivore, or one of those turkey things."

Walls nodded, his eyes dancing in their sockets.

"You alright?"

Walls nodded and glanced down at his pouch. "A sip of whiskey every two days just isn't cutting it. My nerves are frayed."

Drew could see the big man coming apart. Physically, he was fine. The guy was a rock, but mentally... He'd gotten very quiet over the last day or so, and it concerned Drew because Walls had been in some serious shit, and for him to be down, or depressed, didn't bode well for the future.

"What's that stink?" Walls said. "Smells like oil or gasoline."

"I picked that up a ways back," Drew said. "Probably a tar pit."

The land fell away and the trees thinned, and the partners arrived at a junction where two animal paths forked in different directions, one south and one north.

"Looks like the beasts were smart enough to go around whatever's ahead," Walls said.

"Let's go north."

The pair hadn't gone far when the trees to the east thinned and gave way entirely, the path sculpted into the side of a steep incline that fell away to a pond as black as night.

Bubbles popped in the thick tar, the scent sticking in Drew's nose like glue.

Walls said, "Incredible."

Drew nodded. "What's really incredible is this exact tar pit could still be around in our time."

"Yeah, I've seen La Brea and Pitch Lake, but still. The time involved."

"Geological events are sometimes extremely slow. This pit was formed because there must be oil below the surface here. The crude seeps upward through the porous sedimentary rock layers and pools up."

"Crazy that back in the day they used this stuff for roads and such," Walls said.

"Not crazy at all, really," Drew said. "See those darker sections around the edges there. The portions that look denser than the bubbling tar?"

Walls nodded.

"That's because when the lighter components in the crude oil evaporate into the atmosphere they leave behind the sticky asphalt."

"Great for preserving fossils."

"More than that," Drew said. "Not only do tar pits preserve fossils because of the chemical makeup of the tar, and the trap-like qualities these types of pits possess, but also, like water, we know from the fossil record that predators often laid in wait along the edges of tar pits hoping to find screaming prey trapped in the sludge."

The partners continued down the narrow path, swatting at tiny green gnat-like insects that clouded the air. They put their helmets on to help ward off the insects, and Drew felt confined. He liked being able to smell the scent of the air, which provided all types of warnings, and feel the wind on his face.

To the east, the steep incline ran down to the pit, and trees and bushes filled the western side of the trail.

"These things!" Walls was punching the air, slapping his chest and legs, tiny insects alighting all over his exposed skin.

As is often the case before an accident or unforeseen event, time slowed, and Drew saw what was going to happen before it occurred. He screamed, "Walls! Back up!"

Walls danced about swatting bugs, his feet shuffling dangerously close to the edge of the path and the sheer incline beyond. A chunk of the hardpan broke away and took a piece of the path with it, and Walls was gone in a cloud of dust and grit. He tumbled down the incline, grabbing at vegetation to stop his fall, but the slope was too steep and he too heavy. He crashed feet first into the sticky thick blackness of the tar pit.

The harder he fought to free himself, the deeper Walls sank into the tar.

When Walls had sunk to his waist Drew found his voice. "Don't struggle!" he yelled. "It'll make it worse!"

The big man stopped thrashing, his tar-speckled white torso and head like a stick protruding from a dark chocolate creamsicle. "At least the flies are leaving me alone," Walls said.

Drew had to laugh. "Stay still. I'll be right down ."

Walls was at the edge of the tar pit and was no longer sinking, so Drew searched for a vine to use as a rope. They'd seen a few candidates along the way, but had decided they had enough to carry and finding more should prove easy—except when you needed it in a hurry.

Drew said, "I can't find any vines here, and the slope is too steep to climb down without risking me ending up right next to you. I'm going to backtrack a bit. Sit tight."

"You're leaving me?" If it wasn't for the jovial tone in the big man's voice Drew might have reconsidered.

Finding vines proved as easy as expected, and Drew was climbing down to the edge of the tar pit with a twenty-foot length of sturdy vine when three gunshots broke the calm. He couldn't see Walls because of the underbrush, but he heard the man yelling.

"Go away. Yo dinosaur. Yoooooooo!!!!"

Knowing he couldn't help his friend if he wasn't by his side, Drew scrambled down to the edge of the tar pit where he discovered the source of his partner's distress.

Two raptor-like beasts stood twenty feet from Walls, their claws in the thick tar, eyes aglow with opportunity.

Walls was having a hard time aiming the gun, because when he moved or shifted his position, he sank deeper.

Knife in hand, Drew bounded through the underbrush, screaming in an attempt to scare off the creatures.

The dinosaurs stared, eyes blinking, as if waiting for this second newcomer to fall prey to the tar trap.

An explosion of muscle and teeth surged from the thicket of ferns to Drew's left, a beast hitting him with a glancing blow and knocking him to the ground. His face landed in tar, the black ooze creeping up his nose and into his mouth. He coughed and sputtered as he rolled onto his back, expecting to feel the bone shattering bite of the dinosaur's powerful jaws clamping down on him.

No such attack came. Through eyes slitted with fear, Drew gazed up at the dinosaur, which stood frozen, staring at something he couldn't see.

There was yelling and screaming, and it took a few seconds for Drew to realize there were two voices.

The raptor-like beast looked down at Drew, its mouth hanging open revealing sawblade teeth. With a jerk of its head and a whimper, the beast bounced away into the underbrush.

Drew's heart hammered as he stared at the blue cloud-streaked sky. Had that just happened? He sat up and pushed to his feet.

Pop. Pop. Pop. Pop.

Four gunshots followed by the thump of bullets hitting flesh, and the whimper and cries of a dying beast.

Drew fought through the thick vegetation to the edge of the tar pit, and when he finally could see what had occurred the warmth of elation spread through him.

Gina stood holding a gun in a double-handed grip, and the two raptors that had started the party lay dead in the tar before Walls, who had sunk to his armpits.

Branches snapped as Drew burst from the foliage, and Gina swung the gun in his direction.

The weapon fell to her side, and Gina shrieked, "Drew!" Then she seemed to deflate, like every ounce of energy she possessed had been used to get her to this time and place.

Gina stood wide-eyed as Drew tossed an end of the vine to her and inched out onto the blackened asphalt along the edge of the tar pit toward Walls.

A little slow on the uptake, Gina stood watching Drew and Walls like they were ghosts.

Drew tossed an end of the vine out to Walls, and he snagged it on the first toss.

With Gina's help, Drew pulled Walls from the sludge.

Walls crawled the last stretch, and when he arrived at Drew's feet, he said, "Thanks," and collapsed onto his stomach.

Gina stood watching them, her brown eyes wide with disbelief. Her blue jumpsuit was in tatters, but she wore a backpack, and she had a gun. Her short black hair was greasy and dark bags hung beneath her eyes, tiny scratches covering her normally pristine skin. The jumpsuit bulged in all the right places, though Drew felt no stirrings of arousal, despite Gina being the first woman he'd seen in... How long had it been?

Walls broke the awkward silence. "Good to see you, Gina. Are you O.K.?" He pushed to his feet, his body black with the slick tar.

She stared at him like she still didn't believe he was there.

"Gina?" said Drew.

"I..." She looked from Drew to Walls like a child trying to decide which parent to make a request of. "I heard gunshots." Her voice was low, and it cracked like she was learning to speak again. "I didn't believe it at first, but... here you are." Finally, she smiled.

Gina led Drew and Walls to a nearby stream that babbled and popped through a dense section of tropical forest that looked to be new growth. Drew figured the area was subjected to regular fires thanks to the oil. When he scuffed the ground with his boot, he found black asphalt beneath, and his memory sparked, but yielded nothing.

The trio cleaned up and ate reconstituted rations Gina had lugged in her backpack. She'd found a section of the ship and had been luckier than Walls and Drew in her scavenging efforts.

"Any sign of the professor or the pilots?" Gina asked.

Walls stared at the hardpan as Drew told his tale from the crash to present, and when he reached the part about finding the pilots burned beyond recognition, the body parts he'd found, she looked at the ground.

"So the professor is most likely dead?" Gina said.

Drew kept his suspicion that the professor had used the escape pod to himself.

"Probably," Walls said, then as if reading Drew's mind, he added, "You didn't happen to see the emergency pod, did you?"

She shook her head no as a smile crept over her face.

"Something funny?" Drew said.

"I've been hanging around here because I figured you'd come this way," she said.

Drew pointed toward the mountains. "You saw the ruins?"

She nodded. "But that's not the only reason I'm in the area."

Drew lifted an eyebrow and looked to Walls, who shrugged.

"There's something I have to show you," Gina said, the sparkle in her face washing away all Drew's concerns.

19

As the party sliced their way through the thick underbrush of weeds and scrub pine the scent of oil and grease from the tar pit faded. They stopped at a thin stream and drank their fill, but now that the companions were on the march Drew noted the extra footfalls of Gina, the three crash survivors like a marching band cutting through the forest. Insects filled the air, and Drew noted Gina wasn't wearing her spacesuit. Her blue jumpsuit clung to her shapely figure, a large brown stain on her right forearm.

"What happened to your suit?" Drew asked.

She chuckled. "I was in such a hurry to get it off. It was the first thing I did when I hit the ground and was told the air was O.K. to breathe."

"Me too," Drew and Walls said in unison, their voices muffled by their helmets.

"Thing was, I went hunting, and when I came back the suit was gone. Vanished. Helmet and all. It was a good thing I had my pack with me."

Drew said nothing, and he could almost hear the gears of Walls' brain turning.

"I know," she said as she blew jet black hair from her eyes, her ponytail holder gone. "It sounds crazy, but it's true."

"What do you think happened? Curious animal?" Walls asked.

"Had to be, right?" she said.

"Occam," Walls said, and he and Drew laughed.

"Inside joke?" Gina asked. "You two have been alone together for too long."

Drew chuckled and said, "Maybe, but don't forget he saved my bacon, just like you did."

"Where did you come down?" Walls asked.

"In the jungle," Gina said. "Walls, I saw you, but a gust of wind blew me east and I landed in the tree canopy. Lucky as hell I wasn't impaled by a conifer branch."

"I hear that," Walls said.

"Since then, I've been surviving. I had rations, but not much else, the gun, a flashlight, a blanket, my knife," she said.

"Any sign of the rear of the ship?" Walls asked.

"Nope," she said. "You guys are the first nonnative thing I've seen. Now, the natives..." She looked around at the jungle as she trudged forward. "As a paleontologist that's spent my entire life studying the Cretaceous and the extinction event, I'm still in awe."

"Then you haven't been chased like you're a chicken and it's chow time," Walls said.

"But I have," she said. "In fact, that's one of the theories that has been proven true. We... the bigheads I believe is how you refer to us? We thought the stereotype of dinosaurs being slow moving stupid beasts was inaccurate, and my experience here has proven that."

Drew told of how the T-rex had showed itself to be an ambush predator.

Gina nodded emphatically. "If we ever get back, we're going to blow the doors off dinosaur research."

The finality of their situation laid out in stark words killed the conversation, and the titter of birds, the rustle of mammals darting about in the undergrowth, and the push of the hot wind stirring the tree canopy filled the void.

After they'd trekked a mile or so Drew asked, "So where are we going?"

"You'll see," Gina answered.

"Really?" Drew said. "We need more mystery?"

"I want you to see it and form your own opinion," she said. "Plus... it's a little hard to explain. Kind of like your impossible triangle."

"So you're saying whatever you're going to show us isn't a natural formation?" Walls said. "It's not as if that would be a big deal at this point."

"I'm not giv—"

The ground trembled violently, as if a two second earthquake had rocked the area. A primal squeal of pain pierced the calm, the crack and snap of breaking bones bringing the daylight band to a screeching halt. Even the insects stopped buzzing, the rattle of palm fronds and the tinkle of evergreen leaves the only other sounds.

The three companions stood frozen for a heartbeat, and then Gina was on the move, knifing through the jungle, slipping under tree boughs, around trunks, and through patches of short green plants that looked like Purslane, a noxious annual succulent with red-rimmed oval green leaves.

Gina paused to examine the plants and Drew bumped into her, his pelvis slamming into her butt. He felt a moment of arousal, but it quickly fled.

"What is it?" Walls said. He glanced over his shoulder, the sounds of tearing meat filling the forest.

"These plants," she said. "They look similar to Purslane, which is high in vitamins and can be grown as a crop."

Now she had the boys' attention.

Drew asked, "You mean we can eat this stuff? Like salad?"

"Maybe," she said. "I said it looks like Purslane. I didn't say it was Purslane."

"You seem to know a lot about the stuff," Drew said.

"In our time it's illegal to plant Purslane in public areas because a single plant can produce over 2,000,000 seeds. At home, the plant's tiny black seeds spread in late spring when it gets really hot, and it also can reproduce vegetatively through its leaves, making it very invasive."

She started picking leaves and stuffing them in her bag. The scene was comical; as she picked, the sounds of a bigger animal consuming a smaller beast echoed through the jungle like a slow-moving car crash. When she'd packed her bag with green stuff, the company continued, Gina leading Drew and Walls steadily southeast towards her mystery.

Though he couldn't see it through the dense forest canopy, Drew's gaze strayed to the northeast where he knew the ruins awaited them on the mountainside. Suddenly he was eager to get there, and any minor discovery they found in the jungle would serve what purpose? From a higher elevation they could scan the terrain for the emergency pod using his spacesuit's enhanced helmet display. What would finding more mysteries in the jungle achieve?

Despite his misgivings, Drew said nothing. He wasn't the leader of the expedition, and they had nothing if not time.

Gina pulled her flashlight when the party entered a particularly dense section of forest. The evergreens were packed tight, and Drew sensed they were slowly drifting south as they worked their way through the dense boughs, sharp needles raking their clothes and exposed skin.

"Here we go," she said, as the trio pushed out onto a thin animal trail that cut through the evergreens. Gina drank some water and Drew and Walls followed her lead.

As the boys drank, Gina dropped to a knee, examining a fresh set of prints in the dirt. The tracks were of a bipedal beast, and three flat toes arced away from a central foot pad.

"You have something?" Drew asked.

"I'm not sure, but I th—"

A sharp crack, like stone smashing against stone, rang through the woods.

The trio exchanged glances as the loud popping sounds continued, and below the harsh cracking, the huffs and grunts of beasts could be heard.

Gina's face lit up with excitement. "Follow me and be quiet."

"Shouldn't we—" Walls said, but Gina was gone.

Drew shrugged and trailed after her, and Walls followed.

The path was like a hallway with green spiked leaf walls. There was no leaving the path, and Drew felt confined as he slipped deeper into the thicket of evergreens, the sound of breaking stone rising and falling with each anger-filled grunt and huff.

The path opened up, and a massive boulder jutted from the ground like a rotten tooth, clouds fleeting across the blue sky above. Vines and stunted palm-like trees packed the clearing around the boulder, but it wasn't the upheaval of stone that made Drew's mouth fall open.

"What are they?" Walls whispered.

"Pachycephalosaurus, I think, but..." She stared in amazement like only a scientist can when seeing something heretofore theorized, "...But I can't be totally sure because only skull remains have been found, and we know very little about the creatures, though recent fossil discoveries have shed more light on the beasts."

There were two dinosaurs, and they were ramming their heads together like musk oxen.

Gina's paleontologist teaching gene came forward. "Pachycephalosaurus is famous for having a large, bony dome atop its skull. See it?" The crack and pop of the skulls crashing together resounded off the huge boulder. "Their skulls are ten inches thick and serves as a cushion for their tiny brains."

The dinosaurs' skin was smooth brown streaked with white, and tense muscles rippled beneath as the creatures surged forward, their heads smacking into each other with incredible force. The beasts were the size of a human and were roughly fifteen feet in length from the tip of their bony noses to the end of their heavy tails, which were rigid because of ossified tendons. The beasts stood on long, muscular hind legs, and two short fore limbs hung from their stocky bodies. Oddly shaped heads sat atop short, thick necks, and the rear portion of the creatures' skulls were edged with bony knobs and short spikes that wrapped around a huge bowl-like crest of bone that covered the dinosaurs' foreheads.

The Pachycephalosauruses continued to pound on each other as the trio watched. Drew felt tension creep down his back. The beasts were making so much noise he had to wonder what other creatures might be drawn to the fray.

"What are they fighting over?" Walls asked.

Gina pointed, and Drew followed the line of her finger, but saw nothing but the dense greenery of the evergreens surrounding the boulder.

"I don't—" Then Drew saw it. A beast a bit smaller, but clearly of the same species, stood within the cover of the woods, neck frills ruffled as it watched the battle.

"A female?" Drew asked.

"I'd think," Gina said. "Like I said, we know very little about this species."

"Do they like meat?" Walls joked.

"Actually, I don't know," she said. "We're not sure what these dinosaurs ate. I know it's hard to see with them trying to crack each other's skulls, but do you see their teeth?"

Drew strained to see through the clouds of grit and dust that lifted from the hardpan.

"They have very small, ridged teeth, but we don't think they could've chewed extremely tough, fibrous plants like flowering shrubs as effectively as other dinosaurs of this period. I'm not an expert on this species, but I know it was assumed that Pachycephalosaurs lived on a diet of leaves, seeds, and soft fruits. Its sharp teeth are excellent for eating basic vegetation, but it's also suspected that they may have eaten meat because the most complete fossil jaw shows serrated blade-like front teeth, reminiscent of carnivorous dinosaurs."

With a wail that sounded like an infant throwing up, one of the Pachycephalosaurs coiled and threw itself forward, its head driving into its opponent's face. The strike put the dinosaur's rival on defense, and the creature shook its head as if trying to clear its small brain of the blow as it stepped back.

Both dinosaurs reared back, than clashed with a thunderous *pop* like two huge boulders had smacked together. Head spikes broke free and fell to the ground like shark's teeth, both beasts' fist-sized eyes rolling in their heads as they lunged forward with their cranial domes out front.

The crack of bone pierced the day, and one of the dinosaurs went to the ground before hauling itself up and staggering into the forest like the beast was drunk.

A chill breeze wafted over the clearing, the evergreen leaves tinkling. The victor lifted its head and squeaked, a cry of dominance that sounded like a cow giving birth.

The female Pachycephalosaurus inched from cover, its head bobbing, its erratic lunging strides like that of a bird.

"Might be time to split, no?" Walls said.

"No," Gina responded without taking her eyes off the beasts.

"You don't want to give them some… privacy?" Drew asked.

Gina didn't respond.

The male, in keeping with males of every species, wasted no time taking his spoils and accepting his partner's initial flirtation. As the female Pachycephalosaurus strutted along the edge of the boulder, the male bounded forward, came up behind her, and mounted his mate. Squawking and squeaks of pain and… pleasure? Drew didn't know, but he felt strangely obscene as he watched the awkward dance of dinosaur coitus.

"I'm thinking this is a first?" Drew said.

"Live dinosaur porn?" Walls chuckled. "I would think so."

Also like most males regardless of species, the act of love making was longer in the planning and anticipation than in the making, and after a series of rough thrusts the male Pachycephalosaurus shrieked, dismounted, and walked into the woods as if the female wasn't even there.

Even the female Pachycephalosaurus must have felt the snub because her cool wet eyes followed her partner, but she made no sound. When the male was gone, the female began pulling leaves from a nearby bush, the sounds of her chomping rising above the wind and the rattle of the trees.

"That was amazing," Gina said.

"For them or for you?" Drew said.

Gina made fish lips as she pushed to her feet. "I wish I had a camera."

"I think I saw enough to describe the scene, if necessary," Walls said.

The trio's laughter was cut short by the cacophonous shrieking of birds as they sprayed from the forest. The ground trembled, each step louder, the vibration of the land more intense.

"Looks like our little show has brought on some attention," Drew said.

"Come on," Gina said. "If we push, we can make it to the spot before nightfall."

Walls glanced at Drew, who lifted an eyebrow, but both men followed Gina without a word.

Drew's mind wandered as he walked, the sound of blades hacking through the underbrush cathartic. He saw Kimmy's face, tears streaking down her cheeks. Boy did he miss that kid. Shame leaked through him. He'd put adventure—his needs—above those of his daughter, and as he trekked through the prehistoric jungle, he couldn't help but feel guilty. Again. He figured his stomach would be in knots until he made it back to her, but with each passing second that goal seemed farther away.

Pterosaurs shrieked overhead, though Drew couldn't see them through the dense roof of green. Large brown ants trundled over the needle-covered hardpan, and tiny rodent creatures with scale bones running down their backs scurried about in the vegetation, the glow of their beady black eyes appearing and disappearing in the thick shadows beneath every tree bough and behind every bush.

Drew drank the last of his water, his stomach grumbling, his healing wounds prodding and pulling and complaining. He clipped the water bottle back onto his suit, wiped his sweaty brow with the back of his hand, and gripped his knife-spear, which he'd reassembled, tight as he fought through an immense plant with huge elephant ear leaves.

20

The companions traversed a deep section of conifers as the weather turned nasty and a light rain coated everything with a layer of moisture. It was a dusting compared to the concentrated storm that had struck with the force of a hammer two days ago. The forest tapered away, and an impenetrable stand of bamboo stretched into the distance to the north and south. It was impossible to hack through the stuff with only knives, and they were forced to go south, which Gina said wasn't a problem.

"We'll hit the cut through," she said.

"You're sure?" Drew said. "We're already off course."

"And we're way off for the trail up to the ruins," Walls piled on.

"I'm sorry, do we need to vote? We're almost there," she said, but stopped and looked over her shoulder back the way they'd come. "Or maybe we should've gone north."

"Are you kidding around?" Drew asked.

"No," she said. "I'm not exactly sure where the path into the bamboo is, but it's here."

"Percentage?" Walls said.

"Seventy percent south," she said.

"Then let's keep going," Drew said. "We can always backtrack."

The trio walked the edge of the bamboo patch, the tall stalks rising sixty feet into the sky, tiny shoots running across the ground and creeping into the forest. At the edges of the patch the remnants of trees littered the root-streaked ground, the bamboo eating the forest in its slow crawl. The stalks were deep green with white nodal rings, and some of them were as large as six inches round. The bamboo creaked and popped in the breeze, yellowed leaves fluttering in the air.

Tension crawled up Drew's spine with each step, and he wondered how far they would go before Gina turned them around. He didn't want to be stuck in the bamboo when night came. They'd be too exposed, and there would be little shelter without work.

Walls said, "How much further do you think?"

Drew nodded, his friend having read his mind.

"We're good," she said. "I know where I am. We should start seeing…" She gave up on the sentence, her gaze locked on the jungle to the west.

Drew and Walls waited.

"We should start seeing these," she said as she strode forward and pointed at a fresh nub on a conifer where a limb had been cut off. "I did that. Not far now."

The crack of breaking tree limbs and the crunch of snapping vegetation carried from the jungle, but it sounded far off. Gina doubled her pace, confident now that she was leading them in the right direction.

Wind brought the scent of earthen rot, and the company reached a set of tumbled boulders holding back the bamboo patch, stunted evergreens and pricker vines with two-inch thorns filling every empty space.

A trail was worn into the hardpan, and it wound around the large stones and plunged into the bamboo. The trio stood at the path's entrance, staring into the dark tunnel-like maw, stalks snapping and popping as they swayed in the breeze.

"You've been in there?" Walls said. "Looks safe."

No laughs.

Gina licked her lips, her brown eyes studying the path as if struggling to pull free a memory.

"Problem?" Drew said.

She said, "I'm just trying to recall the path."

Walls pointed sarcastically.

"I mean it's kind of a maze in there, but we should be able to follow my footprints."

Problem was that the rain had washed away Gina's prints and it didn't take long to lose all sense of direction in the green maze. The trail narrowed to three feet across, and it took many twists and turns. When they reached a clearing and found a pile of bones, they hurried on, taking the wider of two paths that appeared to head east.

Thick green canes whispered and sighed in the wind, and bamboo leaves rattled like water rushing over stones. They were forced to choose a path four more times as the intertwined maze of trails crossed over one another, and the party unintentionally backtracked.

"If we had time, we could weave rope from the stringy threads of bamboo like this." Drew reached out a hand and stroked a thick green stalk.

"I should have put cuts on some bamboo, but when I came through the first time it was so easy," Gina said. "Let's take a break and let me think for a second."

The thin storm passed, and daggers of sunlight streaked through the thinning clouds. The crew stood on the path, sipping water as Gina tapped her chin. Her lips moved, but no sounds came out. She nodded slowly. "I know now. I've got my bearings. We need to work toward the center. Go back north."

The trio retraced their steps, then headed north, the narrow trail cutting through walls of green stalks, the ground a tangled mess of looped roots that grabbed at the companions' toes.

"What made you come in here in the first place? I mean, curiosity killed more than the cat," Walls said.

"I was coming from the opposite direction. That's what threw me off."

"How big is this patch?" Drew said, and as the words left his mouth, he thought that question was late in coming.

"Big," she said. "I crashed into the jungle just beyond it, saw the…" She looked at the ground. "Almost got me."

Ahead, blue sky filtered over the landscape, and the bamboo gave way to a clearing not unlike the one that had contained the impossible triangle. The hardpan was dirt brown, and no bamboo roots or shoots marred its lifeless surface. There were no burn marks, no signs at all to explain why the bamboo hadn't consumed the area long ago.

At the center of the clearing sat a large black marble monolith. Like the rectangular stones of the first guidepost they'd seen, the black marker was cut stone. It looked like a large holo screen, flat on two sides and narrow on the others. The dark stone was etched with white dots and short lines that seemed to shift and move as the sunlight reflected off the marble.

Drew was the first to inch from the bamboo, his newly acquired dinosaur alarm silent. The bamboo nipped and squeaked in warning as Drew strode across the hardpan, the uneasy feeling of the unknown crawling into his stomach and lighting a fire. Dirty clouds streaked the sky, but no Pterosaurs knifed through the mist.

Walls and Gina joined Drew, who walked around the stone, examining its features.

"The etchings are only on one side?" Drew half asked, half stated.

Gina nodded. "Why do you say the marks are etchings? They could be the natural patina of the stone from weathering."

Drew shrugged and moved in closer. "The marks look rather uniform, no?" The etchings in the black marble reminded Drew of chisel marks on a tombstone, the sharp edges of a cutting implement evident in the grooves. Despite this, there appeared to be no pattern, no symbol or picture that he could see.

"Could it be a language of some kind?" Walls asked.

Neither Drew nor Gina answered, but a knowing smile spread over Gina's face.

"Something funny?" Drew asked.

"Nope." She sat on the ground ten feet away from the face of the monolith and stared at its surface.

The boys exchanged glances, then joined her.

Drew felt the fool sitting there, the breeze pushing his greasy hair, the bamboo cackling. He studied the marks in the marble, and after a few moments he saw that the etchings consisted of horizontally repeating patterns, all separate images, and as he stared, the patterns appeared to float above the marble background.

"My head hurts," Walls said.

Gina chuckled.

A 3D image emerged from the flat surface, but as Drew's vision blurred, he lost it. "Is... is there something there?"

Gina nodded. "It's a primitive autostereogram."

Walls harrumphed, but said nothing.

"A single image stereogram designed to create the visual illusion of a three-dimensional scene from a two-dimensional picture," Drew said. He recalled reading that the trick photographs had been all the rage a century ago.

"Correct," Gina said. "Most folks have normal binocular vision and are capable of seeing the depth in autostereograms, but first you have to overcome the normally automatic coordination between the focus of your eyes and their angle."

"So... what?" Walls said.

Gina sighed like she was lecturing a student back at university. "The illusion is one of depth perception arising from the different perspective each eye has of a three-dimensional scene, called binocular parallax."

Drew and Walls glanced at each other, but said nothing.

"About 5% of people have disordered binocular vision that prevents them from seeing the depth in autostereograms," she said.

"Guess I'm in the five because I don't see shit except a bunch of white marks on black stone," Walls said.

"That's because adjusting your binocular vision takes time, total concentration, patience, and you have to stare at the image, completely focus. Have you ever done that, Walls? Completely focused on something?"

To his credit, Walls was smart enough to keep his mouth shut.

Drew also held his tongue, but he was tempted to tell her he'd seen Walls completely focused on her ass more than once.

The three companions sat in silence, eyes forward as they stared at the slab of shaped marble.

The marks on the black stone moved and shifted, but Drew couldn't get them to come together. There was an image there, just below the surface, its outline teasing Drew, his temples throbbing with pain.

"Damn," Walls said. "What in the hell is that?"

Gina shushed him. "Give Drew a chance."

Sweat streaked down Drew's back, the heat of shame and embarrassment leaking over him. Walls had seen the image before him. He tossed his head to the side, cracked his neck, and focused, staring hard at the center of the monolith as the white etched marks danced around as if playing with him.

Drew's eyes stayed locked on the stone for two long minutes. Then like an ancient negative of film clearing to form an image as it floated in developing chemicals, the picture on the marble popped out like it had been freshly drawn.

The image wasn't a dinosaur, lizard, or mammal—at least not one Drew had ever seen. A picture of a forgotten beast whose fossil remains had escaped the prying searches of anthropologists stood ten feet tall, the creature's lizard-like body engraved into the granite marker. The beast stood on two legs and looked humanoid, and thin lines that appeared to represent scales covered the creature's body. Each of the beast's four appendages ended in a three-fingered paw, each digit sporting a wide, curved talon that looked like a hoof. Lines streamed from the creature's large round eyes, and they appeared to move and narrow as they examined the trio. Curved white fangs stuck from an extended jaw, and a white froth caked the edges of the creature's mouth like mange.

Drew thought perhaps the animal was a distant relative of a lizard, but the beast had no ears and its arms and legs appeared too short for its massive torso. He shifted his head slightly, and the image pulled apart like pixels dissipating on a holo screen. But getting the image back was easy, and as he stared, Drew said, "That thing looks too human for my taste."

"I think it might be a Dinosauroid," she said.

"I know you joined the mission as scientific support, and you're not being paid to lecture, but…" Walls said.

Drew simply hiked his shoulders and waited.

"There were scientists back in the day that speculated about a possible evolutionary path for Stenonychosaurus, if it didn't go extinct in the Cretaceous–Paleogene extinction event. The theory was that Stenonychosaurus could have evolved into intelligent beings similar to humans. They even went as far as to suggest these creatures may have actually existed, though no fossils resembling what we see here has ever been found."

"It was a long time ago," Walls said.

"And perhaps the population was small?" Drew said as his gaze shifted east toward the mountains where the ruins waited.

"Possible, I suppose," she said, "And given this…" She paused as she gathered her thoughts. "The theory was that over geologic time there had been a steady increase in the relative brain weight of Stenonychosaurus when compared to other species of dinosaurs with roughly the same body weight. The idea was if one extrapolated that brain growth, today... er, when we left, a Stenonychosaurus brain case would be comparable to a human's by now."

"That's pretty thin," Drew said.

"Paper," added Walls.

"That wasn't all of it. There were paleontologists that believed they'd found a type of missing link fossil that proved the Stenonychosaurus evolution theory, and it might not be total craziness, though that's what most experts thought at the time. This..." She pointed at the image on the marker stone. "This changes things."

"What of this link fossil?" Drew said.

"Troodontids, which is a family of bird-like theropod dinosaurs, had semi-manipulative fingers, able to grasp and hold objects, and they may have had binocular vision. Some scientists believed that the Dinosauroid was a human-like member of the Troodontid group." She pointed. "The creature would've had large eyes and three fingers on each hand, one of which would have been partially opposed. Curved white fangs, an extended jaw, and internal genitalia. Just like that." She was still pointing at the pixelated image on the black marble monolith.

"Could they talk? I mean, communicate... oh, forget I asked. How would we know?" Walls said.

"Extrapolation and conjecture mostly, but it was speculated that if the creatures existed their language would have sounded like bird song," Gina said.

As if on cue a chorus of sharp titters and squeals emanated from within the bamboo.

"What's with the arrow?" Walls said, then added, "Oh, it's pointing toward the cliff dwelling. Just call me Mr. Stupid Questions."

"Do you think..." Drew left his thought go unspoken, but it didn't matter because his companion was thinking the same thing.

"Do you think that the Dinosauroids may have been the intelligent life that built the mountain structure, and they were wiped out in the Cretaceous–Paleogene extinction event?" Walls said.

Gina gazed at the ground and didn't answer.

Drew said nothing, but his memory flashed back to him swaying at the top of a great conifer tree, him holding on for his life as he stared at the structure on the mountainside, the dark rectangular window-like holes that hadn't been covered in vines and overgrowth.

When Gina saw Drew's tight lips and squinted eyes, she said, "You look like a cat that's just swallowed a canary."

"More like a goat that's swallowed a porcupine," Drew said.

21

The party made camp in the lee of a large boulder at the outskirts of the bamboo thicket. The fire crackled and popped, and shadows fought at the edges of the flame's glow. Patches of laser-like stars peered through the gaps in the thinning cloud cover, the fly fart of a storm having blown through the area. Drew cooked dinosaur meat as Gina and Walls constructed a primitive fence of spiked bamboo to keep out the smaller riffraff. To the south a stream gurgled through the jungle, the soothing sound of water falling over stones punctuated by the night cries of birds and beasts.

"You know he has whiskey, right?" Drew said.

Gina stopped pounding her final stake of bamboo into the perimeter fence.

"Tonight we finish it," Walls said.

The trio ate and drank, then stripped down and took turns cleaning up in the stream. When they were done, suits and helmets hanging to air out and dry, guns and knife-spears at the ready should an ambush predator exercise their skills, the three crash survivors sat around the smoldering fire passing around the metal flask.

The clicking and chirping of birds leaked from the bamboo and the jungle, and Drew thought of the Dinosauroid, and their bird song speech. "Gina, I assume there's no way to know exactly when we are? I mean, the world isn't a flaming hell, so we're at least sixty-six million years in the past."

"That's the best estimate I could give you without equipment to analyze the rocks and environment. We've seen a very small portion of the post Pangea world, so it's hard to estimate." She passed Drew the flask. "The bend was supposed to drop us seventy-five million years back."

The burn of the whiskey felt so good, not only for its connection to reality, but it brought memories of happy times. His stomach grew hot, and the fuzzy warmth of numbness spread through him. Back home a mouthful of whisky would hardly stir the hair on the back of his neck. Now, after forced sobriety, two mouthfuls had him feeling brave and relaxed.

Walls said, "So, Gina, what brings you to this lovely place?" He glanced at Drew as if to say, "I'm not telling her my depressing tale."

She chuckled, and it was like music.

"Beyond wanting to see the beasts you'd been obsessed with since..." Walls put a finger to his lips, took a pull of whiskey, and passed the flask. "You got hooked on dinosaurs in the fourth grade. A book from the school book fair."

Gina made a flat buzzing sound. "Wrong, though not that far off. My stepfather gave me a set of plastic dinosaur toys. They'd been his son's." She shook her head. "Never met Jerry. He died in World War III."

The fire popped and bitched, and nobody spoke. Transcending time and all races, the three companions were smart enough not to discuss politics, and there was no way to talk about the Third World War without hashing out how the world had gotten there. There were no innocent parties, except those telling the story, and many of the war's open wounds had yet to heal.

She took a drink and shook her head. "I played with those plastic dinosaurs my whole life."

"And now they're on a shelf in your office at the university," Drew said, taking a wild guess that felt right.

"One of them is. My brown T-rex I named Teddy," she said. "The rest are in a box in my bedroom closet. I hoped to one day..." The sentence died on her lips as she stared into the fire.

Walls tipped the flask back and made a show of letting the last few drops drip into his mouth. As he twisted the cap back on, he said, "Well, that's that. Expect me to get much nastier from here on out." Walls rolled onto his side, used his arms as a pillow, closed his eyes, and said, "See you at sunrise."

The next day found the companions fighting their way northeast toward the cut in the mountainside that marked the path that led up to the ruins. Drew still thought of the cliff dwelling as ruins, but after seeing the human-like dinosaur depicted on the stone, the vine-free windows, and the triangle guidepost, he wasn't so sure. If the creatures did exist, and they were killed off by the extinction event, that meant they could be crawling around the jungle now. His tension eased with the thought that if the beasts had wanted to attack and kill them, they'd already had plenty of opportunities.

Drew hadn't shared his reservations, because he had no alternative plan, but he wanted to shed some of his self-imposed sense of responsibility for his mates. "So, I have to ask."

Gina and Walls stayed silent. Walls was on point, pistol in his hand, and Gina had rearguard.

"It does still make sense to go to the ruins, right? I've given up on the professor, at least for now, and the view... From up that high we can search the entire area, maybe find the emergency pod."

Walls and Gina said nothing. This was well trodden ground.

Drew rolled his shoulders. He understood how his companions felt. Regardless of what they found up on the mountainside, there would be nothing there that could help get them home.

The land was steadily rising, the conifers falling away as large boulders covered the hillside like acne, thick tufts of devil grass and primitive sagebrush packing the gaps between the stones. It was slow going, and when the party reached the top of a small rise, they stopped to drink water and rest.

Drew's wounds had mostly closed, but his joints ached from overuse, his stomach always twisting and squirming with angst and hunger. Visions of wine and steak and potatoes danced in his mind like twirling candy canes in the head of a child on Christmas Eve.

"About before," Walls said between pulls of water. "About if we should be going up the mountain."

Drew nodded as he capped his bottle.

"What else is there to do? I mean, what? Did you need to hear me say it?" Walls asked.

Gina cleared her throat. "I think he just wanted to make sure we were in agreement."

Walls' face twisted, and Drew saw a brief flash of what a dried-out Walls was like. But the big man reigned it in. "Sorry... my nerves are jumping a bit."

"Maybe we'll find one of the professor's bottles of wine in the woods," Drew said.

"Don't tease me."

The hilltop fell away to a shallow bowl, and within it a grove of maple trees stood out like a T-rex at a supermarket. A path ran through the forest, and small bat-like beasts circled above the deep green tree canopy like a storm cloud of gnats.

"That's odd," Gina said.

"The trees?" Walls said.

She nodded. "There have been oak tree fossils found from Late Cretaceous deposits in North America and East Asia, however the finds aren't considered definitive. Some scientists believe that the fossils are too poorly preserved and lack critical features needed for certain identification."

"Another find for us, then, huh?" Drew said.

"Guess so," she said. "They're clearly oak trees, and the oldest indisputable records of oaks are pollen from Austria, dating to the Paleocene-Eocene boundary, around 55 million years ago. The oldest records in North America are from Oregon, dating to the Middle Eocene, around 44 million years ago."

"Can we eat the acorns?" Drew asked. His memory was filtering back to his youth. The days when he and his friends would run wild in the woods of North Carolina.

Gina nodded emphatically. "They can be eaten—as nuts, or made into flour or mush. But first we'd have to leach the tannins from the raw acorns. Then we can roast them for fifteen to twenty minutes."

The promise of new sustenance drove the three crash victims forward, the sound of trickling water leaking through the woods.

The oak grove was bigger than it looked from above. Full grown trees with thick trunks and spidery limbs with paw-like leaves packed the floor of the shallow bowl. Lichen hung from many of the tree branches, and large stones dotted the root-tangled hardpan. The leaves whispered and sighed in the wind, gray muted sunlight leaking into the forest, the crackle of tree branches, and the endless green of the oaks bringing Drew back to his youth.

The pop of a firecracker echoed through the forest, a thin cloud of white smoke dissipating in the crisp fall air, the scent of sulfur carrying on the breeze.

Drew hooted. "Don't waste them all!"

"I got five more, don't worry," Ken said. His friend had stolen some basic snap-bangs from his father's Fourth of July stash.

The thick oak forest gave way to a dark pond with underbrush creeping into its shallow depths on all sides. As the boys worked their way through the undergrowth, the sound of breaking branches and the pucker of feet pulling from mud marked their passage.

Ken froze and put out a hand as Drew bumped into him.

"Wha—"

"Ssssshhhhhh," Ken hissed as he pointed.

A frog sat atop a piece of rotted wood at the pond's edge, its buccal cavity filling with air and puffing in and out as its wet eyes looked out on the placid dark surface of the lake.

Ken put down his bucket and motioned for Drew to stay still. The boys had been hunting for boxer turtles, but the availability of a frog had bumped their priorities. Ken crept through the foliage, stealthy as a cat on the prowl.

Drew held his breath as he watched. Catching frogs at the pond's edge was no easy task, and he and his friend had both ended up in the mud numerous times while attempting to capture the slippery beasts.

The wind gusted, the frog croaked, and Ken dove for the creature, arms out, hands cupped. He missed, and the beast leaped from its perch atop the rotted log and landed in the mud at Drew's feet.

Drew stared down at the animal, the frog looking up at him. He bent slow, intending on snatching up the beast, but then a memory pushed its way to the forefront of his brain, screaming and yelling and reminding. Last time he and Ken had caught a frog... He pushed the thought away, his hand shooting out like the head of a viper.

The frog tried to jump, but Drew got him, if only for a second. The slippery creature twisted and fought as Drew brought up his other hand to secure the animal, but he slipped in the mud and fell on his ass. The frog wriggled free, jumped toward the lake, and almost made it.

With a yell of victory, Ken placed the up-side-down bucket over the frog.

"Got you!" Ken yelled as he raised his hand for a high-five.

The tapping and thumping of the frog as it jumped frantically against the sides of the plastic pail turned Drew's stomach, but he gave his friend a weak high-five.

Ken carefully turned the bucket over, keeping the frog secured therein. "Come on," he said.

With the foreknowledge that a bad thing that was about to happen was his fault, Drew followed Ken through the water reeds and underbrush at the edge of the lake until they were back under the cool canopy of oaks.

"Are you going to put him in your backyard?" Drew asked, though he knew the answer was no.

"Naw," Ken said.

The frog jumped around in the bucket, slamming itself against the plastic in its panicked attempts to escape.

Ken took a firecracker from a pocket and brought out the blue Bic lighter he'd found next to a garbage pail at the high school.

"Let see what happens when I drop this in there," Ken said, his eyes alight with mischief and murder.

Drew's heart sank. He was no wimp, but killing for killings sake didn't sit right with him. He didn't go out of his way not to step on ants, but he didn't go out of his way to stomp them either. He said, "Don't do that, man."

"Why not?"

"The question is why?"

"To see its guts," Ken said. His face scrunched. "What? You being a pussy? It's just a frog." Ken stroked the lighter with his thumb and a tiny flame sprouted from the Bic. He lit the small firecracker, a wicked grin spreading over his freckled face.

Drew didn't realize what he'd done until his friend was on the forest floor, the fizzing firework lying on the ground beside him.

Ken stared up at Drew, a thin trickle of blood running from his nose.

The wind laughed and spat, and Drew realized his fists were still clenched.

Drew kicked over the bucket and the frog jumped away.

The lit fuse disappeared into the tiny, red-striped cylinder on the ground and the firework popped, burning Ken's face.

"What the hell was that sound?" Gina said.

Snapped from his reverie, Drew gazed around the forest, the leaves arguing, tree branches creaking.

"I… I'm not sure," Walls said.

A cacophony of breaking branches and fluttering leaves echoed through the woods.

"Something is—"

Drew didn't have time to finish his sentence because the companions were forced to flee the path. A herd of duckbills pounded down the trail in their direction. The beasts squawked and hollered as they ran, their feathers aflutter, legs churning in their primal attempt to escape. There were at least ten of them, but it was hard to count all the bobbing heads. The creatures were clearly panicked and running from something, but Drew was slow on the uptake.

His mind was still back in his ten-year-old body, the heat of anger leaking through him. He and Ken never spoke of the incident by the lake, but from that day forward they'd spent less and less time together, until by the time they hit middle school they barely knew one another, despite living on the same street. Last he'd heard, Ken was in prison for beating his wife. Guilt trickled through Drew, because he knew—had always known-that Ken was damaged, even as a boy, and he'd done nothing, though what could a ten-year-old kid do? Save the frog. The knot in Drew's chest loosened a hair.

The duckbills left a trail of dust hanging over the path, their cries fading as the ground trembled, and the tree boughs rattled. Whatever was chasing the duckbills was big.

"Over here," Gina said. She was hidden behind a massive ancient oak, its gnarled trunk eight feet around.

Walls and Drew shuffled off the path, the footsteps of the oncoming beasts driving out all other sound.

Drew's nerves jumped, and beneath the tumult he thought he heard the bleat of a frog.

22

The alpha T-Rex squeezed its way down the trail, its tail smacking oak trees, the pounding of its enormous feet shaking the ground. Torrents of dust and grit pushed down the path before the beast, leaves dusting the air. The dinosaur's head was low to the ground, forearms dangling, jaws open in a rictus smirk. It clicked and gurgled between gusty breaths, and a stream of snot streaked with dirt dripped from the creature's nostrils.

Drew and his companions pressed their backs to the tree, the pounding of the fleeing beasts fading as the forest went silent with the exception of the trilling insects.

It was a spectacular dinosaur. Other than the Titanosaurus, the beast that stalked before the company was the largest living creature Drew had ever seen, and he wondered if in fact it was a T-rex, or some larger relative that had escaped the fossil record.

The alpha was black with deep scars of red and yellow. White feathers shot from the top of the beast's head at odd angles, its eyes narrow snake-like slits. White mange, like dirty snow, crawled down the beast's chest, and brown mud caked its legs. It limped after the duckbills, and as the T-rex passed, Drew saw that the dinosaur's left hindleg had a large open wound. The cut looked like a long sword had slashed the beast's leg, and Drew recalled how the Triceratops had used their horns as weapons.

When the massive beast was gone and only a dust trail and the vibrating ground remained, the trio eased out from their hiding spot as the jungle symphony cranked it back up to full tilt.

"Before you ask, I'm not sure if that was a T-rex," Gina said. She was the resident PhD expert, and if she didn't know, the odds were good they'd just made another discovery.

"Another new finding for our ever-growing list?" Walls said.

"Could be," she said. "The feathers on the top of the head, the beast's size, its teeth. Everything just seems a little off. Maybe if—"

A booming snarl cut through the jungle, and as the companions jerked their heads in the direction of the sound even the insects took note and stopped buzzing. The sound of breaking bone and slapping meat carried down the trail, and imaginary ants crawled up Drew's spine.

"I'll never get used to that sound no matter how long I'm here," Walls said. His gaze was set on the trail as it twisted into the forest.

"It's not us, so…" Drew said.

"Based on everything I've seen, it's the smaller predators we need to be concerned with. I know you've already tangled with raptors, but there are many more small and mid-sized dinosaurs that are believed to be ambush carnivores."

Drew's back tightened and he instinctively looked around, searching the undergrowth for eyes. He rolled his shoulders, loosening the angst and reminding himself that if there was a beast hiding in the foliage, he most likely wouldn't see it until it had its jaws clamped onto his neck so there was no sense worrying about what he couldn't control.

Control. The party continued on down the wide animal path, enjoying the lack of traffic thanks to the school bus T-rex having plowed through the area, its munching still faintly audible above the push of the wind and the static of the forest's buzz. The idea of control spun in Drew's head. He'd always believed he controlled his life. His decisions and actions. He understood that the universe was constructed with chaos at its foundation, and that random chance played just as much a role in outcomes as advanced planning, but that didn't mean floating through life like a leaf on a breeze was the way to live.

Certain choices are more important than others, like momentary decisions that were often more crucial than a year's work and planning. He remembered walking into The Snail thinking it was his choice to be there, and it had been his choice to abandon his daughter to come here, yet… The professor had contacted him for a reason, and it wasn't because of his skills. It was because he'd known that Drew would be unable to turn down his offer. Unable to exercise what little control he had.

"Are you alright?" Walls asked. "Looks like your face might crack."

Some of the tension fled and Drew chuckled. "Just pondering the what ifs."

"Never smart," Gina said.

"Really?" Drew said and made a show of looking over his shoulder at Walls. "If given it all to do again you would come on the mission? Knowing you'd be stranded here? Most likely for the rest of your life?"

That last part made her stop walking and turn to face him. "I've got people I love back home, just like you. But..." The wind fled from her sails, and she seemed to deflate.

"Yup," Drew said. "You couldn't help yourself. I know the feeling."

"No, you don't," she said. "I'm no adrenaline junkie. I don't care about being the first to go someplace or to get there the fastest." An odd fly with huge yellow eyes and dark green scaly skin alighted on her arm and Gina gently transferred it to her ungloved hand. "This is why I'm here. To see everything I've studied come to life."

"I suppose I can understand that, but still. It might be—"

Gina shrieked, shook her hand, and the fly buzzed away. "It bit me!" she said as she rubbed the bite.

"Like I said..." Drew mocked, and the three companions laughed, the sound like music in the harsh prehistoric forest.

The oak trees gave way to low scrub pines that clung to gray stone, and twisted evergreens of a type not even Gina recognized dotted the open spaces. Though the incline wasn't steep yet, Drew was sucking wind after only a few minutes, and when he looked back and saw that the trio had only climbed a couple of hundred feet in elevation, what little energy he had drained from him.

The mountains rose before them like a wall of stone, the peaks disappearing into the perpetual cloud cover that hung over the entire range, as if the great pinnacles of stone were holding back a massive storm or some impending doom.

They stopped to rest and take care of personal business by a stream that ran into a shallow lake that was strangely devoid of beasts.

"A little quiet, yeah?" Walls said.

"It's midday, and like the savannas back home, creatures big and small hide from the noon sun," Gina said.

As the party trekked higher into the mountains the greenery became sparse, and pricker vines and spiked devil grass filled every gap and crack in the gray stone.

"We've got a good view from here. Let me scan the mountainside for the path," Drew said. He had the only functioning suit helmet. Walls' had died and Gina's was long gone.

Drew was told for the hundredth time that communication hadn't been reestablished with the Triumph, then he increased the magnification of his face shield and searched the slope above.

The stone was gray and black, and shadows filled every crack and crevasse. It was like staring at the odd autostereogram etched into the black marble monolith. Nothing moved, and his neck ached as he slowly adjusted the angle of his vision. He was close to giving up when he saw it. A thin trail through the black rock, with step-like stones arcing up into the mountains.

After getting the confirmation of his direction via the suit computer, the trio pushed themselves to pack up and make a little more distance before nightfall. The sun was dropping behind them, and everyone's stomachs growled as they climbed through a thicket of brambles to a level plateau that looked out over the oak forest, the tall peaks of the mountains in the west.

"I'll get a fire going so we can boil and roast those acorns," Gina said. "And I'll boil those greens."

Camp made, the scent of roasting acorns making Drew's mouth water, the companions sat down to eat within a ring of stones that shielded the trio from the growing wind, a tiny fire crackling before them.

"Smells like another storm," Walls said.

The western horizon was smudged dark, the sun like an egg yolk resting atop its purple albumen.

"Doesn't look anywhere near as bad as that one we got a couple of days ago," Walls said. "Any bighead history on superstorms during this time?"

Drew kept cracking nuts, knowing the question wasn't for him.

Gina washed down her mouthful of acorn sludge, took a sip of water, made a face, and said, "Yes and no. The conjecture was, is, that the breakup of Pangea caused all kinds of strange disturbances in the weather patterns, so it's possible there are a few superstorms floating around that haven't dissipated yet."

"Just our luck," Drew said. "What are the odds?"

He was joking, but in typical academic fashion she answered as if he'd asked a serious question. "Maybe not so bad. There could be a hundred… five hundred of those isolated storms spiraling around the globe."

"Still," Drew said, turning serious. "I just feel like if there's some hardship available, this place is throwing it at us."

"We are outsiders, that's for sure," she said.

With that, the conversation died a natural death and the three survivors ate and drank in silence. There was no reason to rehash their situation.

"I have to take a leak," Walls said as he pushed to his feet. His pistol had been at his side resting on a stone, and he grabbed it and stuffed it into his jumpsuit pocket as he disappeared behind a boulder.

Dusk settled over the primordial forest below, tall black shadows reaching out over the mountains. Drew felt good, his insides squirming with acorns, the throbbing of his sore muscles easing as he rested. He would've paid five thousand credits for a vodka martini in that moment, more than that for some whiskey or a glass of wine, maybe a piece of beef. The dinosaur meat was edible, but barely. They needed to find a better source of protein. He turned to ask Gina what she thought, his mouth falling open, but he didn't speak.

A squeal, like a pig fleeing the butcher's knife, pierced the peace.

Drew surged to his feet, and Gina followed his lead as she grabbed her gun.

A gunshot rang out. Another, then a strangled cry that turned into a wail of pain. It was Walls.

Gina broke into a run, throwing herself forward as she went in search of Walls.

Drew held out a hand, his mind telling his mouth to call after her. Tell her to stop, be careful. Instead, he lurched into motion and raced after her.

Another gunshot pierced the growing darkness, and there was yelling and screaming and cries of pain. The sounds of pounding footfalls and harsh breathing carried up the mountainside, echoing off the hard stone.

Gina's flashlight flicked on, a cone of light falling over Drew's path as he skidded to a halt, his stomach climbing up his throat and getting stuck in his windpipe. He couldn't speak as the heat of horror and fear spread through him like a disease.

Walls lay on his back, Gina bent over him, the flashlight wavering in her hand as she pressed her other hand to the bleeding wound in his chest. When she saw Drew, she screamed, "Get me something to stop the bleeding!"

The remainder of Drew's spacesuit was draped over a pricker vine that stretched between two large stones like a clothesline, and he grabbed it and rushed back to Gina's side. He stood there like a child, his mind racing but unable to process what he was seeing.

Walls bucked and heaved, blood spilling from his mouth and leaking from his nose. His chest heaved with each breath, and the gurgle of blood leaking up his throat sounded like the babble of bad plumbing. The big man stared up at the darkening sky, faint pinpricks of stars peering through the grayness.

"Don't just stand there," Gina wailed. "Cut me some strips and get some water boiling."

Drew stood over his friend, pain crushing his resolve as if it was him that had been bitten by a prehistoric beast. A trail of blood ran away from the scene, but if Walls or Gina had hit the dinosaur with one of the shots it hadn't taken the creature down because it was nowhere to be seen.

"Drew!"

The shrillness of her voice brought him around, and he stumbled backward, eyes locked on his friend. "Yeah," he forced out. Then he was gone in the daze of panic, fear, and procedure. He set water boiling and made several bandages and strips to hold them in place.

Gina cleaned the wound, Walls twisting and fighting the pain as Drew pressed the man's shoulders to the stone ground. When she was done tending the wound, and Walls had stop squirming like he had a snake up his ass, Gina said, "We need kingsfoil. Do you know what it looks like?"

Drew knelt beside Walls, but said nothing.

She sighed. "You didn't pay much attention during our briefings, did you?"

He had, but he didn't remember anything about kingsfoil.

"There's a plant out here that may be of help."

Drew, stunned from his shock by the preposterousness of her statement, began to protest, but Gina put up a hand.

"Computer simulations," she said. "All they need is a seed, or pollen, and the computer geeks can create a complete biological makeup."

"Still I don't remember anything about kingsfoil," he said.

"Because that's not what it's called. That's my name for it. Remember? I joked with you about it during training."

He didn't remember, so he waited.

"It's an herb, like Echinacea. Its leaves, stalks, and roots can be used to treat or prevent colds, flu, and infections, and for wound healing. It has general healing qualities, and supposedly will numb the pain."

Drew didn't know if he believed a computer could possibly know all those things, but at the same time he saw no reason not to try. "Tell me what it looks like and I'll go find some."

She shook her head no, her flashlight beam cutting a cylinder of light through the growing darkness. "I'll go find some. Just keep that water boiling and keep an eye on him. Don't let him fall asleep or choke on blood."

Gina disappeared into the darkness.

Walls moaned like his mother had left his side, and he reached out with both hands, massaging the air, his eyes focused on something Drew couldn't see. His friend spit up more blood, and it seemed like hours slipped away, Drew willing the man to survive despite all the rational thoughts that told Drew he had no chance. With no doctor, medicine, or sterile instruments…

Gina returned with a plant she'd pulled from the hardpan, roots and all. The plant had slender deep green leaves and a purple flower with a yellow cluster of stigmas. She worked quickly, cutting up the roots, the stem, and the flower. When it had all steeped in the hot water for half an hour, she applied the sodden leaves to the wound.

Walls sighed with relief as Gina placed the leaves and the big man opened his eyes.

"Welcome back," Gina said as she fell back onto her butt, her head hanging with exhaustion.

23

Walls died at dawn with a final exhalation of spewing blood that looked darker than normal. Drew had been by the man's side, holding his bear paw of a hand, as Walls sucked and fought for life. But it was not to be, and as Walls fell still, and his chest stopped heaving, Drew couldn't stop the wave of relief that drove through him like a sharpened snowplow. In this environment the man had no chance, and prolonging the inevitable meant only pain.

Gina had gone for water, and she'd returned to find Drew leaning against a stone, tiny rivulets of tears cutting channels through the dirt and grime covering his face. She put a hand on his shoulder, and said, "You O.K.?"

He nodded, but he was anything but O.K. Loneliness, fear, the angst of never getting home, not giving away his daughter at her wedding, not being around when she had a child of her own—it all came down on him with the weight of two lifetimes, and he felt his resolve buckle. Why not just give up? What sense did it make to push forward when all he was doing was throwing himself against hard, immovable stone?

"It was for the best," Gina said. "What could we have done to help him out here? Even if we knew what the hell we were doing we've got no drugs, no—"

"I know!" he yelled, his tone harsher than he'd intended. "I'm sorry. It's just…" Drew felt himself deflate.

"I get it," she said. "Seems like we can't catch a break."

Drew nodded and drank some water.

"Clean him up and lay him out over there in that patch of devil grass. I'll start collecting stones," Gina said.

"Stones?" Drew muttered through the fog of sadness that had consumed him.

"Even if we had shovels there's no way we could dig through stone."

Drew's mind came into focus. She was talking about the corpse. "Yes, of course," he mumbled. "We need to build a tomb, or the beasts will—"

A roar carried up the mountainside from the forest below.

Gina went searching for rocks as Drew did his best to give his dead crewmate the proper respect. He buttoned what was left of the man's jumpsuit, smoothed his hair, and cleaned the dirt from his face. Then he placed tiny colorful stones on each eye, but didn't know why he did it. Drew took Walls' gun, his knife, but the man had nothing else except a necklace with a Saint Jude medal. On the pendant's back the name Helena was engraved.

Drew removed the chain and draped it over his head. If he ever got home, he'd find Helena, whoever she was, and return her saint. Saint Jude was the patron saint of lost causes, and as Drew stared down at his dead friend, he thought the man had been anything but.

Gina returned with two rocks the size of cantaloupes. She dropped them in frustration and said, "Most of the stones are big." She paused to catch her breath. "We're going to have to think of something else. Many of the stones are buried, then there's the devil grass and pricker vines."

Drew nodded, but said nothing.

Her gaze fell on the corpse, and she said, "If we can't bury or cover him, at least we should say something." Gina's eyes drifted to Drew and the look she gave him left no doubts as to who she meant by "we."

"The medallion he wore is Catholic," Drew said.

"Wow," she said. "An old one. I didn't know people practiced that religion anymore."

Drew hiked his shoulders. "No idea if he did or not, but…" He stood and mumbled an awkward prayer about forgiveness, and the hope that if there is an afterlife, Walls would find a peaceful place there where he could rest. Drew didn't believe a word of it as he spoke.

Dead was dead, but respect was respect.

The pair had the entire day in front of them, but the last thing the partners wanted to do was climb, so they sat for a bit, drinking water, eating the last of the roasted acorns, and staring at the bag of decaying skin and evaporating water that had been Walls.

Drew slipped the clip from the gun he'd inherited and thumbed out the bullets into his palm. Nine shots between him and oblivion. As he pushed the cartridges back into the magazine, he said, "How many bullets do you have left?"

"Six," she said, her gaze never leaving the corpse.

"We need to…" He looked around as if every beast of the Cretaceous was eavesdropping on them, "…conserve ammo, right?"

"If possible," she said.

"Can you think of anything we can do to stop…to prevent the beasts from getting to him?"

She shrugged. "What's the point, really? We can't stop the maggots and bugs."

An odd thought fluttered through Drew's head, a lost idea during a sorrow-filled moment. Did maggots exist in the Cretaceous? He searched his mind, came up blank, and said, "Are there maggots… here?"

Gina licked her lips. "Actually, in a technical sense, there is no such thing as a maggot. It's a slang term for insect larvae in general."

"So the mag… larvae will get him."

She nodded.

In lieu of stones, the partners covered their fallen crewmate with a blanket of dead vegetation, and laid his arms across his chest. Walls' blue jumpsuit could be seen through the thin layer of dried moss and twigs, but there was nothing for it. On the trail, this high-up on the mountain, dead brush was scarce, which killed Gina's idea of burning the body. Drew thought cremation was better than the creatures getting him, but without something to burn, setting their teammate ablaze would be difficult.

Drew scratched Walls' name into one of the stones Gina had found. Then with the wind purring, the scent of death filling his nostrils, he placed the marker at the head of the grave and bowed his head.

Undoubtedly it was the scratching of metal on stone and the wails of frustration and loss that brought the beasts.

Four rat-like things the size of dogs nudged from the foliage, mouths hanging open, two thick tusk-like teeth hanging over dark red gums. The beasts got low to the ground, sniffing, the scent of decaying meat promising a meal.

Drew and Gina slowly backed off, putting as much space between them and the creatures as possible.

The beasts had gray leathery skin, and walked on all fours, their rat-like tails swaying, dark eyes shifting from the partners to the corpse. The creatures bared their teeth as they advanced, and Gina pulled her gun.

Drew said, "Are we really looking for a fight? With fifteen bullets left?"

"I think they're a type of Didelphodon," Gina said. "They were… are… the largest Cretaceous mammal. But these… They're huge, and they might be a related unknown species."

Drew kept his "another find" joke in its can and said, "Judging by those teeth, I'm thinking they're carnivores."

She nodded as she slipped behind a boulder, the scree-filled slope falling away behind her. "It's almost impossible to see, but their teeth have specialized bladelike cusps and carnassial notches, which tell us the animal was…" The irony made her chuckle. "Is… a predator."

The creatures hissed as they advanced on the corpse, mouths hanging open, sharp teeth glistening.

Drew was starting to think taking out a couple of the creatures might scare off the beasts, but when five more slunk from the greenery his hope fled.

"We have to do something," Drew said as the creatures began nosing through the vegetation that covered Walls.

"Do what?" Gina said. She sounded angry, but Drew recognized her tense tone for what it was; she didn't want to see her teammate eaten by scavengers. "If we shoot, who knows what else might show up?"

"We're on the mountainside, I don't think—"

"What, Drew? What don't you think? Are we going to stay here and protect him forever?"

"We…" Drew stammered. She was right, and he knew it, yet still he pressed forward like a child unwilling to accept a parental decision. "We can't leave him like this."

"We have to, and, well, he's dead, and we're not," Gina said.

The bluntness of her tone left Drew cold. If it was his corpse lying on the ground like a fallen candy bar surrounded by an army of ants, it would make no difference. She would leave him behind. This wasn't the Marines of old. With more darkness than he intended, Drew said, "We have to at least..." They'd done all they could do, and his eyes drifted skyward.

"Yeah," Gina said. "Let's go."

The pop and snap of one of Walls' hands getting ripped off echoed through the boulders, the murmur, grunts, and titter of the beasts feeding frenzy like the buzz of an ancient mechanical saw. Bones cracked, meat tore, sinew stretched and snapped, and the last sight Drew had of his friend was a mess of the dog-sized creatures climbing over the corpse like flies on a fallen lollipop. Blood splattered the vegetation and surrounding stones as the beasts ate, their cutting teeth tearing flesh, stump-like premolars crushing bone and meat.

Drew said a silent goodbye to his buddy and the pair eased around the huge boulder and slipped into the thin underbrush. The smack and pop of Walls being torn apart and eaten carried up the mountainside and guilt strummed Drew's heartstrings, the thought of leaving his friend behind eating him like a cancer. He was exhausted, starving, and as he stumbled along his mind tried its best to justify his actions, reminding him that dying for someone who was already dead made no sense at all.

Through a haze of grief and shame, a story emerged from the recesses of his memory. A tale his father had told him as a boy, though Drew hadn't believed it then.

His dad told him of the Donner Party, a group of American pioneers traveling to California in a wagon train from the Midwest. Delayed by mishaps and general misfortune, the party spent the winter of 1846 snowbound in a mountain range Drew didn't recall the name of. Some of the desperate people resorted to cannibalism to survive, eating the bodies of those who had succumbed to starvation, sickness, and extreme cold.

The idea of cannibalism sickened him, but some of his undeserved guilt drained away. He could continue in the knowledge that no matter what happened, he didn't eat Walls, and he wouldn't eat Gina. His stomach soured as the rational side of his brain said, "Let's hope we never need to find out."

As the morning waned, the duo continued their climb. It was odd. Without Walls they made very little sound, but up on the mountainside no birds chirped, and an eerie silence settled over everything, a faint breeze whistling and shrieking around sharp edges and through narrow gaps in the rock face.

With the morning's horror fading from his mental screen, the partners stopped to rest. The elevation was making it harder to climb, and as Drew gazed down at the path they'd traversed, he saw they'd only climbed a thousand feet or so.

The path above was difficult to see as it cut between a narrow ledge of stone and a huge boulder. It looked like the boulder could be dislodged in a strong breeze, and the partners gave it a wide berth as they scrambled up the stone steps carved into the cliff face.

"You O.K.?" Gina asked.

"I guess," he said. "You?"

"I'm fine. What happened down there wasn't our fault and there's nothing we could have done."

"Still feel like shit, though."

"Are you up for this?" she asked, pointing at the steps which were as close to vertical and were really no more than a ladder in the stone.

"We could rest here a little," she said. "Spend the night."

"Naw." Drew rolled his shoulders. "You go first, though. That way if I fall, I don't take you down with me."

"If you fall, I'll…" She let the sentence die as she mounted the steps, planting her feet carefully before each movement. "Put your helmet on and see if there's anything to be seen up here," she said.

Drew complied, and as he enhanced the magnification of his face shield, green vines wriggled over the mountainside, blending into the shadows and gray stone.

Gina climbed, and after twenty steps she stopped and looked back at Drew, who still stood at the base of the steps staring up at her. She was fifteen feet above him balancing on the narrow steps embedded in the cliff face.

The cliff dwelling materialized out of the shadows and greenery and Drew started. "Increase magnification to maximum." The face shield blurred, then slowly came into focus. The cliff dwelling was at least five stories high, and it was nestled into the mountain like a natural formation. Dark windows, uncovered by overgrowth and vines, looked out upon the mountain's side. He did a fast count and concluded that there were at least fifty dark windows in the structure.

A dark silhouette filled one of the larger windows, but when Drew focused, there was nothing there.

24

Drew and Gina took turns sleeping, and after an uncomfortable night on the mountainside the pair set off early, pushing up the vertical steps to a plateau, where they discovered a tunnel that sliced into the mountainside. A large precipice of stone jutted from the cliff face above and it stretched to the north and south. Beyond it, higher up on the mountain, the trail could be seen meandering up to the vine-covered cliff dwelling.

The tunnel looked natural, the entrance to the cave a tall triangle with jagged edges. Creeper vines hung over the dark maw like hair, but the air that flowed from within smelled fresh and untainted.

"Not loving this," Gina said. "But I don't see another way."

Drew felt Gina's unease, that feeling of being thrust down a cattle chute to a place you didn't want to go and wouldn't see coming until it was too late to turn back.

Gina pulled her flashlight, flicked it on, and panned the harsh LED light through the dangling vegetation.

The cavern was nothing more than a crack in the mountainside. Unlike caves formed by water or lava, the cave walls were ragged, and flat slabs of stone protruded from the walls before giving way to angled surfaces that zigzagged up into blackness. Tufts of devil grass fought for life just inside the cave mouth, and animal prints could be seen in the dust and grit that covered the slanted ground.

Drew inched aside the vines and stepped into the cool darkness. Sweat dripped down his back, and he felt chilled as the wind whistled through the cave entrance.

Gina joined him and took the lead. "Head on a swivel." Her flashlight beam cut through the gloom, shadows dancing just beyond the reach of the light.

Smooth sections of the cave walls were decorated with what Drew could only describe as pictograms, and exhilaration coursed through him, the tips of his fingers and toes stinging with pain. The realization that the professor had been... was... right. There were no doubts now. Intelligent creatures had lived during the Cretaceous because dinosaurs didn't create the drawings he was looking at.

"Amazing," Gina said as she splashed the light around.

There were a series of squiggles, lines, dots, and slashes that could have been primitive communication symbols, and there were many stick figures performing daily rituals like bathing, cooking, and tending what looked like a fire.

When the duo reached a large triangle etched in the stone, the unmistakable image of a monstrous eye within, Drew's skin crawled with a million imaginary bugs.

Farther down the line a statue of a Dinosauroid blocked the path. It stood eight feet tall, its thick legs chiseled from a boulder that had pushed up through the mountain when the range was formed. Rough cut slashes that represented scales covered the creature's body, and each stone appendage ended in a three-fingered paw, each digit sporting a wide, curved talon. The creature's large round eyes, like the eye inside the triangle, stared defiantly into darkness. Stone fangs curved from an extended jaw, and the beast's narrow face appeared contorted with anger.

"Looks like our intelligent life," Drew said.

Gina nodded. "And this one didn't take extreme patience to see."

The partners pushed on, Drew's unease growing with each step. They'd seen signs of the markers they'd encountered, but not much else, and he thought it was high time to see the sun again.

The wind choked and coughed, and the cave narrowed before opening up into a wide chamber that was roughly round. Here there were signs of water from the distant past, and red gravel covered the ground. Gina panned the light around, and symbols similar to the ones they'd seen on the walls adorned every flat surface.

A stone column, like a skinny totem pole, protruded from the stone floor at the center of the space. Tiny holes pocked the mostly vertical walls, and daggers of light streamed through narrow gaps and holes in the stone ceiling.

Drew eased into the chamber, gun out before him in a double-handed grip as he pretended to know what he was doing. He knew guns, had fired the same weapon he held many times, yet he still felt like an imposter as he swung the weapon around, looking for…

Gina said, "Looks clear to me and there appears to be light at the end of the tunnel down there."

Drew strained to see through the gloom, and he noticed that the pole at the center of the space was made of an odd translucent stone flecked with gold and silver. To Drew it looked like silver and gold flecks were incased in quartz. The silver and gold sparkled under the harsh LED light, and Drew reached out and caressed the smooth pole.

A loud click reverberated through the cave.

The pole began to slide into the floor, and the sound of stone scraping on stone filled the cavern. Two blocks of stone began to lower like massive doors, threatening to trap the partners.

"What do I do?" Drew wailed.

Gina glanced at both exits, which were shrinking as the doors lowered.

Drew grabbed the odd pole, and it slipped through his hands, the smooth stone difficult to grip. He struggled, squeezing tighter, bracing his feet and leaning in, using the leverage of his weight to stop the pole's movement.

The stone pillar screeched to a halt, two feet of the pole having disappeared into the floor.

Gina's sigh of relief was so loud Drew imagined he felt her hot breath on his face. The slabs of stone had stopped descending, and both exits revealed a six-foot ribbon of darkness below where the stone doors had stopped. Rock cracked and popped as the massive chunks of stone fought against the mechanism that held the doors in place.

"Don't let go," Gina said as she made the connection from the pole to the doors.

Drew's arms ached with the strain, but he saw only one solution. Gina should escape before he lost his strength and the primeval trap finished closing. "One of us needs to get out to help the other."

Gina said, "I'm not leaving you."

"Of course you aren't," he said. Drew couldn't let the woman know how relieved he was to hear that. When it came to life and death it was every man... and woman, for themselves, and Gina's loyalty warmed his heart, though it brought little hope.

With an apprehension that was palpable, Gina nodded and inched back the way she'd come, gun out, eyes locked on the dark maw that marked the way they'd entered. She took a hesitant step, then another, but when she was within five feet of the exit, the sing song babble of birds chittering and tapping carried down the cave.

Sharp-tipped spears angled from the holes in the chamber walls, extending outward and pressing Gina back, all the spears inching out at the same pace as if controlled by one mind.

Gina backed up and joined Drew by the pole, and the spears ceased advancing.

"So we're not alone," Gina said.

Understatement of a lifetime. "What now? I can't hold this forever."

"Let me take a turn." Gina stuck her gun in her waistband and gripped the stone column tightly with both hands.

Drew let go as he rolled his shoulders and cracked his neck.

The pole slid an inch during the transfer, and both stone doors screeched as they slid down another inch.

"Everything must be connected to some type of gear mechanism," Drew said.

"Do we have enough time to make a run for it?" Gina asked.

Drew shook his head no. The chamber was roughly forty feet long, but the spears cut the space in half, and there was no way to make a run for the exit without chancing getting impaled before the doors closed.

With no ground left to cover, Gina and Drew took turns holding the pole in place, its clear stone flecked with gold and silver sparkling under the flashlight's beam.

The sound of tittering birds ceased, and the spear points drew back, but not all the way. Outside a beast of the air shrieked, its thin cry distant and forlorn, the faint push of the wind stirring dust and grit from the red rock floor.

"How long can we do this?" Gina said as Drew took over holding the pole. She rubbed her arms, her dirty face twisted in consternation.

Drew's head rang with weariness, his nerves stretched beyond the breaking point. The last few days had been the most challenging of his life, and if it ended here, then so be it. A wave of shame and anger rolled through him, Kimmy's face with pursed lips staring incredulously at him through the void. No, he wouldn't... couldn't give up.

He catalogued every unnatural thing he'd seen in the Cretaceous, searching for any clue, anything that might help him. The triangle gave him the perspective to see the city, and the drawing that had revealed itself showed who lived in it. That had taken patience. What did he need now?

"I need a break," Gina said.

Drew took over. He'd developed a system whereby he leaned against the pole, using his weight, and wedging his arms vertically between his body, which took some of the weight off his hands and arms.

The shards of light streaming into the chamber faded to dusk, then disappeared as the sun dropped to the horizon. Gina turned off the flashlight to save the battery, and she drank some water and held the bottle for Drew.

When impenetrable darkness filled the cave, the sound of wood sliding over stone carried on the breeze and the spears retracted, leaving the decorated stone walls the way they'd been.

A loud click resounded in the enclosed space, and like a lever had been pulled, the pole slid up, back into position, and the giant stone doors retracted.

Gina flicked on the flashlight and the two companions stood staring at each other in amazement, the air filled with dust and grit, the echo of the shrieking stone still hollering in his head.

"What just happened?" Gina said.

"We proved our perseverance," Drew said, but he really had no idea what had happened.

With the passageway open again, the partners pushed into the darkness, Gina's flashlight beam bouncing around. There were no pictograms on the walls here, and the tunnel shrank to a hallway. A hundred feet distant a small triangle of light marked the exit, and as the pair trudged along Gina said, "So you think that was a test? To see how tough we are?"

"Maybe not a test, but a lesson," Drew said. What he left unspoken was that he thought the tests were yet to come.

Gina exited the cave first, gun out as she scouted the area. The mountainside was bleak, tufts of devil grass and creeping juniper-like evergreens the only signs of life. The wind hollered, and it was cold. Above, the dark city jutted from the mountain, and to Drew it looked like there was a faint glow of fire within.

"I'm calling it for the night," Drew said. "That O.K. with you?"

She nodded. "Not out here, though." She pointed back toward the cave.

Drew had no desire to go back into the tunnel, but he agreed with Gina. They needed some protection from the beasts and the cold, and there was nothing to burn up this high so there'd be no fire.

Just inside the cave mouth the partners nestled into each other, sharing body heat as they hugged. Drew felt Gina's hard body against his, felt her breasts pressing against his back, yet he felt no twinge of arousal. Gina was his crewmate... like a sister, yet biology was biology. Was he that tired? That distraught and shot that his body didn't recognize a beautiful woman?

The wind babbled, and Drew would have given anything for another sip of Walls' whiskey. As sleep wrapped him in its cold embrace, he thought of his dead friend, pictured the beasts alighting on him and pulling him apart. Hunger pains, anger, and grief knotted Drew's stomach, but he was so exhausted he fell asleep moments after closing his eyes.

25

Drew awoke to the call of a Pterosaur, its screech grating his nerves and reminding him where he was. He'd been dreaming of a warm beach and a cold beer, and he felt the tingle of carbonation on his tongue, tasted the sweet wheat, relished the soothing warmth as the alcohol coursed through him. He shivered, and when he realized Gina was gone, he pressed to his feet like he was sitting on an ant hill.

Sunlight streamed into the cave mouth, and Drew inched out into daylight, the path and the mountaintop shrouded in mist. Thin rays of sunlight sparked through the fog, the gray stone slick with morning moisture.

The wind was chilled, and as he gazed back down the mountain the oak forest was a green blur. Above, the dark city loomed, its forward edge jutting out from the cliff face. The faint static of running water filled the silence, and Drew figured that's where his partner was, so he followed the sound.

This high up the river would probably be a trickle, but that was all the duo needed. He judged they could reach the city today with a steady climb, so filling the water bottles one last time was crucial. They had no food left, so regardless of what they discovered in the city, finding food would be a priority.

A rock lined culvert ran along the path and a thin stream of water ran therein. The stones were intricately fitted and clearly the work of... He'd given up speculating, and instead gazed up at the precipice of stone above and tried to picture his daughter in his mind's eye.

The trail leveled out, and a thin waterfall shot from the side of the mountain like a broken supply pipe. Mist billowed from the thin falls as the stream of water crashed onto a large flat boulder.

Atop the boulder, wearing only her underwear, was Gina. She stood beneath the stream of water, rinsing off the grime. A small pond, more of a puddle, really, surrounded the boulder and it emptied into the culvert that ran alongside the path.

Again, Drew felt nothing and for the first time he wondered if there was something wrong with him. Gina's muscled body glistened, her hair pulled back, the movement of her body elegant and precise. A wave of shame washed over him, and Drew turned away, keeping her in the extreme of his peripheral vision, and yelled, "Yo. That safe to do by yourself?"

She turned, water cascading over her head. "No, but I didn't want to wake you," she said. "And, well, at this point…"

Yeah. At this point what did it matter? "Let me know when you're done."

"What? You shy?"

Drew said nothing. Was she flirting with him? He felt nothing. Was he dead?

"After everything we've been through together you're uncomfortable seeing my tits?"

"A little." What he'd said was pathetic, not funny. He was single. She was single. Why not go out with a bang?

"You were married, right?" she asked.

"I was."

"Was." She stepped from the water, but with no towel to dry off, and the cold nipping at her, she put her dirty jumpsuit back on. "The water is freezing."

Drew made his way to the pond's edge and cupped his hands under the waterfall.

The screech of Pterosaurs arguing ripped through the stillness, the great beasts streaking through the mists, their sail-like wings fluttering in the wind. The creatures were circling too close for Drew's liking, but as he sucked down water people would pay ten credits a bottle for back home, a chill ran through him, despite the spacesuit. His helmet hung from its carabiner, his knife was in its sheath, its pole gone, and Walls' pistol was in his pocket. He rolled his shoulders, trying to shake whatever was eating at him.

The Pterosaurs wailed again, a thin *reek reek reek* that went through Drew like a nail.

"Amazing, aren't they?" Gina said as she brushed her wet hair aside. She looked like a goddess standing atop the boulder, the waterfall sparkling behind her.

"Amazing isn't the word I wo—"

Reeeeeeeeeeeeeeekkkkkkk!

A Pterosaur the size of an eagle burst from the mist, the reptilian beast's narrow jaws flexing open, needle teeth glinting.

Drew's mind flashed to Walls, the surprise attack, his heart hammering as the weight of being alone again settled on him like a thousand pounds of dinosaur dung.

Gina was faster on the uptake, and she put up a hand to ward off the blow as she dropped and rolled.

The Pterosaur's beak snapped closed as the creature pounded its wings, pulling up short and rearing to make another strike.

Gina rolled off the boulder she'd been using as a shower platform, but like a cat that's been dropped up-side-down, she twisted as she fell and managed to land on her knees in the patch of devil grass wedged between the boulder and the mountainside.

Reek! Reek!

More beasts pushed through the mists. There were more than Drew could count. The order to move was finally answered by his command center, and Drew lurched to his feet, his gaze locked on his partner.

Gina reached her gun, and with one smooth motion she scooped up the pistol, aimed, and blew the Pterosaur off its perch. Blood and bone fragments splattered the mountainside, and for a heartbeat everything went still.

The flock of Pterosaurs squawked and chirped as they came, the sky a mess of fluttering wings and mist.

When Drew turned tail Gina was already jumping down the mountainside, weaving in and out of boulders like a chicken running from the knife. His heart pounded in his chest as he trailed after, the sores on his feet from the spacesuit boots sending daggers of pain knifing up his legs. The shrill cries of the beasts sounded like dying seagulls, and they blocked all other sound as they came on in their fury.

Drew remembered he had a gun and he tried to pull it free, his gaze dripping to his pocket for an instant.

Smack!

Swirling blackness and clouds as Drew bounced off a boulder surrounded by pricker vines and landed in the culvert, cold water shocking him still. He got to his knees and blood ran from a gash in his forehead, dripping into his eyes and momentarily blinding him. He wiped it away with the back of his hand, pain knifing through his head as Gina's chiseled form came into focus.

She hid within a shallow crack in the mountain, her back pressed to stone as she panned her gun around. Why wasn't she firing? Drew shook his head to clear the cobwebs as he sat up and gripped his own weapon. The cold metal felt good in his hand as he pulled the gun free, but as he aimed, he saw there were too many targets and he only had nine bullets left.

One of the beasts streaked from the mist and hit Drew with a glancing blow, and he fell back into the culvert, the water running strong and tugging him away from Gina. A screech made Drew look up, and a Pterosaur was coming right at his face. He rolled, his head dipping below the flowing water as he avoided snapping jaws filled with a double row of sharp teeth.

Drew brought up the gun, his back pressed to the stones of the culvert, water running over his face. He fired and the bullet struck the Pterosaur in its gangly midsection, the force of the bullet knocking the flying reptile backward as if a great gust of wind had torn the creature away. Drew sat up as water eddied around him, his chest pounding, his vision a little blurry.

Pterosaurs filled the sky, a knot of teeth and leathery wings, the beasts' death cries terrible. The flying carpets didn't slow as they cut in and out of boulders like missiles, their sail-like wings folding and spreading with such precision Drew couldn't help but be impressed by their agility.

He pressed to his feet, the knee-deep water pulling at his legs.

Two claws grasped at Drew's shoulders, pain splitting his head as he pulled free and twisted around to face his attacker. The beast crash-landed before him, wings spread, narrow beak-like mouth open, dark eyes gleaming. It snapped its beak and hissed as it came forward, jerking its head back as it prepared to strike.

Drew leveled his gun and put a bullet between the creature's eyes, and the Pterosaur's head exploded with a spray of blood and bone. The animal fell into the culvert, its bony legs pointing up as it floated away.

Another beast came at Drew, and he dodged and avoided the attack. The flying reptiles settled on the boulders all around him, their pounding wings like thunder, their cries fingernails raking over glass.

Gina squeezed off a couple of shots and took out two of the dragons closest to Drew, but the deaths and gunshots didn't scare the creatures and they came on with the furious determination of hunters desperate to get at their prey.

A shriek louder and fiercer than any Drew had heard since arriving cut through the chatter of the Pterosaurs and all the beasts fell still as one.

The mumble of the wind, Drew's harsh breathing, and the soothing sound of water gurgling over stones filled the void. The thinning mists billowed down the mountainside and Drew caught motion in the corner of his eye in Gina's direction. He turned and saw her waving her arms, motioning for him to join her where she hid in a crack in the mountainside.

Drew judged the distance to be forty feet and he was considering making a run for it when another horrible screech pierced the day.

The flock of turkey-sized Pterosaurs scattered like a cloud of gnats in a gust of wind. Wings pounded, but no squeaks and shrieks disturbed the calm.

A creature straight out of a fantasy novel or a children's nightmare descended through the fog, its massive wings spread. The Quetzalcoatlus perched itself atop the boulder Gina had been using as her shower platform, the beast's wings folding down to act as forward legs. Unlike mythical dragons, this dragon-like beast didn't spit fire and had no teeth, yet it's the largest known flying creature to have ever lived. The giraffe-sized reptile's thin limbs jerked and stomped, the creature's terrifyingly long beak hanging open, its wings stretching forty feet.

The Quetzalcoatlus threw its narrow head back, blue head feathers swaying, opened its long yellow beak, and wailed, a thin choking cry that sounded like a massive chicken getting all its feathers pulled out at once.

A mighty wind pushed over the mountainside, driving away the mists. The dragon turned its head, a dark black eye peering at Drew from the side of its narrow head. The black hair-like bristles that ran down the beast's long neck wavered and undulated, the creature's rear legs twisting as if readying to lunge at Drew. It inched forward, its folded wings acting as front legs, the horrific creature spider-like in its movements and appearance.

Gina stepped from her hiding spot, gun leveled. She yelled, waving her hand in an attempt to draw the beast's attention, but the Quetzalcoatlus only had eyes for Drew.

A gunshot rang out, and the beast's head swung wildly, its front appendages transforming back into wings, the creature's rear legs pushing the Quetzalcoatlus into the air. It yelled and bitched as it flew away, and for the first time in what felt like hours Drew took a deep breath and fell onto his ass, the adrenaline fleeing and leaving him with nothing left in the tank. Hunger pains twisted his stomach as he stared up at the precipice of stone that was the front of the cliff dwelling. Suddenly he just didn't give a shit anymore.

"You alright?" Gina stood over him, a ray of sunlight shining on her like a spotlight, her beautiful face smeared with dirt, concern etched into her features.

Drew nodded but couldn't find any words.

"Come on," she said as she held out a hand. "It's not much farther."

He grasped her hand and Gina pulled Drew to his feet, water running around his legs.

Flies had already swarmed the dead Pterosaurs and any thoughts of eating the beasts fled, not that there was any real meat on the overgrown bats. The creatures looked emaciated; all cord-like muscles, long hollow bones, and slick aerodynamic skin. The rusty scent of blood filled the air, blue puddles forming around the dead beasts.

Drew unclipped his water bottle and took a long pull, his nerves jangling, his joints aching with dull pain. He watched Gina as she struggled to get back on the path, the dark maw of the tunnel behind her. He didn't want to continue, and he no longer cared what lay in the city above. Drew wanted to rest, let it all go, but that wasn't in the cards because there was nothing left for him to do except struggle on and see things through.

26

The entrance to the cliff dwelling was more elaborate than Drew had anticipated. A narrow set of steps chiseled into stone delved into a large crack in the mountain, the culvert still running strong beside the path, the clear water rippling and gurgling as it slid over smooth stones. The steps ended on a narrow plateau, the entrance to the city carved into the western cliff face.

"Wow," Gina said as she stopped before the dark entrance, her hands going to her hips as her eyes ranged over the structure.

The face of a Dinosauroid was chiseled into the mountain, the creature's mouth an entranceway. The stone was shaped and contoured, evidence of expert artisans utilizing advanced skills, and the sculpture was more impressive than some of the great Egyptian monuments. Thin trickles of water streamed from the monument's eyes, and beneath them pools stained by time sat almost empty, but Drew figured when it rained the streams of water would be more intense. A precipice of dark rock jutted out from between the creature's eyes like a broken horn obscuring the view of the city above, and no vines hung from it and no vegetation clung to its surface. The rank smell of rot and animal body odor wafted from the tunnel mouth.

Gina took a hesitant step into the great beast's mouth and ranged her flashlight around, hand on her gun.

The faint taps and titters of bird song carried on the rank breeze, and Drew's mind spun backward, searching for some fact, some experience, but he couldn't pull the thought free.

"You coming?" came Gina's voice from within the half-light of the city entrance.

Drew rolled his shoulders, searched for his courage, but it had been replaced with practicality a long time ago. There were so many things in the Cretaceous that could kill him he'd given up worrying on it.

Huge pillar-like fangs of stone marked the sides of the entrance, and an eerie dread crept over Drew as he stepped into the beast's mouth. Gina shined the light in his direction, and pictograms similar to the ones he'd seen prior sparkled with flecks of quartz. There were stick figures doing things, strange letter-like symbols, but it was all gibberish, and nothing stood out.

The short tunnel ended in a large chamber, its walls decorated with intricate etchings, the trickle and pop of running water echoing through the space. A mosaic of dinosaurs, mammals, birds, and everything in-between had been carved into the stone, and again Drew marveled at the craftsmanship. It rivaled the civilizations of old in their detail, and colors had been added. Pastel-like dull shades of natural paints that had most likely been created from stones.

Gina traced a finger over a T-rex head that looked like it had been mounted to the wall like a trophy head of a big game hunter. Dark lines in the stone gave the T-rex angry eyes, and the beast's jaws hung open, the stone teeth glinting with flecks of quartz under the harsh beam of the flashlight.

"This must have taken a long time," Gina said as she played the light around. "Maybe generations."

"I'd like to know what they used to do it," Drew said. "A hard stone?"

"Maybe one of these." Gina shined the flashlight on a stick figure that appeared to be holding a primitive knife. "They… whoever, must have known something about the hardness of stones, or how else would they have made this city?" She shifted the light to a pictogram of several stick figures standing around what looked like a roaring fire.

"It's pretty impressive that the city has running water," Drew said. Like the civilizations of old, bringing water into the dwelling had followed bringing water to the fields and crops, though he doubted whoever had lived in the city farmed up this high, if at all. He'd seen no terraced fields, or any other sign that farming was part of the city's infrastructure. Drew pictured hunting parties spending days away from their families as they hunted and gathered.

The ceiling of the chamber rose into blackness, and when Gina panned the light up the duo saw that though the walls had been intricately hewn, the ceiling was a natural stone slab that slanted upward into blackness, its lower edge fifty feet above the partners' heads. There were no stalagmites or stalactites, the water having been corralled and directed.

"Looks to me like the location for the city was chosen because of the waterflow, which probably helped form the fissure that created this chamber," said Drew.

With only one direction to go, forward, the partners left the large entrance hall behind and eased down the narrow passageway at the opposite end of the chamber. Stale air blew from the triangular entrance way, and close inspection revealed that the opening had been natural, its edges chiseled and refined to be a perfect triangle. At the opening's pinnacle, carved into the rock with great precision, a Dinosauroid head guarded the space.

The crackle of tiny bones crunching underfoot made the duo wary, and they walked slow, Drew putting his feet in the prints Gina left in the thin coating of silt that covered the floor. After twenty paces they came to another triangular-shaped doorway.

Gina and Drew gazed about, waiting for something to surge from the shadows.

No attack came, and the knot of tension holding Drew together released, and for a second he thought he'd gone to the bathroom in his pants. Warmth spread through him, cold sweat dripping down his back, his eyes adjusting to the faint light.

A loud staccato tapping echoed through the chamber, and the sound of stone sliding over stone carried through the city. A stone door slid from a hidden recess in the ceiling, the entrance to the city closing.

Gina ran forward, getting low, and Drew thought she meant to dive through the shrinking opening. She looked back, saw Drew standing frozen, mouth hanging open, and she pulled back.

The stone closed off the triangular doorway with a boom, and the floor vibrated as Gina's sigh rang out like the noon whistle. "This place!" She pulled her gun, spun around looking for something to shoot, but instead screamed.

With the echoes of her frustration still hanging in the dust-filled air, the unmistakable sound of bird-like speech filtered through the chamber.

Gina's eyes went wide, and Drew's stomach went cold.

It was then the partners noticed the holes in the wall beside the doorway. They were all the same size, two inches around, and they pocked the wall like computer generated Swiss cheese.

"Turn off the flashlight," Drew said.

She killed the light.

As his eyes adjusted, pale rays of light streamed from some of the holes and created odd shadows on the far wall. Some of the beams dimmed and grew stronger, as if something was impeding the supply of light. Dust motes danced in the still air, the faint cries of Pterosaurs and the whistle of the wind as it snaked through the chamber the only sounds.

Gina snapped the flashlight back on and said, "So what now?"

"Clearly another test, but of what?" Drew tossed his head side to side and cracked his neck. "Patience, perspective, or perseverance?"

The flashlight beam dipped, and Gina's brow wrinkled.

"Our lessons so far, right? Look at the impossible triangle from a certain angle—perspective—and see the city," Drew said.

Gina added, "And show patience and see the Dinosauroid, perseverance gets you out of a trap. Is this a trap?"

Drew shook his head no as he pointed his pistol at the open doorway on the opposite end of the chamber.

"So perspective." She tossed back her head and chuckled. "Which hole shows the way forward?"

Drew nodded slowly. "Maybe, but where to start? And what's to keep a snake, or who knows what, from biting my eye?"

He counted the holes. They started at ground level and rose to eight feet, so he'd have to boost Gina on his shoulders if they wanted to look through them all. His nerves pulsed at the thought of having his head between her legs, though he didn't feel the slightest tinge of arousal and again he wondered what the hell was wrong with him?

There were twelve vertical rows and eight horizontal rows, but when he counted each hole, he came up with ninety-seven, not ninety-six.

"What are we waiting on?"

Drew explained the hole count.

"So you're thinking the 'missing hole' is the one?"

"It could still be dangerous. What if we trigger a dart or a spear? Or worse?"

Gina took a step back.

Drew dropped to a knee, pulled his knife, and began recreating the hole pattern in the grit that covered the floor. Hole by hole he went, adding each to his drawing, duplicating the pattern on the wall. He worked in silence, Gina's impatient breathing echoing through the room. When he saw the anomaly, he vaulted to his feet and chirped, his heart racing.

"Got something?"

"Let me see the light?" She handed it over and Drew stood before the wall. He counted five rows from the top, then moved to the edge of the door. "This one. See how there's an odd number on this row?"

Gina came forward, her face twisted. "I don't see it."

"Trust me." Drew dropped into a crouch a foot from the wall and shined the flashlight into the odd numbered hole.

A yellow eye blinked within.

Drew yelled, pulled back, and fell on his butt.

Gina snatched up the flashlight and shined it into the hole. "What did you see?"

"An eye," he said.

Gina deflated, the relief evident on her face. "A beast. I thought…" She abandoned the sentence.

"Not a beast," Drew said. "Well, maybe a beast, but the eye looked… human, but much bigger." He recalled the large round eyes of the Dinosauroid.

Gina still had the flashlight focused on the hole, its cone of light disappearing into the wall.

The floor trembled, and stone scraped on stone as the door began to open.

Gina stepped back, the flashlight falling to her side.

With a click and tap of stone, the door shuttered to a stop, and began to fall.

Realizing her error, she placed the head of the flashlight over the hole where the eye had been.

The door ground to a halt. Dust filled the air as the seconds dripped away, the door frozen three feet from the smooth stone floor.

"Maybe we only get one chance," Gina said.

"I don't think so," he said. Drew was now certain he and Gina were being watched.

Two minutes slipped away before the slab of stone began to move again, sliding back into its hiding place above the triangular door. It fell into place with a *crack* and hollow *pop*, and dirt and rock dust sifted down as the floor vibrated.

Gina waited, then slowly arced the flashlight beam away from the hole.

Nothing happened.

Blackness pressed into the chamber, and nothing could be seen within the murky darkness beyond the door. Gina shined the flashlight into the blackness and the darkness consumed the light, nothing visible beyond a few feet.

"Before we go on, I have to tell you something," Gina said.

Drew licked his lips and said nothing.

"There's no way the professor came this way, you know that, right?" Gina said.

Drew had realized that as soon as they entered the main entrance hall. There had been no footprints in the dust and grit coating the floor.

"It's true there have been no signs, but maybe he came in another way?" he said.

Gina made a show of looking around. "Yeah, this was all built to keep creatures out, but they left a backdoor open?"

"There's no telling how long it's been since…" Drew looked at the floor. "Something lives in this city… now. There are no doubts, so there must be other ways in and out." His eyes ranged back to the floor.

"You're worried about the eye you saw?" Gina said. "It could have been any number of beasts."

He knew that was true, but at the same time he knew it could only be one. Dinosauroid. He said, "Thanks for everything, Gina. Really. I don't know what I would've done without you."

"You'd be dead," she joked.

Drew didn't laugh as he sucked in a breath and pushed forward into the darkness.

27

The crunch of bones under foot rattled Drew's nerves, the sound like traipsing over a horde of cockroaches. Were there roaches in the Cretaceous? He thought back and decided no. Roaches and the like were products of man, and they couldn't live without mankind's waste.

Gina kept the flashlight forward, the white light pushing away the blackness and revealing rough, natural cave walls that blended with the sharpened stone.

"Do roaches live in the Cretaceous?" he asked.

"For sure," Gina said.

"Without our garbage?"

"Yup. Only about thirty species out of more than four thousand are associated with humans. They're an ancient group, with ancestors originating during the Carboniferous period three hundred and fifty million years ago. Those early cockroaches, however, lacked the internal egg laying ovipositors of modern roaches."

The passageway gave way to a vast open square. Mountain peaks shrouded in mist dominated the eastern view, and clouds streaked over a blue sky, light slanting into the space. What appeared to be an arena sat at the center of the square, rows of large stadium seating spiraling down. Whatever had lived in the city was big.

Dark windows stood out like eyes on the chiseled cavern walls, pictograms and the odd linguistic symbols dominating every flat surface. A tunnel of sunlight opened to their right and the duo followed the lighted path. There were doorways with no doors and windows opening into dwellings that had no furniture or accoutrements of any kind.

All the spaces were a perfect amalgamation of natural stone and manipulated stone. In most spots no major excavation had been performed. Simply a tap of rock here, the splitting of stone there, the addition of rock walls throughout, and everything was decorated with symbols and pictograms.

The passageway grew brighter, and Drew and Gina exited out onto a wide veranda chiseled from the mountainside. From their position the duo could see the front of the city in all its majesty, as well as the eastern mountain slope and lands beyond.

Green creeper vines that were certainly relatives of arrowroot covered most of the stone, inside and out. Vines snaked up walls and covered what appeared to be statues which were of the same sort they'd seen prior. Lizard men walking on two legs, their tails pressed to the ground for balance.

"Do you want to check for the emergency pod?" Gina asked. "We can see most of the eastern jungle up to the top of the escarpment you climbed."

Drew stared into the cloud-streaked sky, the sun warming his face, the breeze pushing goosebumps up from his damp skin. "That's going to take a while. Let's take a look around first."

The partners headed back into the heart of the city and the great plaza.

"Whoever built this place chipped most of it away, but see that line of brown rock?" Gina shined the flashlight up at the rock walls just below the lip of the opening, the dark star filled sky beyond. "This entire section is a crack in the mountainside. They just smoothed the edges. How all the individual chambers were formed I don't know."

The partners passed two vast halls cut deeper into the mountain, and Drew estimated there were at least one thousand private rooms throughout the cliff dwelling. He saw no signs of cooking, tools, clothing, furniture. There was nothing except piles of dirt, sand, and silt.

"Are those piles what's left of personal belongings?"

"Sure looks like it," Gina said. "What I don't get is the lack of life? Why aren't birds, Pterosaurs, varmints, and all kinds of beasts using the place as a hotel?"

"Too high up on the mountain?"

"For birds? I haven't seen a single nest. Very odd."

A massive arch appeared in the gloom, its edges decorated with Dinosauroid heads carved into the stone.

The partners stopped before the dark maw of the passageway, and Gina shined the light therein.

Something sparkled in the inky blackness. The faint sound of running water overpowered the gentle push of the breeze, and… there was something else… a clicking and tapping.

"Once more unto the breach?" Gina said.

Drew nodded.

The passageway was wide, but the stone walls were black, and they ate light. Ahead, a narrow column of moonlight arced from the ceiling, illuminating a mosaic of tiles on the stone floor.

Gina and Drew had seen this holo story, and without speaking they focused on the pattern of small tile-like stones that spread across the ground.

The stones moved and shifted, waves of motion washing over the floor. A pain knifed through Drew's forehead like a nail, but he continued to stare at the design, the stones moving faster, a picture coming into focus, a low ringing building in his head.

The autostereogram was a map, and it showed the city, its levels, and there were directional signals and a block of text he couldn't understand.

"I think the beings who built this place didn't have binocular vision," Gina said.

"So to them the autostereograms are just normal pictures?"

"Maybe," she said.

Drew said, "What do you make of that lower chamber?"

She hiked her shoulders.

Below the central plaza there was a staircase that descended to a stone box. Within the box were a series of stick figures leaning on their stick forearms in what appeared to be contemplation. Symbols that looked oddly like question marks decorated the edges of the box, and there were smaller boxes within that had lines shooting from them.

"What do you make of the lines?" Drew said.

"Light? The glow of something sparkling?"

"Like gold or jewels?"

"Possibly," she said. "There are many examples of civilizations using jewels and precious metals—shiny shit—as holy items and central pieces of their societal mythology."

"A hall of knowledge preservation?" Drew said. "Maybe a tomb for the revered dead or a vault?"

"I think so."

"That's certainly where the professor would go," Drew said. "I admit I'm intrigued." To that, Drew's muscles sent a dull tremor of pain through him that rattled his bones and settled in his empty stomach.

"I don't like going down into darkness, and..." She stepped forward and traced a spot on the map with the tip of her index finger. "Did you see this staircase when we went through the plaza?"

Drew shook his head no. There'd been some statues, the—

"That arena," he blurted.

Gina nodded slowly in the half-light. "Makes sense, right? They would build a gathering place to commemorate their shrine."

The partners backtracked to the central square, the uneasy feeling that they were being watched seeping through Drew and making him sweat despite the chill air. Shadows danced in the grayness, but nothing moved through the deserted city.

When the partners reached the arena, they saw that there was a round stone stage-like slab at the bottom of the amphitheater, but nothing else adorned the space.

As they helped each other down the large stone benches to the bottom of the arena, Gina said, "You got anything?"

He didn't, so he said nothing.

The rank scent of stale air wafted up from the bottom of the depression, the smell of wet stone, mold, and decay. Specks of quartz danced under the flashlight's beam, but Drew saw no key holes, doors, or possible hiding spots.

Gina mounted the small stone stage and turned three hundred and sixty degrees.

Drew knelt and examined where the stone platform met the floor, and there looked to be a gap. He stood and hopped onto the stone and stood next to Gina. "Perseverance," he muttered.

The duo stood for the first half-hour, and then they sat upon the cold stone, the glow of moonlight seeping into the city painting everything in garish black and white.

Drew was unsure how long they sat there, but when the scrape of stone finally filtered through the city the moonglow had faded as the sun prepared to rise and start a new day.

"I figured it would sink into the floor," Drew said.

The stone they sat upon was rising as if lifted by some massive unseen hand. When it stopped, Drew and Gina were ten feet above the ground.

A debilitating weariness engulfed Drew. The crash survivors had been going nonstop for days, and they'd had no food for over a day. He drank the last of his water as the massive stone rumbled to a stop.

The partners climbed down and found a narrow door two feet wide and eight feet high.

Gina shined the flashlight into the opening and an albino Utahraptor stared back at her, its wet eyes glowing, mouth open, slime dripping through dagger teeth. The beast threw its head back and cackled, muscles flexing beneath white leathery skin.

Drew went for his gun, but it was stuck in his pocket, and he fumbled to pull it free.

Gina was faster. She sprang for cover as she drew down and fired through the open doorway. But she was off balance, in motion, her aim skewed by weariness, sleep deprivation, and lack of food. The gun clicked empty, and her last shot hit stone a foot above the door, shards of stone spraying the passageway beyond.

She dropped the empty gun and pulled her knife, its blade shining under the flashlight's beam as Gina shined the light into the dinosaur's eyes.

The albino raptor swung its narrow head away from the harsh light as it clicked and chuffed, its gaze falling on Drew. It came at him with the suddenness of a heart attack, and as Drew brought up the pistol, he realized he was going to die.

Gina moved like a bullet. She streaked across his field of vision, knife out, her fierce battle cry ringing through the city.

The plunk of the knife plunging into the raptor echoed through the chamber along with Gina's strains of exertion as she twisted the knife.

Drew tried to get a bead on the raptor with the gun, but Gina was in too close. She clung to her knife like she was hanging from a five-hundred-foot cliff ledge, the albino dinosaur thrashing and struggling beneath her.

The raptor tossed Gina from its back. She sailed through the air, the flashlight falling to the ground. It landed with a pop and went out.

Darkness pressed in on Drew, harsh breathing and the chuffs and clicks of the raptor carrying through the blackness.

The beast's glowing eyes thrust up and down, its form a blur deeper than night.

Gina screamed, and the sound of crunching bones and tearing meat made Drew's stomach go cold.

Drew sighted the beast's eyes and squeezed the trigger. The gun bucked slightly, but if the bullet struck home, it had little effect because the sounds of ripping flesh and breaking bones got louder and more extreme.

He moved in closer to ensure his next shot would hit its mark and he kicked the flashlight. It came back to life, and a narrow cone of light spilled across the floor and grew to a cloud as it drove back the darkness.

The raptor had its jaws clamped on Gina's shoulder, the front of her blue jumpsuit drenched crimson, her head lolling to one side from a tattered neck. The dinosaur cocked its head to get better hold of its prey as it eased back into the doorway, the cries of his partner dying away.

Gina's corpse hit the ground and the raptor tore off one of her arms and bolted away.

Drew scooped up the flashlight and trained its fading beam on his dead partner.

Gina was nearly decapitated, and her head rested on a shoulder, the dead woman's spine all that was keeping the skull attached to the body. Blood, bone, and strands of gristle and tendons protruded from the shoulder where the arm had been bitten off, and bloody gashes ran across the corpse's chest.

A trail of blood led into darkness, and the rank scent of human waste carried on the breeze. Drew didn't want to think of Gina shitting her pants as the shock of death took hold. He didn't want to see her pretty face broken and stained with blood, her perfect hourglass figure twisted and melted like a glass bottle that's been thrown in a fire.

He backed away from the open door, his breaths coming in ragged bursts, his vision blurred red and black with rage and fear. Sorrow consumed him and he sat on one of the arena's benches. Despite the danger, he let his head fall to his chest, the spacesuit helmet dangling from its carabiner and tapping against stone. Another teammate lost, yet he remained.

Walls and Gina had saved his bacon multiple times, yet they were dead, and he was alive. He'd had enough. Done. Finished. Kaput. He didn't give two dinosaur asses what the Dinosauroids were or had been or what they were up to and what they might do and when they died. It all meant nothing. He was going to look for the emergency pod and delving deeper into the city wouldn't help the effort.

Drew pushed to his feet and headed for the exit tunnel.

"Drew? Drew? Is that you?"

The voice was frail, yet unmistakable. It was the professor.

28

Drew skidded to a halt, slipped in the grit and grime covering the stone floor, and put out his arms to stop from falling. He stood still, his heart racing. Water dripped, wind sang, but… He went back and stood before the open doorway, listening hard.

"Professor Lokker?" whispered Drew. Through his sorrow and pain a spark of hope ignited the flame of his perseverance, though it made no sense. Was he going crazy? Hearing what he wanted to hear in the chanting of the wind? There was a raptor down there, but maybe the professor was hurt or trapped? He envisioned Dr. Lokker lying at the bottom of a pit with a broken leg, the albino raptor staring down at him with Gina's arm dangling from its jaws.

The rank scent of rodents carried through the doorway, that stale smell of dry animal body odor, dirty hair, and feces. Squeaks and titters and claws scratching stone told Drew what the raptors ate, and for the first time his spinning mind came to a stop on the fact that the dinosaur had been white. Lack of skin pigmentation, specifically the congenital absence of melanin, is usually genetic, but it can also occur when skin cells aren't exposed to light. The raptor's eyes—if that was what the creature was—were huge and almost translucent.

The flashlight was still in one hand, his gun in the other. Drew shined the light into the opening, but there was nothing to be seen on the staircase beyond except Gina's corpse and a trail of blood that led down into darkness.

Drew knew he should turn on his heel and leave, abandon the city and never come back. The idea felt so right he took a step back, putting a few feet between him and the open doorway. His skin crawled with unease, every red flag in his arsenal raised high, warning lights flashing and alarms chiming all over his mental control panel.

The faint scent of Gina's waste filled his nostrils. She was tough—tougher than him—but she was dead, and he was alive. He just couldn't get by the fact that another person had lost their life saving his.

If Professor Lokker, by some unimaginable effort, managed to find his way into the bowels of the city, so what? It was his fault Drew was stuck in this mess. He shook his head. Drew had decided to come on the mission. It had been his choice, and without knowing exactly why the ship had crashed, blaming the professor was akin to a child complaining about not being chosen first for dodgeball. It all came down to what he owed the man, and given the current situation that tally was small in Drew's estimation.

Still, he wasn't without feeling; loyalty, obligation, a propensity to do the right thing even when nobody was watching. He'd done that most of his life, yet he still managed to find himself on the wrong side of relationships. "Shit," he muttered as he rolled his shoulders.

"Help me," came the frail voice of Dr. Lokker.

Drew thrust the flashlight forward as if it would grow brighter with the effort, his bloodshot eyes stinging as he peered into the darkness.

Nothing moved in the blackness, the flashlight beam fading to black beyond ten feet. The staircase looked wide, and the elaborately decorated handrails had many new designs he hadn't seen before. Stone flowers and vines wrapped around the banister, the steps of normal human size. The place looked different, more refined, and Drew thought whoever had constructed the steps had taken significantly more care in the undertaking than the creators of the cliff dwelling. The carved stone here looked to be painted on with a brush, each cut clear and significant. It had taken great skill to hew the stairs from solid stone, and he couldn't imagine the amount of time and effort required to complete the accents and petroglyphs.

"Help me. Drew? Please."

The voice sounded so real, the pleading so genuine, that Drew could only draw one conclusion. Like it or not, the professor was down there, and he couldn't leave him. He descended two steps, the stink of shit filling his nostrils, the stale air tickling his nose.

The flashlight revealed footprints of every size and shape. Tiny three-toed rodent-like prints in pairs of two, as if the small mammals that made them were bipedal. The giant chicken-like prints of the raptor and a winding track that looked to have been made by a snake cut through it all.

He panned the light around and saw that the walls were filled with holes approximately six inches round. Bigger than the gazing holes he'd found prior, but as he bent to press his eye to one of the holes an alarm klaxon wailed in his head.

Drew pulled his knife and plunged it into the nearest hole.

Nothing.

He dropped into a crouch, and shined the light directly into the hole. Only blackness stared back at him. No eye, no beasts, no perspective at all.

As Drew sidestepped Gina's twisted body, thoughts of protecting her remains scuttled through his brain like a thought late in coming and never wanted. There were no stones to cover her. No way to bury her. The heat of sorrow engulfed him as he knelt and closed Gina's eyes with the back of his hand. She was already cold, the dark blood congealing in the cracks of the stone floor.

"Drew? Please. Help me."

Drew started down the steps. He held the flashlight atop the gun as he ranged the weapon back and forth, following the trail of blood. The map he'd seen showed two levels, and as he descended the staircase the designs in the stone became even more refined, and Drew became convinced whatever society had constructed the city above, didn't create the stairs.

Could it be like Earth's known past? Were the ruins of ancient civilizations stacked in layers beneath the new like tree rings? Had there been another intelligent species on Earth before the Dinosauroids evolved?

None of it mattered. Even if he managed to get home, what would change? How would the fact that intelligent beings lived on Earth over sixty-five million years ago change anything in the present? Sure, there'd be papers, research dollars, documentaries, books. But so what? He'd come to the rational conclusion that fundamentally the world he'd left was pretty messed up and learning a distant fact about history wouldn't change anything. Not even a little.

The stairs ended after ten steps on a landing of red stone. A narrow passageway led away to his right and left, and the staircase switched-back and plunged deeper into the mountain.

The hallway looked to be cut from solid stone, but there were no chisel marks, no symbols, no signs that marked the corridor as non-natural. He knew lava caves sometimes had smooth walls, but his elevation and all the right angles told Drew he wasn't standing in a lava tube.

Drew called out for the professor several times as he went right, inching down the passageway with the gun up, sparkles of quartz dancing under the flashlight's beam like tiny diamonds. There were no doors or windows leading into chambers, no statues, no signs of life at all. The footprints in the silt were mostly small, but there were odd bipedal three-toed prints he hadn't seen before. Drew didn't see any raptor prints. Not surprising. The hall was narrow, and based on what he'd seen so far, the raptors—all the beasts, really- didn't like enclosed spaces if they could be avoided.

The passage went on and when Drew arrived back at the staircase the heat of fear and embarrassment stroked his last nerve. He didn't think he'd gone in a circle, but concluded he must have. Brushing aside the purpose for the circular hallway that appeared to lead nowhere, he continued down the steps.

Professor Lokker had been silent for several minutes, and Drew questioned his sanity for what seemed like the thousandth time. Had he heard what he wanted to hear in a moment of extreme stress and loss?

A gurgling followed by the gnashing of teeth carried on the faint breeze, and Drew struggled to determine if the raptor was making the noise, or the smaller beasts. He swung the gun and flashlight around but saw nothing except gray stone as he descended to the next stair landing.

The stairs switched back and plunged deeper into the mountain, but instead of a narrow hallway to nowhere, a vast chamber stretched into blackness around him. The rumble of rushing water echoed through the chamber, the gentle touch of mist cooling his face.

Drew panned the light around and what he saw sent a shiver of elation through him.

Another city, carved from a natural cavern, rose all around him, but instead of intricately carved decorations and accents, bones of every shape and size served as ornaments as well as practical things like door handles and windowsills. The city was much smaller than the one on the surface, but its windows were more widely spaced, as if the chambers beyond were large.

Dinosaur, bird, and varmint tracks crisscrossed the floor, but nothing moved within the gloom. Drew played the light around, shadows gyrating on the walls.

Squeaks and the crackle of snapping bones echoed through the cavern as one of the creatures noshed.

The flashlight beam found a rat-like beast standing on its hindlegs, its huge milky eyes locked on Drew as it nibbled on something. The creature was the size of a standard dog, but without Gina, identifying its specific genus was beyond his knowledge. He did know there had been a series of mammal-like dinosaurs called Orodrominae, but based on the existing fossil record the largest of these creatures should be no bigger than a weasel.

"Another discovery for your list, Gina," Drew said aloud, his sour stomach twisting, hunger pains shooting down his arms and legs. If he ever got home, he'd make sure Gina got the credit for every new discovery they'd made. It would be his way of memorializing her sacrifice, though the thought didn't sooth the pain. Regardless of how everything turned out, Drew would carry the guilt of Walls and Gina's deaths, and their ghosts would haunt him for the rest of his life.

The dog-dinosaur stopped nibbling, its whiskers going still as the beast inched forward. It stood on two legs, two gangly arms hanging by its sides, its slick black hair glistening. Long curved claws scraped the ground as the beast advanced, its fat body undulating, two big teeth sticking from closed jaws.

Drew raised the gun to fire, but paused, the rational side of his brain telling him he only had seven bullets left, and asking if he wanted to draw attention to himself? Pinpoint his position? But hadn't he already done that when he'd screamed the professor's name? Multiple times? In the end he tried to scare the beast off because bullets were too valuable to waste on a creature that wasn't even bothering him... yet.

He screamed and shooed the creature, but the beast just stared at him with sad eyes. There had been no further cries from the professor, and Drew didn't want to consider what that meant.

Something was happening, some unknown Drew had set into motion. He felt it in his bones, and his instincts told him all the answers were in the lower chamber, the one he'd coined the Dinosauroid's Hall of Records.

A horde of the dog-things inched from the darkness as if controlled by one mind, their dark fur standing on end like frightened cats, eyes alight with hunger. The beasts tittered and squeaked as they advanced, like the sound of an orchestra tuning up. There were so many Drew couldn't get a good count. He spun three hundred and sixty degrees, waving the gun around as if he had enough bullets to take out all the creatures. The beasts advanced until Drew stood in the center of the pack, no more than ten feet separating him from the masses.

He pointed the gun up and fired, the report echoing through the enclosed space and bouncing off the walls and ringing in his head. The rat-dog-dinos froze for a heartbeat, then continued to advance.

29

Squeaks and the gnashing of teeth echoed through the chamber, the dinosaurs advancing, Drew's safe zone shrinking.

One of the beasts lunged forward, hissing, its partners pushing in behind their leader.

Drew blew the beast apart, a cloud of blood, muscle, bone fragments, and fat splattering the advancing creatures behind it.

Five bullets left.

The swarm of dinosaurs mounded and crawled on one another as they fought to get closer to Drew, but with their buddy's blood still hot on the stone floor none of the creatures were willing to follow their leader and cross the invisible line of protection that was holding the horde of creatures back.

For the second time in the last hour Drew thought he was done. He pictured Kimmy in his mind, an imaginary encounter during which he made up for all his screw ups and his daughter gave him complete forgiveness and a stack of get out of jail free cards for future stupidity and failures on his part. If he made it back, he'd make things right with Kimmy or die trying, but with a sinking sense of failure and an utter finality that tightened his chest and made it hard to breathe, Drew understood he wasn't going to get the chance.

Several of the creatures sprang forward and pulled back, testing the imaginary boundary, and it was only a matter of seconds before the beasts gathered their collective courage and swarmed Drew like ants on a fallen lollipop.

A ferocious wail of anger that sounded oddly human froze the advancing creatures as if time had been paused. Dust motes danced in the air as Drew frantically panned the flashlight around and found rows of glowing eyes staring back at him.

A bestial call rang through the chamber, followed by a series of barks and clicks that made most of the rat-dog-dinos scuttle backward.

Except one.

The new alpha Orodrominae inched forward, teeth bared, its low mouse-like growl almost comical.

A screech of anger followed by harsh clicking scattered the creatures, leaving the alpha alone before Drew.

The whoosh of a projectile whizzing by Drew's right ear made him tilt his head. A primitive arrow plunked into the dinosaur, catching the beast in the chest and knocking it to the ground. Blood oozed onto the stone floor, the beast's dark eyes already staring into the next world as a small red puddle appeared around its head.

A loud extended series of clicks followed by a chuff.

Drew dropped to a crouch, spun, and sighted the gun. Pain pierced his chest as it tightened, fear, excitement, and bewilderment turning him to stone.

Thirty paces away, bathed in the half-light between darkness and the flashlight's cloud, what Drew could only describe as a lizard man eased into the light, an arrow notched in its primitive bow. As Drew struggled to process what he was seeing, his thoughts went to Gina. She'd missed the biggest discovery of all. The Dinosauroid.

The creature was a sleek amalgamation of homo sapiens and reptiles, but the Dinosauroid's face was more fish-like than lizard. A large round skull was covered with smooth green skin, thick wrinkles over each eye socket. The creature's eyes were the size of hockey pucks, and the twisting yellow and red around thin black pupils gave the eyes a marble-like quality. Ear slits and nose holes were in similar positions to that of humans, but the Dinosauroid's beak-like mouth protruded several inches from its face like a bird, two tusk-like fangs hanging from the mouth like overgrown incisors. Hands hung from long gangly arms, and Drew noted three long flexible fingers on each.

The Dinosauroid pointed its arrow at Drew who instinctively brought up the gun.

Like an old school duel, the two lone figures stood face to face, their weapons trained on each other, millions of years of evolution and thirty paces separating them. Drew saw intelligence in those big eyes. He saw the future of the human race, though he knew the Dinosauroid's reign would be ending soon, along with his own.

Drew's arms trembled and the hand gripping the gun began to shake. Sweat dripped down his face, despite the chill breeze that carried the scents of waste, rot, and animal body odor. In the silence he picked up the faint tinkle and pop of running water, and the scraping of creatures moving about unseen in the darkness, the cone of light from Drew's flashlight the only illumination.

The Dinosauroid stood still as a statue, its left eye closed, its right eyeballing the bow's aim. The bow looked to be made of wood, its line dark and dirty. Drew figured it was pulled muscle sinew. The arrows had a multitude of feathers of different sizes and colors, and stone served as arrowheads.

Drew's mind spun back to when he was a boy and he and his father would go hunting for arrowheads in the shallow riverbed behind their house. He'd found paint pots, large spear heads, along with many notched and chiseled arrowheads. All the basic artifacts had been attributed to Native Americans; tribes of people who had lived in the area now known as the Free Zone. He wondered how many of those arrowheads had been of Dinosauroid creation?

The creature clicked and chuffed, the tip of the arrow moving up and down slightly.

Was the thing trying to communicate?

Drew's shoulder ached, and the tip of the gun barrel moved in small circles. He knew if it came down to a draw, he could win. A primitive bow and arrow were no match for state-of-the-art weaponry, but the creature could get lucky. Getting impaled by an arrow would certainly be the end to his odyssey.

The Dinosauroid clicked louder, jutting out its chin in frustration.

Drew didn't know what to do. He didn't speak dolphin, and his experiences were so different than the creature's he doubted he and the lizard man would be able to find common ground, even with a professional linguist's help.

Time dragged out, like unpleasant experiences often do, and as the seconds dripped away Drew considered shooting the beast and being done with it. Yet something deep inside, some failsafe that took over his mental control center when rationality, logic, and self-preservation were debating a course of action, stopped him from pulling the trigger.

Killing was a crime against nature. Drew believed that with all his being. Killing an animal for food, or murdering in self-defense—these things were understandable, yet still unpleasant, but necessary. But killing another human… another sentient creature, for no reason was beyond him.

As if reading his mind, the Dinosauroid slowly lowered its bow, the low murmur of its speech echoing through the chamber.

Drew searched his memory for what Gina had taught him, about how there had been scientists back in the day that speculated about a possible evolutionary path for Stenonychosaurus, had it not gone extinct in the Cretaceous–Paleogene extinction event. The theory was that Stenonychosaurus could have evolved into intelligent beings similar to humans and now that theory, which seemed so crazy to Drew as he listened to Gina explain it, now made sense. The creature that stood before him was intelligent and had just made the decision to stand down in the face of an unknown threat.

The Dinosauroid's beak-like mouth opened, and a red tongue lolled out. The creature clicked, the bow coming back up, the arrow trained on Drew again, only to be lowered the next second.

Drew slowly lowered his gun.

The Dinosauroid's eyes grew wider, its mouth clicking closed. Muscles undulated beneath the creature's green and yellow scaly skin, and the Dinosauroid purred like a cat.

Drew felt himself tense, then relax. When cats made that sound that meant they were content, so with nothing else to do, Drew mimicked the sound. He closed his lips tight, pushed his tongue against his teeth, and blew out a thin stream of air. At first it sounded like he was farting, but he evened out the rhythm, easing back on the air and hitting a steady vibration.

Then the Dinosauroid did something Drew would never have expected. The creature smiled. Leathery skin wrinkled and drew back, the beak falling open a crack. The purring ceased and a harsh clicking sound that sounded a lot like laughter filled the chamber.

The knot in Drew's chest loosened, but the pain was replaced by hunger pains, his joints, neck, and head throbbing with a dull pain that he hardly had the energy to notice. He stared at the Dinosauroid and the beast stared back. With internal genitalia Drew's mind wandered where men's minds often get lost, sex. How did the creature reproduce? Did it have a mate? Little lizard men and girls? Where did they live? Nothing Drew had seen so far said active living space, and Drew surmised the city was a shrine of some kind, or something so far in the Dinosauroid's distant past that memory of the place had become legend.

The Dinosauroid pointed at the fallen Orodrominae, its blood now dark red, the puddle thickening on the old stone.

Drew knew the creature was asking a question, but it took him a few seconds to figure out the message. The Dinosauroid was offering Drew its kill.

Hunger pains knifed through him, but Drew slowly shook his head no.

Understanding bloomed in the Dinosauroid's eyes as millions of years washed away. The universal sign for "no" had worked.

Drew felt motion to his right and he shifted his gaze.

Two Dinosauroids strolled from the darkness, arrows pointed down.

Without thought, Drew brought up his weapon.

The original Dinosauroid screeched, the sound of its clicking and clucking freezing the newcomers in place. The creature brought its own weapon up, then down, then up, then down again.

Drew got the message and lowered his weapon. He watched with strange fascination, cold sweat chilling him to the bone. The new arrivals each took an end of the dead dino, its head lolling, blood dripping as they carried the corpse away into darkness.

The Dinosauroid clicked, its beak-mouth opening wide, fangs hanging through two natural channels. It was clear the creature was trying to tell Drew something. Maybe it was offering help? Inviting him to dinner? He didn't know, and he never would.

A rank stink carried on the stale breeze, and the strong scent of body odor filled Drew's nostrils. Was it the creatures? Did they bath? Had the Dinosauroid before him ever bathed? The creature wasn't caked in dirt, but ribbons of dried black mud climbed up its muscular legs like the creature had been traipsing around a swamp.

Drew had exercised great patience since arriving in the Cretaceous, and he was convinced that attribute was revered by the Dinosauroids based on his experiences thus far. He could be patient. He had all the time in the world. He worried that if he attempted to break away from the communal waiting session, the creature might interpret it as disrespect, or worse yet, aggression. Drew rolled his shoulders, lifted his legs, and stretched his arms. He could wait.

After what felt like an hour, but was only ten minutes, the Dinosauroid took a hesitant step forward.

Drew didn't move, the gun in his hand pressed to his side, flashlight trained on the creature.

The Dinosauroid locked eyes with him as it slowly lifted its right arm, the other gripping the bow and arrow. The gangly appendage was scaly green on top, with yellow snake-like skin beneath. Slowly, never taking its eyes from Drew, the Dinosauroid raised its hand and pointed toward the staircase.

Drew spared a glance in the direction of the stairs, and he thought he saw boot prints in the dust and dirt that covered the steps, a trail of footprints leading down into darkness.

When he looked back to the Dinosauroid, the creature was gone.

30

The temperature dropped as Drew descended into darkness, the glow of his flashlight driving away the blackness. He walked in a daze, gun at his side, the reality of what had just happened burrowing into him like an itch he couldn't scratch or a creeping pain he couldn't drive back. The inhabitants of Earth had been waiting for the arrival of extraterrestrial visitors for all of known history to no avail. But the creature he'd just met could easily be described as not of this Earth. Could that be the answer? Could it be that simple? Had aliens visited Earth prior to the Cretaceous–Paleogene extinction event? And if so, could they help him get home?

The scuttering of small claws scratching stone echoing up the stairwell stirred him from his unrealistic daydreams. The Dinosauroid may have displayed intelligence, but not time travel level intelligence. He reminded himself appearances could be deceiving.

Small bird-like tracks crossed the dust-covered steps, boot prints mixed within. The stale air smelled like dirty socks, and beneath it a crisp scent that reminded Drew of bleach.

After ten steps a landing hadn't appeared and he paused, panning the light back the way he'd come. Shadows gyrated and swayed under the flashlight beam, the cloud of harsh light fading into blackness. Drew could no longer see the landing above, but he didn't consider turning around. That ship had sailed.

He counted thirty-one more steps before the staircase ended in a narrow passageway that led to a closed stone door.

There were no markings on the walls, no clues, and no footprints appeared in the silt that covered the stone floor. No human had come this way. At least not for a very long time. Suspicion played his spine like a xylophone, needles of pain spreading through him like the warmth from a shot of alcohol. Thoughts of whiskey led him to Walls, and Drew wished his battle-hardened partner was with him now.

He saw no holes in the walls like above, and there were no seams in the floor, no indication at all that a trap might lay before him. Had a trap already gotten the professor? Was that why his prints disappeared like he'd been transported somewhere else while in midstride? If so, it had been a silent affair.

Nerves jangling, Drew inched down the passageway until he stood before the stone door. Squiggly lines and symbols he hadn't seen before decorated the door. Perhaps a warning? Instructions? The Dinosauroid had sent him this way, so he assumed the symbols were directions or a blessing.

He pressed his palm to the stone door and pushed, and to his surprise it gave way easily, as if the thick slab was somehow perfectly counterbalanced. Drew slipped through the opening, gun out, and when he'd passed through the door it closed behind him with a rumble.

The chamber beyond dazzled the eyes, the flashlight beam bouncing back in Drew's face. He saw an infinite number of duplicate Drews staring back at him, and for a heartbeat Drew thought he was dead. As his eyes adjusted to the bright light, he realized he was in a funhouse of a kind, and all the surfaces that made up the space were reflective like a mirror. The walls were polished obsidian and tiny flecks of quartz sparkled therein. He took a step into the maze of reflected Drews and stopped short, a wall blocking his way. The surface was cold to the touch, and he felt a steady breeze coming from his left, so he went in that direction.

A steady drumbeat built in his head, stress squeezing his spinal cord. It was hard to concentrate, and he felt like someone was pounding a nail into his forehead. His own face stared back at him in the harsh light, and the dark bags beneath his eyes and the carelines etched into his face made him look much older than he was.

How many days had it been since the crash? How many near death situations had he avoided or been lucky enough to escape? His stomach twisted with hunger, and he lifted his water bottle, remembered it was empty, and threw it as hard as he could.

The stainless-steel bottle bounced off a wall Drew didn't realize was there and crashed to the floor. He was beginning to feel like he'd been caught in a trap, and no sooner had that thought plowed through his subconscious when he recalled the reason he wasn't initially able to see the pictures of the Dinosauroid and the map. He had binocular vision, and whatever built the markers—the impossible triangle, the maps, and images-perhaps didn't. What type of vision did the Dinosauroids have? Would they be able to traverse the hall of black mirrors? Was the maze created to keep them out? Were the beasts using him to find a way through?

Having actually been in a funhouse while attending a retro attraction called a carnival with Kimmy, he knew patience was all that was needed to get through the maze of trickery. Going slowly, feeling along the walls as he went, eyes down, he shuffled through the dizzying maze.

He'd survived the crash of the spaceship, lived without food, water, the basic necessities that made him human. As he searched for a way through the maze, his own image staring back at him, he thought back to all the close encounters, all the dead crewmates. The spacesuit boots squeaked, each step sending shards of pain climbing up his legs. His feet were covered in blisters, though his two major wounds had scabbed over and weren't red around the edges. It was a miracle the wounds hadn't become infected, and he hadn't been felled by a microbe or disease that his modern drug-enhanced immune system couldn't handle.

The spacesuit helmet still dangled from its carabiner, and his knife was secure in its sheath around his ankle. He still held the gun and flashlight, but he had nothing else in the world. In some ways that was freeing, not being burdened by the expectations of tomorrow, the worries of another day.

Perhaps he could live happily in this time, but that thought soured his stomach. Staying in the Cretaceous meant he'd never see his daughter again, and even if he discovered a supply of everything he could ever want or need he'd never be able to fill that void. He needed to find a new perspective, or he was doomed.

The flow of air grew stronger, the fresh scent of earthen moisture drawing him on. Drew was forced to backtrack several times, but after half-an-hour of exploration he exited the polished obsidian maze into a vast natural cavern.

No footprints marred the grit-covered floor, but there were vertical slashes in the dust, like a stick figure had crawled through the space.

A massive black vine thicker than a tree trunk protruded from a crack in the dark stone. It clung to the walls and floor, a series of offshoots gripping every inch of rock, deep yellow leaves the size of bear paws fluttering in the faint breeze.

Beneath the covering of vines, the chamber walls were a shattered mess of various types of stone except in one area where a flat surface free of greenery stood out like a holo screen. Drew panned the light around and judged the cavern was a hundred yards long by fifty yards wide. At its far end there was a large depression carved into red stone, a series of detailed images around its edge. Next to it a stone door stood closed.

A gentle hiss, like air escaping a balloon, stroked his last nerve, the image of the Titanoboa slithering through his overburdened mind. But it was no giant snake that cast a huge spastic shadow on the floor before him.

In the harsh glow of the flashlight beam a monstrosity of legs and teeth stared at Drew.

The beast looked like a giant cave cricket. It stood ten feet tall, and the frog-like legs that bent at its back rose to fifteen feet. Yellow stripes cut across a black carapace, and two eyes darker than the darkest night focused on Drew. Tall antennas swayed and undulated, the beast's array of smaller legs cycling and shifting. A narrow mouth hung open, spiked teeth glinting under the artificial light, and its armored back was rounded and ended in what looked like a stinger tail.

Hissing and squeaking, the beast jumped toward Drew with a speed and agility that made him step back a pace. The flashlight shook in his hand, and he brought up the gun and fired, the report like thunder in the confined space.

The crack of the bullet hitting one of the cave cricket's legs was accompanied by a squeal that made Drew shiver. The creature's skeletal-like leg snapped, and the beast fell on its side, its hard-shell smacking stone.

Still the creature came on. It pushed across the floor with its good legs, a red and blue viscus fluid staining the stone floor. With its rear right leg half gone, the beast couldn't move in a straight line, and it arced to its right as it fought to get to Drew.

He rolled his shoulders, sighted the gun, and squeezed the trigger twice.

The bullets thumped into the creature's carapace above its left eye, but the beast trundled on, its good rear leg pistoning as it tried to hop, the bug's torso rising and falling, its chaotic movements stirring dirt and dust.

Drew spread his legs and grasped the gun in a two-handed grip. The giant bug was twenty feet away, its jaws flexed open, its fury palpable. He aimed for the right eye, took a deep breath, and fired.

The shot missed by a foot, but Drew didn't hesitate. He adjusted his aim, steadied himself, and fired his last bullet.

He missed the eye, but the cartridge disappeared into the giant cave cricket's mouth. The creature staggered and fell in slow motion as it collapsed.

Drew threw the empty gun at the bug.

The dead creature spasmed, its legs flexing as the beast's brain issued final orders. The foul stink of rot and decay wafted through the cavern, and with an exhalation that blew back Drew's dirty hair, the massive bug fell still.

With a renewed sense of urgency he didn't fully understand, Drew slipped around the dead animal, examining it with the flashlight as he went. When he was past the creature he headed for the far end of the chamber where he'd seen the flat area of stone free of vegetation.

No great consternation was needed to figure out what the flat area on the wall was. He stared hard at it, totally focused, and the tiny lines and squiggles chiseled into the rock began to shift and move, forming a picture.

Several stick figures crouched around what could only be a roaring fire. One of the figures held a stone, another sticks, and a third something Drew couldn't identify.

Drew glanced at the fireplace-like depression in the red stone, the door beside it, and everything became clear. To prove his worth, his intelligence, and gain entrance to the chamber beyond, he needed to make fire. But how could he do that without the proper supplies?

A gentle breeze brushed his face and stroked the many yellow leaves clinging to the thick black vine. Rocks of many different colors stood out beneath the vegetation, some darker, therefore harder, than others. The warmth of excitement twisted his stomach. He had everything he needed to make a fire right here.

The main vine was too thick to break or cut with the saw back of his blade, but there were several sections that had died off and given way to younger offshoots, and he was able to break free several pieces of seasoned wood. Creating a spark wouldn't be an issue for him because Drew had a knife. Even without a blade he figured with enough patience and persistence two of the correct stones could be used to generate a spark, and some of the layers of rock that made up the cavern walls were thin, tight lines of quartz that could be used to make a sharp implement to slice shavings from dried wood.

With growing anticipation, he used the carbon fiber blade to make wood shavings, and to his delight he saw that the vine-wood was dense with sap that he guessed, based on the situation, might be flammable.

Drew worked like a man who was at the end of a task that had spanned a lifetime, and he slowly built a pile of wood shavings in the depression in the red stone wall. When he was done, he carefully stacked his sticks in a tee pee formation over the shavings and sat back.

The black stone he'd used as a flint was long gone, Drew having lost it in one of his scrambles to survive. He selected a flat black stone with no imperfections and set the flashlight down, using a stone to angle its beam upward. Then he chopped at the stone with the blade of his knife, and sparks flew, but the fire didn't ignite.

He worked for several minutes, his arm aching, firefly sparks skidding over stone into the pile of wood. Nothing. Not even a little smoke. Drew was beginning to despair, the odds that the sap being flammable falling like the value of a credit after he invests, when the scent of the dead cave cricket filled his nostrils.

Drew stopped hacking at the stone, picked up the flashlight, and trained it on the fallen beast. The carcass looked like an empty bag, the stick-like legs the only things still standing upright. The broken appendage looked like dry rotted fiberglass, and as Drew stared, an idea bloomed in his overtaxed mind. Perhaps using the dead creature was part of the puzzle?

With the last of his energy draining from his heavy limbs, Drew cut off a few pieces of the bug's broken hindleg. He added them to the firewood and went back to work chopping at the stone. It took several minutes, sweat dripping into his eyes, but finally a flame sparked at the frayed end of one of the pieces of bug leg.

Soon the fire was raging and the depression in the red stone wall filled with flames. Smoke rolled through the cavern, and as Drew watched, the stone around the fire slowly faded to white as the rock was heated.

A loud *pop-crack* echoed through the cave, and the stone door beside the fire opened a crack, a golden glow leaking from within.

With a strange pleasure that triggered paranoia, Drew eased open the door and stepped into the golden glow of victory.

31

Drew came awake to the buzz of a hydraulic motor as he was lifted from the soup. The blackness was fading, shadows gyrating against a white background of expanding light. There was chatter, laughter, snorts, and huffs. He felt the tug on his limbs as he dangled in his harness, all his pains receding as he was dried off and placed in a soft bed.

"Drew?" came the distant voice of Julie, his wife.

"Daddy?" cooed Kimmy.

Drew forced his eyes into focus, his head splitting with pain.

Julie and Kimmy hovered over him, their smiling faces warming his heart. He reached up and felt the Saint Jude medal that hung around his neck. It brought him comfort as it had been a gift.

The face of an old man in a white lab coat edged his way between the girls. The man's name tag read: Oscar Nille, Travel Liaison Technician. "We feeling O.K.?" the man asked. "Your vitals are fine, and you had no issues during the trip. The neural stimulators causing your simulated wounds to hurt should have worn off."

Drew's adventures in the Cretaceous were still fresh in his mind—the giant cave cricket, the fire, the golden glow. He asked, "Ho.." His throat didn't want to work.

"The intubation may have inflamed your vocal cords. Give the drugs a second to get into you," said the technician.

Drew felt good as he stared up at his family, the memory of his time in the past something he would never forget, the good and the bad, the ghosts and the losses.

"How long?" Drew finally pushed out. "Work..."

"The time compression algorithm is amazing, isn't it? You lived almost a week in four hours. That alone is worth the credits."

He felt his chest loosen. Everything was fine. His time as a fossil mercenary was done and it was time to get back to work, the trip a memory he could relive for the rest of his life.

Julie stroked Drew's hair and kissed his forehead.

"Protocol dictates that we monitor you for half an hour after a trip, so hang here for a bit and then we'll get you out of here," the technician said.

"So, how was it?" came the excited voice of Kimmy.

"Boy do I have a story to tell you guys," Drew said.

EPILOGUE

He'd heard about Remcal Adventures from a friend, the guy going on and on about his service in the US Civil War. It hadn't taken much research to learn the company was real, and his buddy's claims appeared genuine.

A tall slender man with light green skin and wearing a black suit ushered him into a sales pod and motioned for him to sit in a large comfortable chair. A holo screen filled the wall before him.

"I apologize for being crass, but I need to complete the legal disclaimer procedure," said the attendant. The man wore no name tag.

He'd agreed to this, so he said nothing.

"Some people who travel with us, very few, mind you, a mere one in five hundred who participate report having minor dissociative issues including, at times, not being able to distinguish reality from illusion."

The room was so still the beating of his heart pounded in his head, excitement growing in him like a disease.

"Remcal Adventures and all parties associated therewith accept no responsibility for the aforementioned possible side effects, which also sometimes includes the loss of conflicting memories. Thanks to the neural blocker you agreed to take, which was placed in your welcome drink, you will have no recollection of this advertisement, and if you decide to travel with us the memory of your adventure will be so real your friends won't be able to get you to shut up about it."

He was eager to see the pitch, so he said nothing.

"At this point I'll leave you to it," the attendant said. "I hope you decide to travel with us."

The attendant left as the lights dimmed and the holo screen came to life, the Remcal Adventures logo dancing in the air.

A beautiful woman appeared, her long black hair shining, the blue of her dress so pure it made him think of the ocean.

"Welcome to Remcal Adventures, where dreams really do come true," said the soothing voice. The woman stood on Mars, the red-striped mountain Olympus Mons behind her.

"Have you ever wanted to travel to Mars? Serve on a generation ship or travel the paths of history? Now you can!"

The scene shifted and the saleswoman stood in ancient Egypt, a pyramid being constructed behind her. "Experience and participate in the greatest moments in history or play one of our many games. We offer a variety of crime dramas, survival quests, and puzzle games that allow you to actually *live* the action and put the memory away to enjoy for the rest of your life. Skeptical? Let me explain how it works."

Now the surface of the Moon filled the background.

"Using virtual reality technology, neural stimulators, and a series of drugs and memory implants, Remcal Adventures' travel method is a unique melding of reality, false memory, and real memories indistinguishable from the actual experience. The memory of the trip of a lifetime."

The scene shifted to a gun range. "Concerned your adventure skills aren't up to par? Afraid to challenge yourself with one of our games? Don't worry. Though the pain and injuries you experience will feel real, it's only the neural stimulators tricking your brain. Looking for love? There are a variety of erotic options. Happily married? Choose our new non-flirt option so you don't create any memories you'd rather forget."

The background blurred and the saleswoman stepped from the screen, her hologram standing before him. "And you choose how many lives you want. That's right. You can buy more travel or game time by including companions, who will arrive and pull you out of the fire at the perfect moment. If you do die while traveling no worries, you'll wake and remember most of your trip, minus the scrubbing of the unfortunate incident that ended your vacation early."

Silence filled the pod.

The attendant finished, "There is a complete list of possible destinations and adventures following this presentation. In addition, take the opportunity now to review the preview of our newest vacation destination. Agree to play Predators & Prey now and get a discount and future memory enhancers included! Just mention promotion code McClane when you speak with your sales representative."

THE END

Other Severed Press novels by Edward J. McFadden III: Wolves of the Sea, Fortune's Cypher, Crimson Falls, Hell Creek, Barracuda Swarm, The Cryptid Club, Dinosaur Red, Drop Off, Jurassic Ark, Keepers of the Flame, Throwback, Sea Tremors, Primeval Valley, Shadow of the Abyss (#1 Amazon Bestseller Tag), Awake, and The Breach (#1 Amazon Bestseller Tag, Amazon #1 Hot New Audio Release Tag). His other novels include: Terror Peak, the Theo Ramage Thriller series: Quick Sands, Sandbagged, and Too Much Grit, Dogs Get Ten Lives, The Black Death of Babylon, and HOAXERS. Ed lives on Long Island with his wife Dawn, and their daughter Samantha.

Check out other great

Dinosaur Thrillers!

Gustavo Bondoni

TEST SITE HORROR

Lieutenant Max Alexeyev is a Russian Special Forces soldier. His job is to protect his country's interests at home and abroad, not to rescue overly ambitious reporters who have bitten off stories too big to chew. But when his unit gets called to a press event at a laboratory that has been invaded by dinosaurs, that's exactly what he finds himself doing. Fighting both prehistoric nightmares and the products of modern genetic experiments in the forests of the Ural Mountains, he battles for his own survival as well as that of alluring journalist Marianne Caruso and her peers.Unbeknownst to him, however, shadowy human forces are at work to ensure that no one spills the secrets of the research being done in the area.Will they live to tell the story of the Test Site Horror?

John Lee Schneider

AGE OF MONSTERS

Once upon a time, Dinosaurs ruled the Earth.But the Mesozoic era – the Age of Reptiles – came to its cataclysmic end sixty-five million years ago.The Age of Monsters begins tonight.And the world of humankind will crumble. Some will call it Judgment. Some will attempt to fight. Others will simply run. Most will just try and survive. But no one will escape.In the mountains. In the oceans. In the cities and towns. Even up in space.Where were YOU when the world ended?

@severedpress
/severedpress

Check out other great
Dinosaur Thrillers!

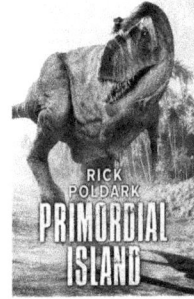

Rick Poldark
PRIMORDIAL ISLAND

During a violent storm Flight 207 crash-lands in the South China Sea. Poseidon Tech tracks the wreckage to an uncharted island and dispatches a curious salvage team—two paleontologists, a biologist specializing in animal behavior, a botanist, and a nefarious big game hunter. Escorted by a heavily-armed security team, they cut through the jungle and quickly find themselves in a terrifying fight for survival, running a deadly gauntlet of prehistoric predators. In their quest for the flight recorder, they uncover the mystery of the island's existence and discover an arcane force that will tip the balance of power on the primordial island. Things are not as they seem as they race against time to survive the island's man-eating dinosaurs and make it back home in one piece.

P.K. Hawkins
SUBTERRANEA

Fall, 1985. The small town of Kettle Hollow barely shows up on any maps, and four young friends are used to taking their BMX's outside of town in an effort to find anything interesting to do. But tonight their tendency to go off by themselves may have saved them, and also forced them into the adventure of a lifetime. While they were away, Kettle Hollow has been locked down by the government, and a portal to another world has opened on Main Street. It's a world deep below the ground, a world where dinosaurs roam free, where giant plants and mutant insects hunt for prey. It's also a world where all their family and friends have been kidnapped for sinister purposes. Now, with time running out before the portal closes, the four friends must brave the unknown to save their loved ones. Time is running out, and in the darkened tunnels of Subterranea, something is hunting them.

SEVEREDPRESS

🐦 @severedpress
f /severedpress

Check out other great

Dinosaur Thrillers!

Greig Beck

PRIMORDIA: IN SEARCH OF THE LOST WORLD

Ben Cartwright, former soldier, home to mourn the loss of his father stumbles upon cryptic letters from the past between the author, Arthur Conan Doyle and his great, great grandfather who vanished while exploring the Amazon jungle in 1908. Amazingly, these letters lead Ben to believe that his ancestor's expedition was the basis for Doyle's fantastical tale of a lost world inhabited by long extinct creatures. As Ben digs some more he finds clues to the whereabouts of a lost notebook that might contain a map to a place that is home to creatures that would rewrite everything known about history, biology and evolution. But other parties now know about the notebook, and will do anything to obtain it. For Ben and his friends, it becomes a race against time and against ruthless rivals. In the remotest corners of Venezuela, along winding river trails known only to lost tribes, and through near impenetrable jungle, Ben and his novice team find a forbidden place more terrifying and dangerous than anything they could ever have imagined.

William Meikle

THE LOST VALLEY

A remote high valley in the Canadian Rockies hides an ecosystem that has been lost in time. A small team of prospectors and their local guides are looking for gold. What they find is blood and terror and death.The valley's monstrous inhabitants are not about to let go of its secrets lightly.

Check out other great

Dinosaur Thrillers!

Doug Goodman

HUNTING WITH DINOSAURS

A hunting party is sent to catch and kill raptors that have escaped Dinosaur Falls Restricted Area and murdered nearby hikers. But the hunters find the raptors are unlike any creature they've ever hunted, and soon one lone bowhunter is running for his life through the Perdidos Mountains. He discovers an old wilderness survival trench and burrows in deep, but eventually the raptors come for him. His only salvation is to befriend a wolf hellbent on destroying the raptors. If they can come together, they can form a pack the world has never seen, but if they fail, the raptors are waiting with their sharp teeth and elongated claws...

Edward J. McFadden III

DINOSAUR RED

There's a doorway on Mars that has mankind's greatest minds perplexed. Deep beneath Aeolis Mons an ancient secret is revealed, and a team of explorers led by Forest Judge, Deputy Commander of Gale Base Alpha, are dispatched to investigate. The prehistoric gateway reveals a biosphere preserving Earth's distant past, and as Judge and crew stand on the threshold of mankind's greatest discovery the Martian ground trembles. A roar thunders from within, the doorway closes, and the team is trapped. Six mission specialists, each with unique skills, each with different reasons for wanting to break free of the primordial trap. To get home Judge is forced to choose between escape and changing the course of humanity. What will he do?